CHICAGO NOIR

THE CLASSICS

EDITED BY JOE MENO

Published by Akashic Books
©2015 Akashic Books

Series concept by Tim McLoughlin and Johnny Temple
Chicago map by Sohrab Habibion

Cover photo courtesy of the Newberry Library, Chicago. Call #: CBQ Granger 2170.

Hardcover ISBN: 978-1-61775-377-0
Paperback ISBN: 978-1-61775-294-0
Library of Congress Control Number: 2015934076
All rights reserved

First printing

Grateful acknowledgment is made for permission to reprint the stories in this anthology. See page 254 for details.

Akashic Books
Twitter: @AkashicBooks
Facebook: AkashicBooks
E-mail: info@akashicbooks.com
Website: www.akashicbooks.com

ALSO IN THE AKASHIC NOIR SERIES

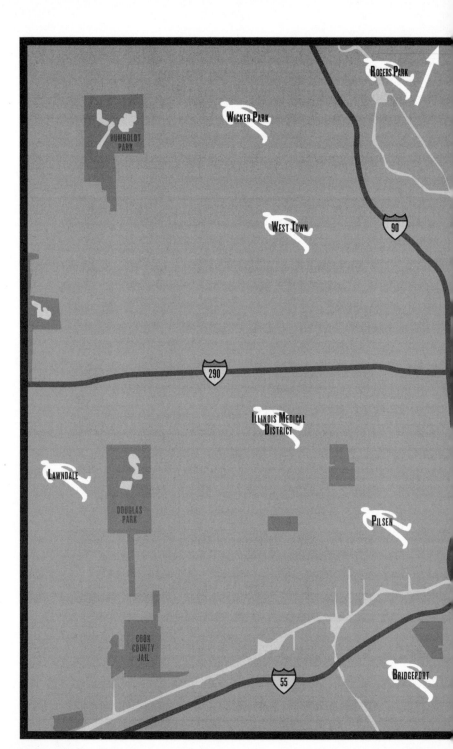

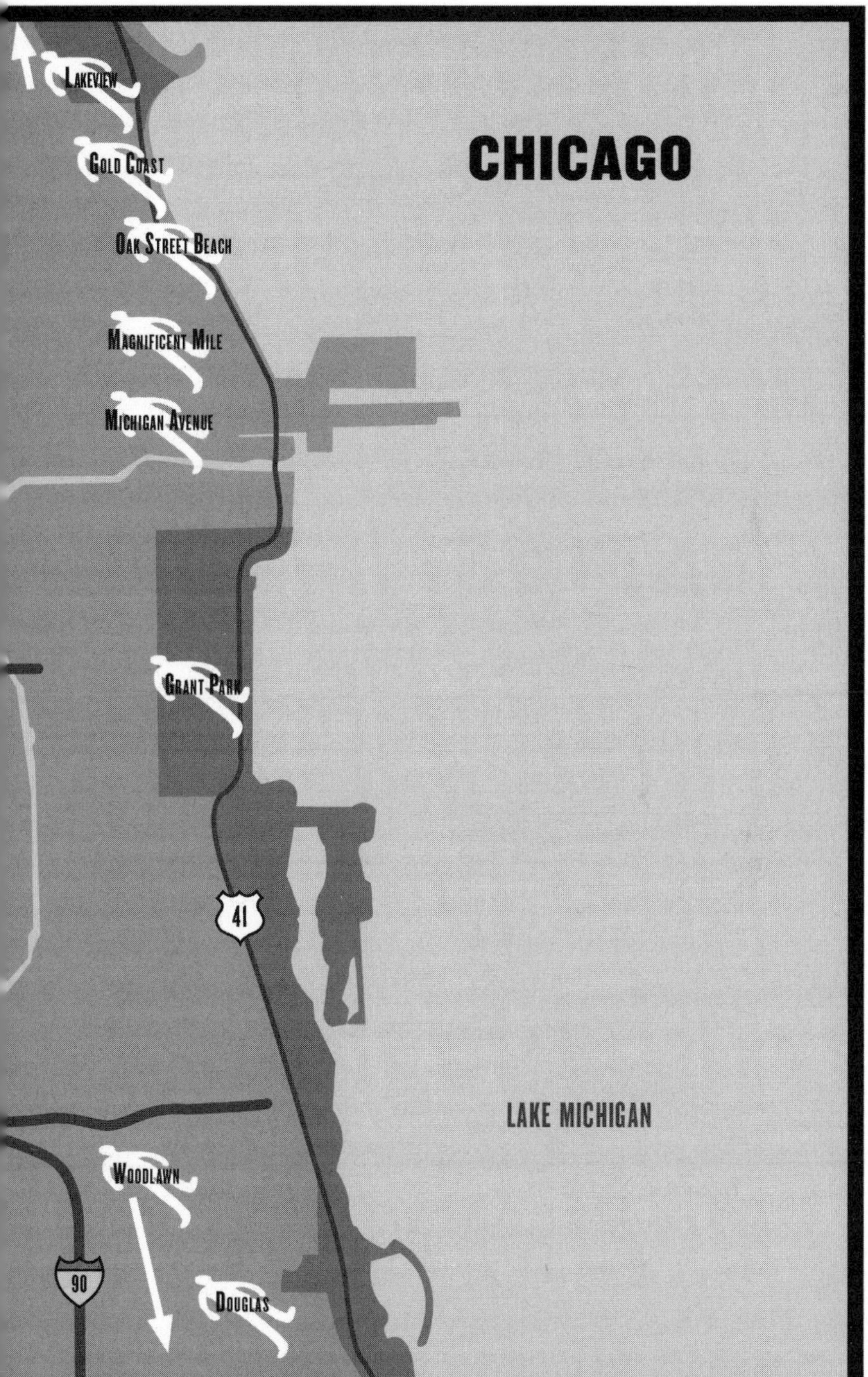
CHICAGO
Lakeview
Gold Coast
Oak Street Beach
Magnificent Mile
Michigan Avenue
Grant Park
41
Lake Michigan
Woodlawn
90
Douglas

TABLE OF CONTENTS

PART III: MODERN CRIME

INTRODUCTION

Noir is the language of shadows, of the world in-between. The shape a stranger's mouth makes murmuring in the dark, the color of a knife flashing in a dead-end alley, the sound of an elevator rising to an unlit floor; noir is the language of stark contrasts, life and death, good and evil, day and night.

First defined in the 1940s and '50s by French academics to describe a specific kind of bleak, black-and-white crime film produced by Hollywood in that era, the term gained popular relevancy in the 1970s and since then has also been applied to various works of literature as well: crime novels, detective stories, mysteries, suspense thrillers, each with elements of the gothic or traditional tragedy. Raymond Chandler's *The Big Sleep*, Dashiell Hammett's *Red Harvest,* and James M. Cain's *The Postman Always Rings Twice* all defined the genre with their conflicted heroes and antiheroes, mysterious plots, murky atmospheres, and punchy, stylized writing. These novelists and their counterparts who published short fiction in pulp magazines like *Black Mask* depicted the moral uncertainty of the modern age—the human struggle to find meaning in a world that by its nature is necessarily obscure.

Noir writing, like the night, is also, by its very definition, somewhat borderless. The history of crime writing in America bears this out. *Black Mask*, the pulp magazine that first exposed these sorts of stories to the public, was initially created by journalist H.L. Mencken and drama critic George Jean Nathan to help finance their literary journal, the *Smart Set*. This dynamic tension between the "highbrow" and the "lowbrow"—between the literary elite and the man on the street—is one of noir's most enduring qualities. Recent award-winning books by the likes of Michael Chabon, Denis Johnson, Jonathan Lethem, Roberto Bolaño, and Cormac McCarthy attest to this liminal phenomenon.

Over the years, the literature of noir has proven to be as essential as any other writing genre. Although highly riveting, it's much more than mere entertainment. It's modern mythology at its most powerful. Like its musical equivalent, jazz, I believe it may be one of America's most enduring cultural contributions.

Considering these aspects of the literature of noir, the city of Chicago is arguably its truest embodiment; more corrupt than New York, less glamorous than LA, Chicago has more murders per capita than any other city its size. With its sleek skyscrapers bisecting the fading sky like an unspoken threat, Chicago is the closest metropolis to the mythical city of shadows as first described in the work of Chandler, Hammett, and Cain. Only in Chicago do instituted color lines offer generation after generation of poverty and violence, only in Chicago do the majority of recent governors do prison time, only in Chicago do the dead actually vote twice. With its public record of bribery, cronyism, and fraud, this is a metropolis so deeply divided—by race, ethnicity, and class—that sociologists had to develop a new term to describe this unfortunate bifurcation. As Nelson Algren best put it, Chicago is and has always been a "city on the make."

The stories collected in this volume all explore this city of shadows, of high contrasts, spanning nearly a century, tracing the earliest explorations into the form. Harry Stephen Keeler's

"30 Seconds of Darkness," first published in 1916, demonstrates both the influence of Edgar Allan Poe and the high-minded formality of Charles Dickens. In the 1910s and '20s, Sherwood Anderson—a uniquely American writer with his interest in crime, the grotesque, and the underrepresented—influenced the still-developing genre with *Winesburg, Ohio* and his popular literary stories including "Brothers." Andersons' work alone would go on to inspire William Faulkner, Ernest Hemingway, and Nelson Algren, whose story "He Swung and He Missed" echoes much of Anderson's character-driven fiction. Midcentury writing like Richard Wright's "The Man Who Went to Chicago" and Patricia Highsmith's *The Price of Salt* depict the outsider's view of an ambiguous, foreign place where anonymity reigns and racial and sexual mores are less constrained. Several modern pieces, like Stuart Dybek's "We Didn't," with its poetic repetition and lyrical imagery, and Hugh Holton's "The Thirtieth Amendment," with its dystopian elements, help to expand and redefine the form in new and surprising ways.

Chicago's history of crime writing is extensive, perhaps deserving an encyclopedia all its own. Many fine writers were not included in this collection, though their work has been no less influential: pulp writers like Edgar Rice Burroughs, with his dedication to horror and science fiction, mingling crime with decidedly otherworldly elements; newspaper reporters and fiction writers like Ben Hecht and Ring Lardner, who explored noir in their daily columns and stories (though both of them, well aware of the preferences of the New York publishing apparatus, chose to set most of their noirs in New York City); memorable literary novelists like James T. Farrell and Leon Forrest, who both depicted the grim lives of citizens on the city's South Side. Other important crime writers like Eugene Izzi, with his brand of raw, late-'80s noir, seemed less interested in the short story form, preferring instead to produce unflinching novel after unflinching novel.

Chicago—more than the metropolis that gave the world Al Capone, the Saint Valentine's Day Massacre, the death of John Dillinger, the crimes of Leopold and Loeb, the horrors of John Wayne Gacy, the unprecedented institutional corruption of so many recent public officials, more than the birthplace of Raymond Chandler—is a city of darkness. This darkness is not an act of overimagination. It's the unadulterated truth. It's a pointed though necessary reminder of the grave tragedies of the past and the failed possibilities of the present. Fifty years in the future, I hope these stories are read only as fiction, as somewhat distant fantasy. Here's hoping for some light.

Joe Meno
Chicago, IL
June 2015

PART I

THE JAZZ AGE

PART I

30 SECONDS OF DARKNESS

BY HARRY STEPHEN KEELER

Rogers Park

(Originally published in 1916)

Tomorrow evening, my dear T.B.," DeLancey suddenly remarked, "I intend to be the cause of a little excitement at old Garrard Bascom's dinner party. In simpler language, my dear fellow, I propose to steal the Countess of Cordova's $100,000 diamond necklace. What do you think of the project?"

With surprise I stiffened up suddenly in my chair. My newspaper dropped from my fingers and I stared unbelievingly at the immaculately clad figure that was seated across from me. But his pair of brown eyes returned my gaze unflinchingly.

"Do you mean to assert, DeLancey," I managed finally to ask, "that you intend to try such a feat as that at a dinner table surrounded by thirty or more people—and the usual two or three Pinkerton detectives present?"

"Precisely," he smiled, blowing a few smoke rings ceilingward. "I've had the thing in mind ever since our invitations arrived. But, my dear fellow, you haven't yet given me your opinion."

"I think you are bereft of your senses. The chances that you take will land us both in a state penitentiary one of these days, if not in some European rat-infested dungeon."

But DeLancey only smiled more enigmatically, and commenced smoothing back the black hair that was turning slightly gray at his temples.

I confess that I invariably slumped into a feeling of profound dismay whenever DeLancey proposed to perform one of his apparently impossible exploits. Yet, time and again, he had achieved the seemingly unachievable—and I had been able to go my way rejoicing, knowing that liberty was ours for a while longer. But always, down in my heart, the dread feeling existed that sooner or later was to come the one mistake, the one misstep in DeLancey's almost perfect plans, that would carry us both inside the dull gray walls for many years.

Across Europe we had gone, DeLancey leaving in his wake a series of mystifying thefts—thefts that to this day are riddles to the Continental police. Petrograd, Berlin, Rome, Madrid, Paris, London, even New York, had contributed their toll to the man's super-cunning brain and his magnetic personality. So for the last few months, while we were living in our Chicago bachelor apartments, I felt that we were assuredly to refrain from any more of these feats—at least for an appreciable time to come. It seemed to me that in justice to ourselves, to the pleasure that we took in each other's company, to the joy of existence itself, we should continue to live quietly on the proceeds of DeLancey's last feat—the theft of Castor and Pollux, the famous red and green twin diamonds, from the vault of Simon et Cie in the Rue Royale, Paris. Success had crowned that performance, I had good reason to know, for it was into my hands that DeLancey had sent the stones in the custody of Von Berghem. And Von Berghem, traveling as an invalid in company with his small son from Paris to Calais, from Calais to Dover, from Dover to Liverpool, from Liverpool to New York, suspected finally of having had something to do with that inexplicable crime, arrested at the docks in New York and searched for three long hours, had come through unscathed, not an inspector nor a police officer discovering that he was blind and that the diamonds were concealed behind his spectacles—concealed back of his hollow glass eyes themselves.

True, that particular success had been due in a great measure to the skill and cunning of Von Berghem himself, yet it was DeLancey's genius that had first seen the possibilities that lay in the blind beggar whom he had found wandering in the Montmartre cemetery.

I pulled myself together with a start and turned to DeLancey, watching the inscrutable smile that still lingered on his face.

"Are you able to tell me, DeLancey, just how you expect to remove a $100,000 necklace at old Bascom's dinner table under the glare of that big electric chandelier? What do you intend to do if he orders a search? Who the Countess of Cordova is, and how you know she's going to be there? How you know this necklace is to be around her neck? What part I am to play in the affair? How—"

"Enough, T.B.," he chuckled. "Stop your restless pacing back and forth. If you'll sit down I'll answer your questions one at a time."

I dropped back on the edge of my chair and waited to hear what he had to say.

"Now," he began slowly, "it is only fair to tell you, my dear fellow, that our exchequer is low—extremely so. The amount paid over to us by old Moses Stein for Castor and Pollux a year and a half ago was hopelessly out of proportion to the value of those two stones." He shrugged his shoulders and frowned for the first time. "But that, T.B., is the unfortunate part of this exciting game of ours. The legitimate profits are cut to a half—to a third—even to a fourth.

"And so," he went on, "the time has come for one last coup—one big coup; and then, lad, South Australia for you and me. What do you say?"

"Anything," I replied fervently, "is preferable to this continual living in fear of a slip-up of your plans. I like you, DeLancey, and I can't endure the thought of—" I stopped, for a picture of DeLancey being dragged away to suffer the ignoble fate of a prison sentence began to swim before my eyes.

"No doubt you do," he returned, after a pause. "But, nevertheless, the fact remains that our scale of living, the exorbitant rent of this apartment, our club dues, theatres, bachelor dinners, taxicabs, the gifts to that little dark-eyed love of yours, have all helped to consume our capital far too swiftly. But I don't regret it, T.B., for it has been capital well invested, since it has secured us two invitations already to Garrard Bascom's home in Rogers Park."

"I'm inclined to credit that to your strange winning personality," I returned.

"Personality, bah!" he snorted. "We've put up a bluff—we've jingled the money—we've belonged to the best clubs in the city; and those are the stunts that have made us welcome in such circles. But tomorrow night," he added savagely, "we'll try to reap the profits."

He paused a moment, and the smile that had so suddenly left his face slowly reappeared. For DeLancey was always genial, always in good humor, seldom ruffled.

"So as I said before," he went on, "it is up to us to make what you native born Americans—you real Yankees—call a killing. But it must be a decent killing, lad, such as the Cordova necklace, for after that episode the name of DeLancey will always be looked upon with a very slight—perhaps an appreciable—degree of suspicion and distrust. But I'll explain.

"Among several questions you asked me was how I know that this Countess of Cordova is to be present at old Bascom's dinner tomorrow evening. That, T.B., is simplicity itself. The countess, before she married old Count Cordova of Madrid, was Amelie Bascom of Chicago. And her arrival in this city was chronicled in the *Tribune* four days ago. Quite elemental reasoning, is it not?

"Have I never told you, my dear fellow, that I met the countess when you and I were in Madrid a year and a half ago? That the good lady, married to that old crustacean, was not at all averse to a violent flirtation? That—if I may be pardoned for any seeming egotism in the statement—I made quite an impression on her?"

I nodded, for now I dimly remembered having heard him mention something about the matter at some obscure time in the past.

"Now," he continued, "when she glances over her estimable papa's list of guests invited to that dinner party, you may rest assured that she is going to arrange to have—er—DeLancey for a partner. Have I made this quite plain?"

"You have. You seem to have a genius for paving your way—months and years ahead."

"Specialization in crime, T.B., merely specialization such as characterizes success in any line of endeavor. But enough of that. I'll now step to another one of your questions: how do I expect to remove a $100,000 necklace at a dinner table under the glare of a huge electric chandelier?"

"Yes. How—"

"By the use of a tiny pair of well-sharpened manicure scissors which, replaced in their black leather case, will be tossed clear across the room and remain unnoticed till the servants are cleaning the dining room several hours afterward."

"But you haven't answer—"

He raised his hand. "Of course I haven't answered your question. It happens that I'm not going to perform that simple operation in the glare of any hanging electric lights. I have sent in an order for thirty seconds of darkness."

"Thirty seconds of darkness!"

"Exactly. You remember Tzhorka?"

I surely did. Tzhorka was the little dwarfed Russian electrician whom DeLancey had met in the great world of crookdom. On more than occasion the latter had vaguely hinted to me that Tzhorka had worked with him once before. And this instance, I felt certain, was the night that old Count Ivan Yarosloff's safe in his palace on the Nevski-Prospekt at St. Petersburg was burned open by a pair of carbon electrodes and several thousand amperes of current stolen from the lighting feeders that led to the Russian Admiralty Building at the farther end of the Nevski-Prospekt. So since I, no doubt, had helped to spend part of old Yarosloff's 83,000 missing rubles, I became interested at once.

"Yes," he said, "Tzhorka has been in Chicago for some time on plans of his own. And he has agreed to supply me with thirty seconds of darkness at any time I shall indicate."

My face must have shown my bewilderment, for DeLancey hastened to explain his statement.

"Did you notice, the last time we were at the Bascom mansion, how the house was lighted?"

I shook my head.

"Which goes to show, T.B., that your faculties need considerable sharpening before you can stand alone on your legs in this game. If you had taken cognizance of this fact, however, you would have discovered that the current which lights up the mansion and outlying buildings at the center of that great estate is brought over the ground from the Commonwealth Edison Company's feeders which skirt the eastern edge of the property. And in saying that it is brought over the ground, I am referring, of course, to the line of poles which carry two thick cables tapped on the Commonwealth Edison's feeders."

This time I nodded, for I was dimly beginning to comprehend that DeLancey, through the help of Tzhorka, contemplated tampering with this pair of suspended cables, thus interfering with the light supply of the Bascom residence.

"Late last night," DeLancey went on, "Tzhorka, dressed in a complete lineman's outfit, went up the pole that stands on the outer edge of the Bascom estate and spliced on to one of these cables a so-called single-pole, single-throw switch with carbon contacts. Then, after lashing the inner span to the crossarm by means of a small block-and-tackle and what he terms a come-along, Tzhorka cut the cable completely through with a hacksaw. The whole arrangement, quite inconspicuous in itself, is in addition hidden by the foliage of a nearby tree."

"Then the current that feeds the Bascom estate," I exclaimed triumphantly, "is now passing through this switch. But how—"

"Yes. And if you had used those latent—nay, dormant—faculties of observation that are in you, you would have noticed also that the great French latticed windows of the Bascom dining room are in direct line with that outermost pole. In other words, my dear fellow, if Tzhorka should be astride that crossarm in the darkness of tomorrow night, watching our dinner table intently through a pair of high-power field glasses, and he should see—er—a certain individual, myself for instance, raise his hand to his head and pat down his hair—say—twice in succession, he might easily slip on a pair of blue goggles and pull the handles of that switch. The house, stable, garage, kitchens, and everything would be without electric light, instantly, until such time that—"

"For thirty seconds—"

"After which," DeLancey concluded coolly, "Tzhorka, consulting the second hand of his watch, would throw back the switch. Then the lights would go on and—"

"You idiot, you rash, foolhardy numbskull," I raged, rising up from my chair in agitation, "a search would be immediately ordered by Bascom when anywhere from one to twenty-nine of those guests, not counting the countess herself, discovers that this necklace that adorns her neck is missing. You can't—"

"Which brings us face to face with another one of your questions, T.B. What can I do if one or two of those guests prove to be the usual Pinkertons and lock the doors in order to make a thorough search? A neat problem, isn't it?"

"Far, far too neat," I replied bitterly. "DeLancey, get this project out of your mind. You can't do it, I tell you. If you kept the necklace on your person—they would get it sure. And even if you were able to hide it some place during the thirty seconds that Tzhorka, five hundred yards away, holds open the switch, everyone would be watched so closely that you could not dare to regain it." I stopped, disheartened. "And what part am I to play in this affair, as I asked you once?"

"Nothing, this time, lad. All that you need to do in the darkness is to draw back your chair and rise, as no doubt some of the men and most of the ladies will. You might rattle a dish or two, if handy. Just add to the general confusion, for beyond that I have no definite part for you to play."

I leaned forward and placed my hand on DeLancey's shoulder. "DeLancey, give up this mad idea. I tell you the thing is impossible. Your arrangements are characteristic of the thoroughness that always surrounds your work, and to a certain degree admirable. But I tell you frankly this particular feat cannot be accomplished. It cannot." I leaned forward still farther. "Listen to me, old man. Give it up. Why must you take these chances? Why—"

"Enough, T.B.," he calmly interrupted me. "I've been planning this for several days. When I first studied that Cordova necklace in Madrid, just after the old count parted with it for a wedding gift, I felt a strange desire—almost a hope—that I might place my fingers on it within another ten years. I tell you I counted every stone: I feasted my eyes on their pureness, their scintillations, their unusual brilliancy. I studied even the clasp, so obsessed did I become with the thing and the possibilities for removing it. Not content with that, I looked up the records and valuation of the necklace in the Spanish Royal Archives of the Library Madrid. And then and there I determined that the Cordova line—money lenders, interest sharks, blood suckers as they have been for the past five generations—should pay toll at least to the thousandth part of what they themselves have stolen."

I knew that DeLancey's decision was final, for there, in his last statement, was his whole philosophy of theft summed up. Never yet had I known him to lay a finger on the property of anyone except those scattered individuals who amassed their wealth by extortion and trickery. So I saw full well that all the arguments in the world would prove to be useless now.

I made no more attempts at dissuading him from his purpose. Instead, I tried with all my ability to induce him to tell me just what method he expected to follow in order to leave Bascom's house with this $100,000 necklace in his possession. Did he intend, perhaps, to toss it from the French window? No, he claimed, for the coolness of the late fall weather was too great to count on the possibility of those windows being open. More than that he refused to say. And yet it seemed that some scheme, some rational, logical procedure, was mapped out in his brain, if he had gone to the trouble of securing Tzhorka's services in tampering with the electric cables that fed the Bascom estate.

After a quarter of an hour of vain questioning, I gave it up, for he proved adamantine this time in his resolve not to allow me to enter his plans. He persisted in arguing that, since I could be of no assistance whatever in this instance, it was best that I remain in total ignorance of what was to take place. And finally he seized his silk hat and ordered me to drop the whole subject and come for a stroll along Michigan Boulevard.

I confess that I did not sleep very well that night, for something seemed to tell me that tomorrow was the last day that we should be together; that the following evening was to end disastrously for DeLancey. But as I slipped into a bathrobe in the morning, I met DeLancey himself, emerging from his cold plunge, pink cheeked, smiling, totally lacking the slightest shadow under his eyes. Truly, it seemed as though there was nothing in the world that could disturb the man's equanimity.

After finishing the breakfast that was brought up to our suite, DeLancey donned his cape, took up his hat and walking stick, and pressed the button that summoned a taxicab.

"Now, my dear fellow," he said, "I may be away all day today as I have been during the past two days. Can you exist without me?"

"I thought that perhaps we should have this last day together—a trip to the country, for instance. But here you go off again—on that mysterious business that's been keeping you for two days now. If something unusual should develop, where could I find you?"

He wrinkled up his brows. "Well—I may as well tell you my whereabouts are uncertain. But for the present I'm off to old Moses Stein's shop on Halsted Street, ostensibly to make a purchase, but in reality to conclude the details for disposing of this necklace before we leave for Australia. I may be gone for—"

"Old Stein, the jewel shark? The fence?"

"Yes."

"Then you're still confident that you are to have everything your own way in stealing this necklace? That you can deliberately walk out of the house with it? That you will not make a single mistake?"

"Not absolutely confident," he said simply. "But old Stein knows that necklace as he knows pretty nearly everything of value in the world of jewels, and he has agreed to pay over 60 percent of the intrinsic value of those stones. And I, in turn, have agreed to place it in his hands by midnight tonight. So you see, T.B., there is no recrossing of the Rubicon." He paused a moment. "I may be gone the greater part of the day. Since we dare not employ a valet, you might, if you will, lay out my evening clothes, studs, and gloves at six o'clock tonight—and order the taxicab for seven thirty. The dinner is scheduled for nine, and we must allow at least an hour and a half to reach Rogers Park."

And without even allowing me to put forth one last argument, he slipped from our apartment. A second later I heard the clang of the descending elevator in the outer hallway.

That day was surely an unpleasant one for me. It seemed as though the fear of a slip-up haunted me this time far more than it had in all DeLancey's previous affairs in which I had participated. I tried to read, but my attention failed utterly to stay with the printed page. I tried to smoke, but invariably my cigar grew cold in my fingers while I became lost in my own abstractions.

What plans DeLancey had contrived I could not imagine. Why had he been so rash as to take the old jewel fence, Moses Stein, into his confidence on the subject of the Cordova necklace? Yet I knew, too, that on more than one occasion DeLancey had consulted with the old man on various jobs. One thing, at least, was certain: in dealing with old Stein he was dealing with an individual who knew the exact value and description of every piece of jewelry in the world of any historical value. In fact, it was Stein who outbid Ranseer, the mad gem collector, for possession of Castor and Pollux, a year or more before, and that without ever having seen the stones, so well did he know their size, color, shape, cutting, and purity. So no doubt he knew the Cordova necklace as well, if he had agreed on a finite sum to be paid over for it.

The day dragged by interminably.

I spent the afternoon walking along Michigan Boulevard and returning to the apartment at intervals of an hour, feverishly looking for DeLancey to put in an appearance. Came two o'clock, three o'clock, four o'clock. At five o'clock the afternoon light faded. As darkness came on, I laid out his evening clothes and his studs. Then I ordered the taxicab for seven thirty. And when this was done, I heard six o'clock tinkle from the tiny onyx clock on our mantel.

What in heaven's name, I wondered vaguely, could be keeping him? Mysterious as his movements had been in the last two days, he not yet remained away so late as this. Where had he gone after leaving Moses Stein's? Or was he still lolling in the old man's Halsted Street shop?

Came six thirty o'clock—and DeLancey!

He bustled into the apartment and quickly locked the door behind him. I was making a poor attempt at dressing for the Bascom dinner. He glanced hurriedly at his watch and slipped into his own bedroom without a word, where I heard him splashing about in his tub a few moments later.

But just as I looked from the boulevard window at seven thirty and saw the lights of our taxicab as it drew up to the curbing far down in the darkness below, he emerged from his room, dressed in his immaculate evening clothes, debonair as ever, smiling as though the fortunes of the night meant nothing to him one way or the other.

We descended to the taxicab and started out on the long journey to Rogers Park. DeLancey persisted, however, in chatting about a host of trivial subjects, the very discussion of which required all my self-restraint and composure. But when I touched ever so lightly on the subject of the Cordova necklace, he frowned and quickly changed the subject.

It was a quarter to nine when we rolled up Sheridan Road and turned in between the two great ornamental iron fence posts that marked the entrance to the Bascom grounds. A short drive farther over a gravel road between two tall blackthorn hedges brought us to a grating stop at the steps of the mansion itself. A second later an obsequious footman was opening the door of the cab.

So now the die was cast, for no more that evening—perhaps forever—could I have even a single secret word with DeLancey.

As I mingled with the guests in the drawing room, I tried my best to appear composed and completely at ease. Old Garrard Bascom passed from group to group, and shortly catching sight of me, standing alone and forlorn, introduced me to a pretty debutante who was to be my partner at the table. And I confess that my conversation held forth little promise of an entertaining evening for her, for my attention persisted in straying around the great room, from one individual to another.

Jewels there were a-plenty. They flashed from the earlobes of most of the women, and from the shirt bosoms of some of the men. Here and there a pearl necklace could be seen, and once I caught sight of a flashing diamond stomacher adorning the person of a huge, powdered, beruffled dowager. The Cordova necklace, however, was the one object which I seemed unable to locate.

But suddenly I caught sight of both it and its owner—and DeLancey as well, seated on a divan which was almost concealed from my view by a huge fern. Truly, there could be no doubt that the rather faded woman who sat looking up at DeLancey was the Countess of Cordova, for when she tossed her head coquettishly at his no doubt complimentary sallies, the sinuous coil around her white throat seemed to emit a veritable stream of colored fire. As for him, however, he seemed quite oblivious to it. All preliminaries, though, must come to an end. Yet, when the butler appeared in the wide doorway and announced dinner, my heart persisted in giving a strange leap. But I gave my arm to my partner and I followed the guests to the dining room.

Matters there were just as DeLancey had stated they would be. The French latticed windows were tightly shut. Plainly, then, he must carry the Cordova necklace out of the house himself if it were to be carried away at all. As I dropped into my chair I could see far, far off through the window the twinkling lights of a passing automobile on Sheridan Road, and I found myself wondering what thoughts were running through Tzhorka's head as he crouched on the wooden crossarm at the outermost edge of the estate and surveyed this laughing, chatting assemblage through the field glasses that DeLancey had mentioned.

As chance would have it, I found myself seated across from DeLancey and the countess. Several times during the first few moments I tried to catch his eye, but his whole attention seemed to be concentrated on arousing the inherent vanity of the woman who sat at his side. And since I could not hear a word of what he was saying, so great was the babble of conversation and the chink of glasses, I determined to conceal my nervousness to the best of my ability and to pay more attention to my partner.

Course after course proceeded with clockwork regularity. That the preliminary cocktails had mounted to the heads of some of the younger members was plain, for their laughter grew stronger and more strident. Old Bascom, from his position at the head of the table, beamed in turn on everyone, and the servants passed mechanically and noiselessly from chair to chair. And as nothing happened, I commenced wondering whether DeLancey had changed his plans at the last moment.

My gaze kept up a rather rapid circuit from the chattering young woman at my side, to the top of DeLancey's smoothly brushed black hair, to the string of sparkling brilliants around the countess's neck, to two of the guests who sat at the very end of the long table. Somehow I felt instinctively that they were not of the same world as the rest of those people, for the man's jaws were too strong, and his close-cropped mustache seemed to proclaim the plainclothes man to such an extent that his perfect evening dress was considerably out of keeping with the rest of him. As for the young woman at his side, she had too much of an alert, businesslike air about her, and complexion that showed too well the absence of the trained masseur—and the French maid.

Yet nothing happened.

The last course was brought to the table, and a few moments later its empty dishes were removed. Then the tinkling glasses of iced crême-de-menthe were carried in and distributed. And just as I had concluded with a sigh of relief that DeLancey had given up his scheme, he performed precisely the gesture that I had been seeing in my mind's eye for the past twenty-four hours.

He raised his right hand carelessly to the top of his head and patted his hair twice.

Almost automatically I turned my own head and gazed in the direction of the latticed window—only far out and beyond, into the darkness. It seemed that several long seconds elapsed. But when I detected a bright point of light breaking into being a quarter mile distant, I knew that Tzhorka was playing his part. Almost on the heels of this momentary flash, the lights on the chandelier above the table, as well as the tiny frosted bulbs along the fresco work on the walls, dimmed—and went completely dark.

In the profound blackness that ensued, only an intense stillness, the stillness of utter surprise, followed. Then came a chorus of exclamations, which, with a ripple or two of laughter, served to break the silence. On top of this, a number of chairs were drawn hastily back from the table, and I heard a rumble of anger from the direction of old Bascom's place.

At this juncture, a succession of peculiar, almost indistinguishable sounds struck my ear, for I, of all that assemblage, was expecting them. I heard a slight snip, then a sharp sound as though some light object had struck the opposite wall of the room. Following this came the faintest suggestion of a metallic tinkle. But on top of that a woman's alarming scream sounded forth: "My necklace—"

Almost instantly, it seemed, a match was struck on the underside of a chair, and as it flared up I saw with surprise that it was in DeLancey's hand, and that he was standing erect looking dumbfoundedly down at the countess.

"Get matches—or lights—or something, some of you men," he commanded sharply. "The countess has fainted—and her necklace is gone from her throat. Bascom, lock the doors. Don't let a man—"

But his words were interrupted by the instantaneous bursting into radiance of the great chandelier above the table.

The thirty seconds were over.

And it was just as DeLancey had cleverly announced, for, as far as I could see, he had deliberately drawn suspicion to himself in order to bolster up his own unpleasant position. The countess sat slumped up in her chair, in a dead faint. DeLancey stood above her, still holding the blackened match stub. And every guest, without exception, was staring open-mouthed at her white throat, now utterly devoid of a single diamond.

This last tableau lasted for only an instant. Then the man with the close-cropped mustache, whom I had suspected all along of being an employee of the Pinkerton system, crossed the floor rapidly and planted his back to the door, at the same time throwing back his coat and displaying a shining steel badge. Almost as quickly, a young society man next to him crossed to the French latticed window and took up a position there.

Now we were in for it. Fool, fool, fool of a DeLancey, I reflected bitterly.

Old Bascom, who had been standing bewildered at the head of the table, looking stupidly from his daughter's crumpled-up form to the man posted at the door, ejaculated: "God bless my soul, O'Rourke, what's the matter? What—"

"There's been crooked work pulled off here, Mr. Bascom," retorted that individual quickly. "Can't you see that your daughter's necklace is gone?" He turned to the group around the table. "Two of you ladies help to bring the countess out of her faint. Some of you men look under her chair. If that necklace isn't found, you'll have to step in the next room one by one and be searched." He looked down the table to the young woman who had been his partner. "Miss Kelly, I'll detail you to search the ladies if the necklace isn't on the floor."

A chorus of indignant protests arose from the ladies. The men gasped and looked from one to the other with manifest suspicion written on their faces. A number of the guests stared at DeLancey, who still stood where he was, passing his hand over his brow.

"I feel," he stammered feebly, "that this puts me in a rather peculiar light. If—if there's to be any search made, I suggest that it be made on me first. I—"

But he was interrupted by one of the male guests who pointed down the table and exclaimed: "The countess's glass of cre—"

That gentleman, however, had no opportunity to finish his statement, for the female detective suddenly broke in: "Look, ladies and gentlemen." She, too, pointed at the countess's untouched glass of crême-de-menthe. "The lady's glass of cordial is the only one on the table that's been spilled all over the cloth. It might be that—"

"God bless my soul," said old Bascom again, still trying to collect his wits, "what are you all driving at?"

I lost no time in staring at the point which Miss Kelly was indicating, and I saw what she was trying to call everyone's attention to. Just as she had announced, the green cordial in the countess's glass had slopped down the side of the fragile vessel and had made a great sticky stain around the base. And I daresay that everyone else saw it at the same time. Miss Kelly, however, hurriedly crossed around the end of the long table and hooked a businesslike finger to the bottom of the glass. A fraction of a second later I found myself picturing DeLancey's inward rage when he saw that he had been outwitted by a woman.

For as she raised her hand, something was hanging from the crook of her finger; something that might once have held all the colors of the rainbow, but which now, covered as it was with sticky green syrup, hanging pendant with the clasp opened, covered from one end to the other with crême-de-menthe, dripping green drops that seemed like emeralds being born from more emeralds, showed plainly where the Cordova necklace had gone. With no regard for the white tablecloth, she held it up so that everyone could see.

"The necklace," she stated slowly and triumphantly, "has not been stolen." She looked toward Bascom. "An apology is due your guests, Mr. Bascom."

"God bless my—" he started to say faintly for the third time. But suddenly he seemed to collect his senses. He snatched up a napkin and, unfolding it, leaned over and held it under Miss Kelly's outstretched hand. Without a word she dropped the necklace into it, and he hurriedly folded it up and placed it safely in his breast pocket. Then he turned to the stupefied butler.

"Harkins, get the countess's maid and help her to her room." He glanced angrily at O'Rourke. "O'Rourke, you've made a nasty mistake." He looked at the rest of the assemblage. "I trust, ladies and gentlemen, that you will pardon this affront to your honesty here tonight. This is surely a deplorable happening. Something seemed to have interrupted the city current supply, and in the excitement my daughter must have leaned over, with the result that the clasp of her necklace loosened and it dropped into her glass of cordial. I humbly ask the pardon of one and all of you for the whole occurrence."

With the sudden entrance of the countess's maid, the guests quickly adjourned to the drawing room, the gentlemen, apparently by mutual understanding, giving up the usual coffee and cigars. On the way out of the dining room I caught sight of DeLancey and his face appeared as black as a thundercloud. Perhaps the abrupt disclosure that Pinkerton employees were at the table, or else their crude methods in handling the situation, aroused some ire among the ladies, for cabs were called for shortly after and one by one the guests melted away.

With DeLancey I climbed into our vehicle, but nothing was said by either of us until we were rolling out of the Bascom grounds and down Sheridan Road. Then he remarked glumly: "Well?"

"Well, I consider that you were mighty lucky to escape with your liberty. Your deal proved a fiasco—just as I felt it would all the time. In fact, you might just as well have taken a megaphone and called the attention of the whole company to the countess's crême-de-menthe glass, for the stuff was slopped all over the cloth. But one thing I'd like to ask, DeLancey. Did you honestly intend to drop the necklace into the cordial glass—or was that an accident?"

He spoke fully for the first time since leaving the Bascom estate. "My dear T.B.," he said slowly, "how very, very obtuse you are. Is it possible that you don't yet know that the necklace which was fished from the countess's crême-de-menthe glass, and held up dripping and covered with the green syrup for everyone to see, was a paste duplicate that was put together by old Stein and myself in the last three days? Is it—"

But there was no need of his explaining further, for as we passed an arc-lamp and its rays flashed into the carriage, I saw something gleaming and sparkling in the palm of his hand— something that seemed to hold in leash the colors of a thousand rainbows.

BROTHERS

BY SHERWOOD ANDERSON

Douglas

(Originally published in 1921)

I am at my house in the country and it is late October. It rains. Back of my house is a forest and in front there is a road and beyond that open fields. The country is one of low hills, flattening suddenly into plains. Some twenty miles away, across the flat country, lies the huge city Chicago.

On this rainy day the leaves of the trees that line the road before my window are falling like rain, the yellow, red, and golden leaves fall straight down heavily. The rain beats them brutally down. They are denied a last golden flash across the sky. In October leaves should be carried away, out over the plains, in a wind. They should go dancing away.

Yesterday morning I arose at daybreak and went for a walk. There was a heavy fog and I lost myself in it. I went down into the plains and returned to the hills, and everywhere the fog was as a wall before me. Out of it trees sprang suddenly, grotesquely, as in a city street late at night people come suddenly out of the darkness into the circle of light under a streetlamp. Above there was the light of day forcing itself slowly into the fog. The fog moved slowly. The tops of trees moved slowly. Under the trees the fog was dense, purple. It was like smoke lying in the streets of a factory town.

An old man came up to me in the fog. I know him well. The people here call him insane. "He is a little cracked," they say.

He lives alone in a little house buried deep in the forest and has a small dog he carries always in his arms. On many mornings I have met him walking on the road and he has told me of men and women who are his brothers and sisters, his cousins, aunts, uncles, brothers-in-law. It is confusing. He cannot draw close to people near at hand so he gets hold of a name out of a newspaper and his mind plays with it. On one morning he told me he was a cousin to the man named Cox who at the time when I write is a candidate for the presidency. On another morning he told me that Caruso the singer had married a woman who was his sister-in-law. "She is my wife's sister," he said, holding the little dog close. His gray watery eyes looked appealing up to me. He wanted me to believe. "My wife was a sweet slim girl," he declared. "We lived together in a big house and in the morning walked about arm in arm. Now her sister has married Caruso the singer. He is of my family now."

As someone had told me the old man had never married, I went away wondering. One morning in early September I came upon him sitting under a tree beside a path near his house. The dog barked at me and then ran and crept into his arms. At that time the Chicago newspapers were filled with the story of a millionaire who had got into trouble with his wife because of an intimacy with an actress. The old man told me that the actress was his sister. He is sixty years old and the actress whose story appeared in the newspapers is twenty but he spoke of their childhood together. "You would not realize it to see us now but we were poor then," he said. "It's true. We lived in a little house on the side of a hill. Once when there was a storm, the wind nearly swept our house away. How the wind blew! Our father was a carpenter and he built strong houses for other people but our own house he did not build very strong!" He shook his head sorrowfully. "My sister the actress has got into trouble.

Our house is not built very strongly," he said as I went away along the path.

For a month, two months, the Chicago newspapers, which are delivered every morning in our village, have been filled with the story of a murder. A man there has murdered his wife and there seems no reason for the deed. The tale runs something like this—

The man, who is now on trial in the courts and will no doubt be hanged, worked in a bicycle factory where he was a foreman and lived with his wife and his wife's mother in an apartment on 32nd Street. He loved a girl who worked in the office of the factory where he was employed. She came from a town in Iowa and when she first got to the city lived with her aunt who has since died. To the foreman, a heavy stolid-looking man with gray eyes, she seemed the most beautiful woman in the world. Her desk was by a window at an angle of the factory, a sort of wing of the building, and the foreman, down in the shop, had a desk by another window. He sat at his desk making out sheets containing the record of the work done by each man in his department. When he looked up he could see the girl sitting at work at her desk. The notion got into his head that she was peculiarly lovely. He did not think of trying to draw close to her or of winning her love. He looked at her as one might look at a star or across a country of low hills in October when the leaves of the trees are all red and yellow gold. *She is a pure, virginal thing,* he thought vaguely. *What can she be thinking about as she sits there by the window at work?*

In fancy the foreman took the girl from Iowa home with him to his apartment on 32nd Street and into the presence of his wife and his mother-in-law. All day in the shop and during the evening at home he carried her figure about with him in his mind. As he stood by a window in his apartment and looked out toward the Illinois Central railroad tracks and beyond the tracks to the lake, the girl was there beside him. Down below women walked in the street and in every woman he saw there was something of the Iowa girl. One woman walked as she did, another made a gesture with her hand that reminded of her. All the women he saw except his wife and his mother-in-law were like the girl he had taken inside himself.

The two women in his own house puzzled and confused him. They became suddenly unlovely and commonplace. His wife in particular was like some strange unlovely growth that had attached itself to his body.

In the evening after the day at the factory he went home to his own place and had dinner. He had always been a silent man and when he did not talk no one minded. After dinner he with his wife went to a picture show. There were two children and his wife expected another. They came into the apartment and sat down. The climb up two flights of stairs had wearied his wife. She sat in a chair beside her mother groaning with weariness.

The mother-in-law was the soul of goodness. She took the place of a servant in the home and got no pay. When her daughter wanted to go to a picture show she waved her hand and smiled. "Go on," she said. "I don't want to go. I'd rather sit here." She got a book and sat reading. The little boy of nine awoke and cried. He wanted to sit on the po-po. The mother-in-law attended to that.

After the man and his wife came home the three people sat in silence for an hour or two before bedtime. The man pretended to read a newspaper. He looked at his hands. Although he had washed them carefully, grease from the bicycle frames left dark stains under the nails. He thought of the Iowa girl and of her white quick hands playing over the keys of a typewriter. He felt dirty and uncomfortable.

The girl at the factory knew the foreman had fallen in love with her and the thought excited her a little. Since her aunt's death she had gone to live in a rooming house and had nothing to do in the evening. Although the foreman meant nothing to her she could in a way use him. To her he became a symbol. Sometimes he came into the office and stood for a moment by the door. His large hands were covered with black grease. She looked at him without seeing. In his place in her imagination stood a tall slender young man. Of the foreman she saw only the gray eyes that began to burn with a strange fire. The eyes expressed eagerness, a humble and devout eagerness. In the presence of a man with such eyes she felt she need not be afraid.

She wanted a lover who would come to her with such a look in his eyes. Occasionally, perhaps once in two weeks, she stayed a little late at the office, pretending to have work that must be finished. Through the window she could see the foreman waiting. When everyone had gone she closed her desk and went into the street. At the same moment the foreman came out at the factory door.

They walked together along the street a half-dozen blocks to where she got aboard her car. The factory was in a place called South Chicago and as they went along evening was coming on. The streets were lined with small unpainted frame houses and dirty-faced children ran screaming in the dusty roadway. They crossed over a bridge. Two abandoned coal barges lay rotting in the stream.

He went by her side walking heavily and striving to conceal his hands. He had scrubbed them carefully before leaving the factory but they seemed to him like heavy dirty pieces of waste matter hanging at his side. Their walking together happened but a few times and during one summer. "It's hot," he said. He never spoke to her of anything but the weather. "It's hot," he said. "I think it may rain."

She dreamed of the lover who would some time come, a tall fair young man, a rich man owning houses and lands. The workingman who walked beside her had nothing to do with her conception of love. She walked with him, stayed at the office until the others had gone to walk unobserved with him because of his eyes, because of the eager thing in his eyes that was at the same time humble, that bowed down to her. In his presence there was no danger, could be no danger. He would never attempt to approach too closely, to touch her with his hands. She was safe with him.

In his apartment in the evening the man sat under the electric light with his wife and his mother-in-law. In the next room his two children were asleep. In a short time his wife would have another child. He had been with her to a picture show and in a short time they would get into bed together.

He would lie awake thinking, would hear the creaking of the springs of a bed where, in another room, his mother-in-law was crawling between the sheets. Life was too intimate. He would lie awake eager, expectant—expecting what?

Nothing. Presently one of the children would cry. It wanted to get out of bed and sit on the po-po. Nothing strange or unusual or lovely would or could happen. Life was too close, intimate. Nothing that could happen in the apartment could in any way stir him; the things his wife might say, her occasional half-hearted outbursts of passion, the goodness of his mother-in-law who did the work of a servant without pay—

He sat in the apartment under the electric light pretending to read a newspaper—thinking. He looked at his hands. They were large, shapeless, a workingman's hands.

The figure of the girl from Iowa walked about the room. With her he went out of the apartment and walked in silence through miles of streets. It was not necessary to say words. He walked with her by a sea, along the crest of a mountain. The night was clear and silent and the stars shone. She also was a star. It was not necessary to say words.

Her eyes were like stars and her lips were like soft hills rising out of dim, starlit plains. *She is unattainable, she is far off like the stars,* he thought. *She is unattainable like the stars but unlike the stars she breathes, she lives, like myself she has being.*

One evening, some six weeks ago, the man who worked as foreman in the bicycle factory killed his wife and he is now in the courts being tried for murder. Every day the newspapers are filled with the story. On the evening of the murder he had taken his wife as usual to a picture show and they started home at nine. On 32nd Street, at a corner near their apartment building, the figure of a man darted suddenly out of an alleyway and then darted back again. The incident may have put the idea of killing his wife into the man's head.

They got to the entrance to the apartment building and stepped into a dark hallway. Then quite suddenly and apparently without thought the man took a knife out of his pocket. *Suppose that man who darted into the alleyway had intended to kill us,* he thought. Opening the knife he whirled about and struck at his wife. He struck twice, a dozen times—madly. There was a scream and his wife's body fell.

The janitor had neglected to light the gas in the lower hallway. Afterwards, the foreman decided that was the reason he did it, that and the fact that the dark slinking figure of a man darted out of an alleyway and then darted back again. *Surely,* he told himself, *I could never have done it had the gas been lighted.*

He stood in the hallway thinking. His wife was dead and

with her had died her unborn child. There was a sound of doors opening in the apartments above. For several minutes nothing happened. His wife and her unborn child were dead—that was all.

He ran upstairs thinking quickly. In the darkness on the lower stairway he had put the knife back into his pocket and, as it turned out later, there was no blood on his hands or on his clothes. The knife he later washed carefully in the bathroom, when the excitement had died down a little. He told everyone the same story. "There has been a holdup," he explained. "A man came slinking out of an alleyway and followed me and my wife home. He followed us into the hallway of the building and there was no light. The janitor has neglected to light the gas." Well—there had been a struggle and in the darkness his wife had been killed. He could not tell how it had happened. "There was no light. The janitor has neglected to light the gas," he kept saying.

For a day or two they did not question him specially and he had time to get rid of the knife. He took a long walk and threw it away into the river in South Chicago where the two abandoned coal barges lay rotting under the bridge, the bridge he had crossed when on the summer evenings he walked to the streetcar with the girl who was virginal and pure, who was far off and unattainable, like a star and yet not like a star.

And then he was arrested and right away he confessed— told everything. He said he did not know why he killed his wife and was careful to say nothing of the girl at the office. The newspapers tried to discover the motive for the crime. They are still trying. Someone had seen him on the few evenings when he walked with the girl and she was dragged into the affair and had her picture printed in the papers. That has been annoying for her as of course she has been able to prove she had nothing to do with the man.

* * *

Yesterday morning a heavy fog lay over our village here at the edge of the city and I went for a long walk in the early morning. As I returned out of the lowlands into our hill country I met the old man whose family has so many and such strange ramifications. For a time he walked beside me holding the little dog in his arms. It was cold and the dog whined and shivered. In the fog the old man's face was indistinct. It moved slowly back and forth with the fog banks of the upper air and with the tops of trees. He spoke of the man who has killed his wife and whose name is being shouted in the pages of the city newspapers that come to our village each morning. As he walked beside me he launched into a long tale concerning a life he and his brother, who has now become a murderer, once lived together. "He is my brother," he said over and over, shaking his head. He seemed afraid I would not believe. There was a fact that must be established. "We were boys together, that man and I," he began again. "You see, we played together in a barn back of our father's house. Our father went away to sea in a ship. That is the way our names became confused. You understand that. We have different names, but we are brothers. We had the same father. We played together in a barn back of our father's house. For hours we lay together in the hay in the barn and it was warm there."

In the fog the slender body of the old man became like a little gnarled tree. Then it became a thing suspended in air. It swung back and forth like a body hanging on the gallows. The face beseeched me to believe the story the lips were trying to tell. In my mind everything concerning the relationship of men and women became confused, a muddle. The spirit of the man who had killed his wife came into the body of the little old man there by the roadside.

It was striving to tell me the story it would never be able to tell in the courtroom in the city, in the presence of the judge. The whole story of mankind's loneliness, of the effort to reach out to unattainable beauty, tried to get itself expressed from the lips of a mumbling old man, crazed with loneliness, who stood by the side of a country road on a foggy morning holding a little dog in his arms.

The arms of the old man held the dog so closely that it began to whine with pain. A sort of convulsion shook his body. The soul seemed striving to wrench itself out of the body, to fly away through the fog, down across the plain to the city, to the singer, the politician, the millionaire, the murderer, to its brothers, cousins, sisters, down in the city. The intensity of the old man's desire was terrible and in sympathy my body began to tremble. His arms tightened about the body of the little dog so that it cried with pain. I stepped forward and tore the arms away and the dog fell to the ground and lay whining. No doubt it had been injured. Perhaps ribs had been crushed. The old man stared at the dog lying at his feet as in the hallway of the apartment building the worker from the bicycle factory had stared at his dead wife. "We are brothers," he said again. "We have different names but we are brothers. Our father, you understand, went off to sea."

I am sitting in my house in the country and it rains. Before my eyes the hills fall suddenly away and there are the flat plains and beyond the plains the city. An hour ago the old man of the house in the forest went past my door and the little dog was not with him. It may be that as we talked in the fog he crushed the life out of his companion. It may be that the dog like the workman's wife and her unborn child is now dead. The leaves of the trees that line the road before my window are falling like rain—the yellow, red, and golden leaves fall straight down, heavily. The rain beat them brutally down. They are denied a last golden flash across the sky. In October leaves should be carried away, out over the plains, in a wind. They should go dancing away.

KADDISH FOR THE KID

BY MAX ALLAN COLLINS

West Town

(Originally published in 1998)

The first operative I ever took on in the A-1 Detective Agency was Stanley Gross. I hadn't been in business for even a year—it was summer of '33—and was in no shape to be adding help. But the thing was—Stanley had a car.

Stanley had a '28 Ford coupe, to be exact, and a yen to be a detective. I had a paying assignment, requiring wheels, and a yen to make a living.

So it was that at three o'clock in the morning, on that unseasonably cool summer evening, I was sitting in the front seat of Stanley's Ford, in front of Goldblatt's department store on West Chicago Avenue, sipping coffee out of a paper cup, waiting to see if anybody came along with a brick or a gun.

I'd been hired two weeks before by the manager of the downtown Goldblatt's on State, just two blocks from my office at Van Buren and Plymouth. Goldblatt's was sort of a working-class Marshall Field's, with six department stores scattered around the Chicago area in various white ethnic neighborhoods.

The stores were good-size—two floors taking up as much as half a block—and the display windows were impressive enough; but once you got inside, it was like the pushcarts of Maxwell Street had been emptied and organized.

I bought my socks and underwear at the downtown Goldblatt's, but that wasn't how Nathan Heller—me—got hired.

I knew Katie Mulhaney, the manager's secretary; I'd bumped into her on one of my socks-and-underwear-buying expeditions, and it blossomed into a friendship. A warm friendship.

Anyway, the manager—Herman Cohen—had summoned me to his office, where he filled me in. His desk was cluttered, but he was neat—moon-faced, mustached, bow- (and fit-to-be) tied.

"Maybe you've seen the stories in the papers," he said in a machine-gun burst of words, "about this reign of terror we've been suffering."

"Sure," I said.

Goldblatt's wasn't alone; every leading department store was getting hit—stench bombs set off, acid sprayed over merchandise, bricks tossed from cars to shatter plate-glass windows.

He thumbed his mustache; frowned. "Have you heard of 'Boss' Rooney? John Rooney?"

"No."

"Well, he's secretary of the Circular Distributors Union. Over the past two years, Mr. Goldblatt has provided Rooney's union with over three thousand dollars of business—primarily to discourage trouble at our stores."

"This union—these are guys that hand out ad fliers?"

"Yes. Yes, and now Rooney has demanded that Mr. Goldblatt order three hundred of our own sales and ad people to join his union—at a rate of twenty-five cents a day."

My late father had been a die-hard union guy, so I knew a little bit about this sort of thing. "Mr. Cohen, none of the unions in town collect daily dues."

"This one does. They've even been outlawed by the AFL, Mr. Heller. Mr. Goldblatt feels Rooney is nothing short of a racketeer."

"It's an extortion scam, all right. What do you want me to do?"

"Our own security staff is stretched to the limit. We're getting *some* support from State's Attorney Courtney and his people. But they can only do so much. So we've taken on a small army of night watchmen, and are fleshing out the team with private detectives. Miss Mulhaney recommended you."

Katie knew a good dick when she saw one.

"Swell. When do I start?"

"Immediately. Of course, you do have a car?"

"Of course," I lied. I also said I'd like to put one of my "top" operatives on the assignment with me, and that was fine with Cohen, who was in a more-the-merrier mood where beefing up security was concerned.

Stanley Gross was from Douglas Park, my old neighborhood. His parents were bakers two doors down from my father's bookstore on South Homan. Stanley was a good eight years younger than me, so I remembered him mostly as a pestering kid.

But he'd grown into a tall, good-looking young man—a brown-haired, brown-eyed six-footer who'd been a star football and basketball player in high school. Like me, he went to Crane Junior College; unlike me, he finished.

I guess I'd always been sort of a hero to him. About six months before, he'd started dropping by my office to chew the fat. Business was so lousy, a little company—even from a fresh-faced college boy—was welcome.

We'd sit in the deli restaurant below my office and sip coffee and gnaw on bagels and he'd tell me this embarrassing shit about my being somebody he'd always looked up to.

"Gosh, Nate, when you made the police force, I thought that was just about the keenest thing."

He really did talk that way—*gosh, keen*. I told you I was desperate for company.

He brushed a thick comma of brown hair away and grinned in a goofy boyish way; it was endearing, and nauseating. "When I was a kid, coming into your pop's bookstore, you pointed me toward those Nick Carters, and Sherlock Holmes books. Gave me the bug. I *had* to be a detective!"

But the kid was too young to get on the force, and his family didn't have the kind of money or connections it took to get a slot on the PD.

"When you quit," he said, "I admired you so. Standing up to corruption—and in *this* town! Imagine."

Imagine. My leaving the force had little to do with my "standing up to corruption"—after all, graft was high on my list of reasons for joining in the first place—but I said nothing, not wanting to shatter the child's dreams.

"If you ever need an op, I'm your man!"

He said this thousands of times in those six months or so. And he actually did get some security work, through a couple of other, larger agencies. But his dream was to be my partner.

Owning that Ford made his dream come temporarily true.

For two weeks, we'd been living the exciting life of the private eye: sitting in the coupe in front of the Goldblatt's store at Ashland and Chicago, waiting for window smashers to show. Or not.

The massive gray-stone department store was like the courthouse of commerce on this endless street of storefronts; the other businesses were smaller—resale shops, hardware stores, pawn shops, your occasional Polish deli. During the day, things were popping here. Now, there was just us—me draped across the front seat, Stanley draped across the back—and the glow of neons and a few pools of light on the sidewalks from streetlamps.

"You know," Stanley said, "this isn't as exciting as I pictured."

"Just a week ago you were all excited about 'packing a rod.'"

"You're making fun of me."

"That's right." I finished my coffee, crumpled the cup, tossed it on the floor.

"I guess a gun is nothing to feel good about."

"Right again."

I was stretched out with my shoulders against the rider's door; in back, he was stretched out just the opposite. This enabled us to maintain eye contact. Not that I wanted to, particularly.

"Nate . . . if you hear me snoring, wake me up."

"You tired, kid?"

"Yeah. Ate too much. Today . . . well, today was my birthday."

"No kidding! Well, happy birthday, kid."

"My pa made the keenest cake. Say, I . . . I'm sorry I didn't you invite you or anything."

"That's okay."

"It was a surprise party. Just my family—a few friends I went to high school and college with."

"It's okay."

"But there's cake left. You want to stop by Pa's store tomorrow and have a slice with me?"

"We'll see, kid."

"You remember my pa's pastries. Can't beat 'em."

I grinned. "Best on the West Side. You talked me into it. Go ahead and catch a few winks. Nothing's happening."

And nothing was. The street was an empty ribbon of concrete. But about five minutes later, a car came barreling down that concrete ribbon, right down the middle; I sat up.

"What is it, Nate?"

"A drunk, I think. He's weaving a little . . ."

It was a maroon Plymouth coupe; and it was headed right our way.

"Christ!" I said, and dug under my arm for the nine millimeter.

The driver was leaning out the window of the coupe, but whether man or woman I couldn't tell—the headlights of the car, still a good thirty feet away, were blinding.

The night exploded and so did our windshield.

Glass rained on me as I hit the floor; I could hear the roar of the Plymouth's engine, and came back up, gun in hand, saw the maroon coupe bearing down on us, saw a silver swan on the radiator cap, and cream-colored wheels, but people in the car going by were a blur, and as I tried to get a better look, orange fire burst from a gun and I ducked down, hitting the glass-littered floor. Another four shots riddled the car and the night, the side windows cracking, and behind us the plate glass of display windows was fragmenting, falling to the pavement like sheets of ice.

Then the Plymouth was gone.

So was Stanley.

The first bullet must have got him. He must have sat up to get a look at the oncoming car and took the slug head-on; it threw him back, and now he still seemed to be lounging there, against the now-spiderwebbed window, precious "rod" tucked under his arm; his brown eyes were open, his mouth too, and his expression was almost—not quite—surprised.

I don't think he had time to be truly surprised before he died.

There'd been only time enough for him to take the bullet in the head, the dime-size entry wound parting the comma of brown hair, streaking the birthday boy's boyish face with blood.

Within an hour I was being questioned by Sergeant Charles

Pribyl, who was attached to the state's attorney's office. Pribyl was a decent enough guy, even if he did work under Captain Daniel "Tubbo" Gilbert, who was probably the crookedest cop in town. Which in this town was saying something.

Pribyl had a good reputation, however; and I'd encountered him, from time to time, back when I was working the pickpocket detail. He had soft, gentle features and dark alert eyes.

Normally, he was an almost dapper dresser, but his tie seemed hastily knotted, his suit and hat looked as if he'd thrown them on—which he probably had; he was responding to a call at four in the morning, after all.

He was looking in at Stanley, who hadn't been moved; we were waiting for a coroner's physician to show. Several other plainclothes officers and half a dozen uniformed cops were milling around, footsteps crunching on the glass-strewn sidewalk.

"Just a kid," Pribyl said, stepping away from the Ford. "Just a damn kid." He shook his head. He nodded to me and I followed him over by a shattered display window.

He cocked his head. "How'd you happen to have such a young operative working with you?"

I explained about the car being Stanley's.

He had an expression you only see on cops: sad and yet detached. His eyes tightened.

"How—and why—did stink bombs and window smashing escalate into bloody murder?"

"You expect me to answer that, sergeant?"

"No. I expect you to tell me what happened. And, Heller— I don't go into this with any preconceived notions about you. Some people on the force—even some good ones, like John Stege—hold it against you, the Lang and Miller business."

They were two crooked cops I'd recently testified against.

"Not me," he said firmly. "Apples don't come rottener than those two bastards. I just want you to know what kind of footing we're on."

"I appreciate that."

I filled him in, including a description of the murder vehicle, but couldn't describe the people within at all. I wasn't even sure how many of them there were.

"You get the license number?"

"No, damnit."

"Why not? You saw the car well enough."

"Them shooting at me interfered."

He nodded. "Fair enough. Shit. Too bad you didn't get a look at 'em."

"Too bad. But you know who to go calling on."

"How's that?"

I thrust a finger toward the car. "That's Boss Rooney's work—maybe not personally, but he had it done. You know about the Circular Union and the hassles they been giving Goldblatt's, right?"

Pribyl nodded, somewhat reluctantly; he liked me well enough, but I was a private detective. He didn't like having me in the middle of police business.

"Heller, we've been keeping the union headquarters under surveillance for six weeks now. I saw Rooney there today, myself, from the apartment across the way we rented."

"So did anyone leave the union hall tonight? Before the shooting, say around three?"

He shook his head glumly. "We've only been maintaining our watch during department-store business hours. The problem of night attacks is where hired hands like you come in."

"Okay." I sighed. "I won't blame you if you don't blame me."

"Deal."

"So what's next?"

"You can go on home." He glanced toward the Ford. "We'll take care of this."

"You want me to tell the family?"

"Were you close to them?"

"Not really. They're from my old neighborhood, is all."

"I'll handle it."

"You sure?"

"I'm sure." He patted my shoulder. "Go home."

I started to go, then turned back. "When are you going to pick up Rooney?"

"I'll have to talk to the state's attorney, first. But my guess? Tomorrow. We'll raid the union hall tomorrow."

"Mind if I come along?"

"Wouldn't be appropriate, Heller."

"The kid worked for me. He got killed working for me."

"No. We'll handle it. Go home! Get some sleep."

"I'll go home," I said.

A chill breeze was whispering.

"But the sleep part," I said, "that I can't promise you."

The next afternoon I was having a beer in a booth in the bar next to the deli below my office. Formerly a blind pig—a speakeasy that looked shuttered from the street (even now, you entered through the deli)—it was a business investment of fighter Barney Ross, as was reflected by the framed boxing photos decorating the dark, smoky little joint.

I grew up with Barney on the West Side. Since my family hadn't practiced Judaism in several generations, I was shabbas goy for Barney's very Orthodox folks, a kid doing chores and errands for them from Friday sundown through Saturday.

But we didn't become really good friends, Barney and me,

till we worked Maxwell Street as pullers—teenage street bark-
ers who literally pulled customers into stores for bargains they
had no interest in.

Barney, a roughneck made good, was a real Chicago success story. He owned this entire building, and my office—
which, with its Murphy bed, was also my residence—was space
he traded me for keeping an eye on the place. I was his night
watchman, unless a paying job like Goldblatt's came along to
take precedence.

The lightweight champion of the world was having a beer,
too, in that back booth; he wore a cheerful blue and white
sportshirt and a dour expression.

"I'm sorry about your young pal," Barney said.

"He wasn't a 'pal,' really. Just an acquaintance."

"I don't know that Douglas Park crowd myself. But to think
of a kid, on his twenty-first birthday . . ." His mildly battered
bulldog countenance looked woeful. "He have a girl?"

"Yeah."

"What's her name?"

"I don't remember."

"Poor little bastard. When's the funeral?"

"I don't know."

"You're going, aren't you?"

"No. I don't really know the family that well. I'm sending
flowers."

He looked at me with as long a face as a round-faced guy
could muster. "You oughta go. He was working for you when
he got it."

"I'd be intruding. I'd be out of place."

"You should do kaddish for the kid, Nate."

A mourner's prayer.

"Jesus Christ, Barney, I'm no Jew. I haven't been in a synagogue more than half a dozen times in my life, and then it was social occasions."

"Maybe you don't consider yourself a Jew, with that Irish mug of yours your ma bequeathed you . . . but you're gonna have a rude awakening one of these days, boyo."

"What do you mean?"

"There's plenty of people you're just another 'kike' to, believe you me."

I sipped the beer. "Nudge me when you get to the point."

"You owe this kid kaddish, Nate."

"Hell, doesn't that go on for months? I don't know the lingo. And if you think I'm putting on some stupid beanie and . . ."

There was a tap on my shoulder. Buddy Gold, the bartender, an ex-pug, leaned in to say, "You got a call."

I went behind the bar to use the phone. It was Sergeant Lou Sapperstein at Central Headquarters in the Loop; Lou had been my boss on the pickpocket detail. I'd called him this morning with a request.

"Tubbo's coppers made their raid this morning, around nine," Lou said. Sapperstein was a hard-nosed, balding cop of about forty-five and one of the few friends I had left on the PD.

"And?"

"And the union hall was empty, 'cept for a bartender. Pribyl and his partner Bert Gray took a whole squad up there, but Rooney and his boys had flew the coop."

"Fuck. Somebody tipped them."

"Are you surprised?"

"Yeah. Surprised I expected the cops to play it straight for a change. You wouldn't have the address of that union, by any chance?"

"No, but I can get it. Hold a second."

A sweet union scam like the Circular Distributors had *Out-*

fit written all over it—and Captain Tubbo Gilbert, head of the state prosecutor's police, was known as the richest cop in Chicago. Tubbo was a bagman and police fixer so deep in Frank Nitti's pocket he had Nitti's lint up his nose.

Lou was back: "It's at 7 North Racine. That's Madison and Racine."

"Well, hell—that's spitting distance from Skid Row."

"Yeah. So?"

"So that explains the scam—that 'union' takes hobos and makes day laborers out of them. No wonder they charge daily dues. It's just bums handing out ad circulars . . ."

"I'd say that's a good guess, Nate."

I thanked Lou and went back to the booth, where Barney was brooding about what a louse his friend Heller was.

"I got something to do," I told him.

"What?"

"My kind of kaddish."

Less than two miles from the prominent department stores of the Loop they'd been fleecing, the Circular Distributors Union had their headquarters on the doorstep of Skid Row and various Hoovervilles. This Madison Street area, just north of Greek Town, was a seedy mix of flophouses, marginal apartment buildings, and storefront businesses, mostly bars. Union headquarters was on the second floor of a two-story brick building whose bottom floor was a plumbing supply outlet.

I went up the squeaking stairs and into the union hall, a big high-ceilinged open room with a few glassed-in offices toward the front, to the left and right. Ceiling fans whirred lazily, stirring stale smoky air; folding chairs and card tables were scattered everywhere on the scuffed wooden floor, and seated at some were unshaven, tattered "members" of the union. Across the far end stretched a bar, behind which a burly blond guy in rolled-up white shirt sleeves was polishing a glass. More hobos leaned against the bar, having beers.

I ordered a mug from the bartender, who had a massive skull and tiny dark eyes and a sullen kiss of a mouth.

I salted the brew as I tossed him a nickel. "Hear you had a raid here this morning."

He ignored the question. "This hall's for union members only."

"Jeez, it looks like a saloon."

"Well, it's a union hall. Drink up and move along."

"There's a fin in it for you, if you answer a few questions."

He thought that over; leaned in. "Are you a cop?"

"No. Private."

"Who hired you?"

"Goldblatt's."

He thought some more. The tiny eyes narrowed. "Let's hear the questions."

"What do you know about the Gross kid's murder?"

"Not a damn thing."

"Was Rooney here last night?"

"Far as I know, he was home in bed asleep."

"Know where he lives?"

"No."

"You don't know where your boss lives."

"No. All I know is he's a swell guy. He don't have nothin' to do with these department-store shakedowns the cops are tryin' to pin on him. It's union-busting, is what it is."

"Union-busting." I had a look around at the bleary-eyed clientele in their patched clothes. "You have to be a union first, 'fore you can get busted up."

"What's *that* supposed to mean?"

"It means this is a scam. Rooney pulls in winos, gets 'em

day-labor jobs for $3.25 a day, then they come up here to pay their daily dues of a quarter, and blow the rest on beer or booze. In other words, first the bums pass out ad fliers, then they come here and just plain pass out."

"I think you better scram. Otherwise I'm gonna have to throw you down the stairs."

I finished the beer. "I'm leaving. But you know what? I'm not gonna give you that fin. I'm afraid you'd just drink it up."

I could feel his eyes on my back as I left, but I'd have heard him if he came out from around the bar. I was starting down the stairs when the door below opened and Sergeant Pribyl, looking irritated, came up to meet me on the landing, halfway. He looked more his usual dapper self, but his eyes were black-bagged.

"What's the idea, Heller?"

"I just wanted to come bask in the reflected glory of your triumphant raid this morning."

"What's that supposed to mean?"

"It means when Tubbo's boys are on the case, the Outfit gets advance notice."

He winced. "That's not the way it was. I don't know why Rooney and Berry and the others blew. But nobody in our office warned 'em off."

"Are you sure?"

He clearly wasn't. "Look, I can't have you messing in this. We're on the damn case, okay? We're maintaining surveillance from across the way . . . that's how we spotted you."

"Peachy. Twenty-four-hour surveillance now?"

"No." He seemed embarrassed. "Just day shift."

"You want some help?"

"What do you mean?"

"Loan me the key to your stakeout crib. I'll keep night-watch. Got a phone in there?"

"Yeah."

"I'll call you if Rooney shows. You got pictures of him and the others you can give me?"

"Well . . ."

"What's the harm? Or would Tubbo lower the boom on you, if you really did your job?"

He sighed. Scratched his head and came to a decision. "This is unofficial, okay? But there's a possibility the door to that apartment's gonna be left unlocked tonight."

"Do tell."

"Third floor—301." He raised a cautionary finger. "We'll try this for one night . . . no showboating, okay? Call me if one of 'em shows."

"Sure. You tried their homes?"

He nodded. "Nothing. Rooney lives on North Ridgeland in Oak Park. Four kids. Wife's a pleasant, matronly type."

"Fat, you mean."

"She hasn't seen Rooney for several weeks. She says he's away from home a lot."

"Keeping a guard posted there?"

"Yeah. And that *is* twenty-four-hour." He sighed, shook his head. "Heller, there's a lot about this case that doesn't make sense."

"Such as?"

"That maroon Plymouth. We never saw a car like that in the entire six weeks we had the union hall under surveillance. Rooney drives a blue LaSalle coupe."

"Any maroon Plymouths reported stolen?"

He shook his head. "And it hasn't turned up abandoned, either. They must still have the car."

"Is Rooney *that* stupid?"

"We can always hope," Pribyl said.

* * *

I sat in an easy chair with sprung springs by the window in room 301 of the residential hotel across from the union hall. It wasn't a flophouse cage, but it wasn't a suite at the Drake, either. Anyway, in the dark it looked fine. I had a flask of rum to keep me company, and the breeze fluttering the sheer, frayed curtains remained unseasonably cool.

Thanks to some photos Pribyl left me, I now knew what Rooney looked like: a good-looking, oval-faced smoothie, in his midforties, just starting to lose his dark, slicked-back hair; his eyes were hooded, his mouth soft, sensual, sullen. There were also photos of the union's so-called business agent Henry Berry, a mousy little guy with glasses, and pockmarked, cold-eyed Herbert Arnold, VP of the union.

But none of them stopped by the union hall—only a steady stream of winos and bums went in and out.

Then, around seven, I spotted somebody who didn't fit the profile. It was a guy I knew—a fellow private op, Eddie McGowan, a Pinkerton man, in uniform, meaning he was on night-watchman duty. A number of the merchants along Madison must have pitched in for his services.

I left the stakeout and waited down on the street, in front of the plumbing supply store, for Eddie to come back out. It didn't take long—maybe ten minutes.

"Heller!" he said. He was a skinny, tow-haired guy in his late twenties with a bad complexion and a good outlook. "What no good are you up to?"

"The Goldblatt's shooting. That kid they killed was working with me."

"Oh! I didn't know! Heard about the shooting, of course, but didn't read the papers or anything. So you were involved in that? No kidding."

"No kidding. You on watchman duty?"

"Yeah. Up and down the street here, all night."

"Including the union hall?"

"Sure." He grinned. "I usually stop up for a free drink 'bout this time of night."

"Can you knock off for a couple of minutes? For another free drink?"

"Sure!"

Soon we were in a smoky booth in back of a bar and Eddie was having a boilermaker on me.

"See anything unusual last night," I asked, "around the union hall?"

"Well . . . I had a drink there, around two o'clock in the morning. *That* was a first."

"A drink? Don't they close earlier than that?"

"Yeah. Around eleven. That's all the longer it takes for their 'members' to lap up their daily dough."

"So what were you doing up there at two?"

He shrugged. "Well, I noticed the lights was on upstairs, so I unlocked the street-level door and went up. Figured Alex . . . that's the bartender, Alex Davidson . . . might have forgot to turn out the lights, 'fore he left. The door up there was locked, but then Mr. Rooney opened it up and told me to come on in."

"Why would he do that?"

"He was feelin' pretty good. Looked like he was workin' on a bender. Anyway, he insists I have a drink with him. I says sure. Turns out Davidson is still there."

"No kidding?"

"No kidding. So Alex serves me a beer. Berry—the union's business agent—he was there too. He was in his cups, also. So was Rooney's wife—she was there, and also feeling giddy."

I thought about Pribyl's description of Mrs. Rooney as a

matronly woman with four kids. "His *wife* was there?"

"Yeah, the lucky stiff."

"Lucky?"

"You should see the dame! Good-lookin' tomato with big dark eyes and a nice shape on her."

"About how old?"

"Young. Twenties. It'd take the sting out of a ball and chain, I can tell you that."

"Eddie . . . here's a fin."

"Heller, the beer's enough!"

"The fin is for telling this same story to Sergeant Pribyl of the state's attorney's coppers."

"Oh. Okay."

"But do it tomorrow."

He smirked. "Okay. I got rounds to make, anyway."

So did I.

At around eleven fifteen, bartender Alex Davidson was leaving the union hall; his back was turned, as he was locking the street-level door, and I put my nine millimeter in it.

"Hi, Alex," I said. "Don't turn around, unless you prefer being gut-shot."

"If it's a stickup, all I got's a couple bucks. Take 'em and bug off!"

"No such luck. Leave that door unlocked. We're gonna step back inside."

He grunted and opened the door and we stepped inside.

"Now we're going up the stairs," I said, and we did, in the dark, the wooden steps whining under our weight. He was a big man; I'd have had my work cut out for me—if I hadn't had the gun.

We stopped at the landing where earlier I had spoken to Sergeant Pribyl. "Here's fine," I said.

I allowed him to face me in the near-dark.

He sneered. "You're that private dick."

"I'm sure you mean that in the nicest way. Let me tell you a little more about me. See, we're going to get to know each other, Alex."

"Like hell."

I slapped him with the nine millimeter.

He wiped blood off his mouth and looked at me with hate, but also with fear. And he made no more smart-ass remarks.

"I'm the private dick whose twenty-one-year-old partner got shot in the head last night."

Now the fear was edging out the hate; he knew he might die in this dark stairwell.

"I know you were here with Rooney and Berry and the broad, last night, serving up drinks as late as two in the morning," I said. "Now, you're going to tell me the whole story—or you're the one who's getting tossed down the fucking stairs."

He was trembling now; a big hulk of a man trembling with fear. "I didn't have anything to do with the murder. Not a damn thing!"

"Then why cover for Rooney and the rest?"

"You saw what they're capable of!"

"Take it easy, Alex. Just tell the story."

Rooney had come into the office about noon the day of the shooting; he had started drinking and never stopped. Berry and several other union "officers" arrived and angry discussions about being under surveillance by the state's attorney's cops were accompanied by a lot more drinking.

"The other guys left around five, but Rooney and Berry, they just hung around drinking all evening. Around midnight, Rooney handed me a phone number he jotted on a matchbook and gave it to me to call for him. It was a Berwyn number. A woman answered. I handed him the phone and he said to her, *Bring one.*"

"One what?" I asked.

"I'm gettin' to that. She showed up around one o'clock— good-looking dame with black hair and eyes so dark they coulda been black too."

"Who was she?"

"I don't know. Never saw her before. She took a gun out of her purse and gave it to Rooney."

"That was what he asked her to bring."

"I guess. It was a thirty-eight revolver, a Colt, I think. Any-way, Rooney and Berry were both pretty drunk; I don't know what *her* excuse was. So Rooney takes the gun and says, *We got a job to pull at Goldblatt's. We're gonna throw some slugs at the windows and watchmen.*"

"How did the girl react?"

He swallowed. "She laughed. She said, *I'll go along and watch the fun.* Then they all went out."

Jesus.

Finally I said, "What did you do?"

"They told me to wait for 'em. Keep the bar open. They came back in, laughing like hyenas. Rooney says to me, *You want to see the way he keeled over?* And I says, *Who?* And he says, *The guard at Goldblatt's.* Berry laughs and says, *We really let him have it.*"

"That kid was twenty-one, Alex. It was his goddamn birthday."

The bartender was looking down. "They laughed and joked about it till Berry passed out. About six in the morning, Rooney has me pile Berry in a cab. Rooney and the twist slept in his of-fice for maybe an hour. Then they came out, looking sober and kind of . . . scared. He warned me not to tell anybody what I seen, unless I wanted to trade my job for a morgue slab."

"Colorful. Tell me, Alex. You got that girl's phone number in Berwyn?"

"I think it's upstairs. You can put that gun away. I'll help you."

It was dark, but I could see his face well enough; the big man's eyes looked damp. The fear was gone. Something else was in its place. Shame? Something.

We went upstairs, he unlocked the union hall and, under the bar, found the matchbook with the number written inside: *Berwyn 2981.*

"You want a drink before you go?" he asked.

"You know," I said, "I think I'll pass."

I went back to my office to use the reverse-listing phone book that told me Berwyn 2981 was Rosalie Rizzo's number; and that Rosalie Rizzo lived at 6348 West 13th Street in Berwyn.

First thing the next morning, I borrowed Barney's Hupmobile and drove out to Berwyn, the clean, tidy hunky suburb populated in part by the late Mayor Cermak's patronage people. But finding a Rosalie Rizzo in this largely Czech and Bohemian area came as no surprise: Capone's Cicero was a stone's throw away.

The woman's address was a three-story brick apartment building, but none of the mailboxes in the vestibule bore her name. I found the janitor and gave him Rosalie Rizzo's description. It sounded like Mrs. Riggs to him.

"She's a doll," the janitor said. He was heavy-set and needed a shave; he licked his thick lips as he thought about her. "Ain't seen her since yesterday noon."

That was about nine hours after Stanley was killed.

He continued: "Her and her husband was going to the

country, she said. Didn't expect to be back for a couple of weeks."

Her husband.

"What'll a look around their apartment cost me?"

He licked his lips again. "Two bucks?"

Two bucks it was; the janitor used his passkey and left me to it. The well-appointed little apartment included a canary that sang in its gilded cage, a framed photo of slick Boss Rooney on an end table, and a closet containing two sawed-off shotguns and a repeating rifle.

I had barely started to poke around when I had company: a slender, gray-haired woman in a flowered print dress.

"Oh!" she said, coming in the door she'd unlocked.

"Can I help you?" I asked.

"Who are you?" Her voice had the lilt of an Italian accent.

Under the circumstances, the truth seemed prudent. "A private detective."

"My daughter is not here! She and her-a husband, they go to vacation. Up north some-a-where. I just-a come to feed the canary!"

"Please don't be frightened. Do you know where she's gone, exactly?"

"No. But . . . maybe my husband do. He is-a downstairs . . ."

She went to a window, threw it open, and yelled something frantically down in Italian.

I eased her aside in time to see a heavy-set man jump into a maroon Plymouth with a silver swan on the radiator cap, and cream-colored wheels, and squeal away.

And when I turned, the slight gray-haired woman was just as gone. Only she hadn't squealed.

The difference, this time, was a license number for the maroon coupe; I'd seen it: 519-836. In a diner I made a call to Lou Sapperstein, who made a call to the motor vehicle bureau, and phoned back with the scoop: the Plymouth was licensed to Rosalie Rizzo, but the address was different—2848 South Cuyler Avenue, in Berwyn.

The bungalow was typical for Berwyn—a tidy little frame house on a small, perfect lawn. My guess was this was her folks' place. In back was a small matching, but unattached garage, on the alley. Peeking in the garage windows, I saw the maroon coupe and smiled.

"Is Rosalie in trouble again?"

The voice was female, sweet, young.

I turned and saw a slender, almost beautiful teenage girl with dark eyes and bouncy, dark, shoulder-length hair. She wore a navy-blue sailor-ish playsuit. Her pretty white legs were bare.

"Are you Rosalie's sister?"

"Yes. Is she in trouble?"

"What makes you say that?"

"I just know Rosalie, that's all. That man isn't really her husband, is he? That Mr. Riggs."

"No."

"Are you here about her accident?"

"No. Where is she?"

"Are you a police officer?"

"I'm a detective. Where did she go?"

"Papa's inside. He's afraid he's going to be in trouble."

"Why's that?"

"Rosalie put her car in our garage yesterday. She said she was in an accident and it was damaged and not to use it. She's going to have it repaired when she gets back from vacation."

"What does that have to do with your papa being scared?"

"Rosalie's going to be mad as h at him, that he used her car." She shrugged. "He said he looked at it and it didn't look damaged to him, and if Mama was going to have to look after Rosalie's g.d. canary, well, he'd sure as h use *her* gas not his."

"I can see his point. Where did your sister go on vacation?"

"She didn't say. Up north someplace. Someplace she and Mr. Riggs like to go to, to . . . you know. To get away?"

I called Sergeant Pribyl from a gas station where I was getting Barney's Hupmobile tank refilled: I suggested he have another talk with bartender Alex Davidson, gave him the address of "Mr. and Mrs. Riggs," and told him where he could find the maroon Plymouth.

He was grateful but a little miffed about all I had done on my own. "So much for not showboating," he said, almost huffily. "You've found everything but the damn suspects."

"They've gone up north somewhere," I said.

"Where up north?"

"They don't seem to've told anybody. Look, I have a piece of evidence you may need."

"What?"

"When you talk to Davidson, he'll tell you about a matchbook Rooney wrote the girl's number on. I got the matchbook."

It was still in my pocket. I took it out, idly, and shut the girl's number away, revealing the picture on the matchbook cover: a blue moon hovered surrealistically over a white lake on which two blue lovers paddled in a blue canoe—*Eagle River Lodge, Wisconsin.*

"I suppose we'll need that," Pribyl's voice over the phone said, "when the time comes."

"I suppose," I said, and hung up.

Eagle River was a town of 1,386 (so said the sign) just inside the

Vilas County line at the junction of US 45 and Wisconsin State Highway 70. The country was beyond beautiful, green pines towering higher than Chicago skyscrapers, glittering blue lakes nestling in woodland pockets.

The lodge I was looking for was on Silver Lake, a gas station attendant told me. A beautiful dusk was settling on the woods as I drew into the parking of the large resort sporting a red city-style neon sign saying: *DINING AND DANCE*. Log-cabin cottages were flung here and there around the periphery like Paul Bunyan's Tinkertoys. Each one was just secluded enough—ideal for couples, married or un-.

Even if Rooney and his dark-haired honey weren't staying here, it was time to find a room: I'd been driving all day. When Barney loaned me his Hupmobile, he'd had no idea the kind of miles I'd put on it. Dead tired, I went to the desk and paid for a cabin.

The guy behind the counter had a plaid shirt on, but he was small and squinty and Hitler-mustached, smoking a stogie, and looked more like a bookie than a lumberjack.

I told him some friends of mine were supposed to be staying here.

"We don't have anybody named Riggs registered."

"How 'bout Mr. and Mrs. Rooney?"

"Them either. How many friends you got, anyway?"

"Why, did I already catch the limit?"

Before I headed to my cabin, I grabbed some supper in the rustic restaurant. I placed my order with a friendly brunette girl of about nineteen with plenty of personality and makeup. A road-company Paul Whiteman outfit was playing "Sophisticated Lady" in the adjacent dance hall, and I went over and peeked in, to look for familiar faces. A number of couples were cutting a rug, but not Rooney and Rosalie. Or Henry Berry or

Herbert Arnold, either. I went back and had my green salad and fried trout and well-buttered baked potato; I was full and sleepy when I stumbled toward my guest cottage under the light of a moon that bathed the woods ivory.

Walking along the path, I spotted something: snuggled next to one of the secluded cabins was a blue LaSalle coupe with Cook County plates.

Suddenly I wasn't sleepy. I walked briskly back to the lodge check-in desk and batted the bell to summon the stogie-chewing clerk.

"Cabin 7," I said. "I think that blue LaSalle is my friends' car."

His smirk turned his Hitler mustache Chaplinesque. "You want I should break out the champagne?"

"I just want to make sure it's them. Dark-haired doll and an older guy, good-looking, kinda sleepy-eyed, just starting to go bald?"

"That's them." He checked his register. "That's the Ridges." He frowned. "Are they usin' a phony name?"

"Does a bear shit in the woods?"

He squinted. "You sure they're friends of yours?"

"Positive. Don't call their room and tell 'em I'm here, though—I want to surprise 'em . . ."

I knocked with my left hand; my right was filled with the nine millimeter. Nothing. I knocked again.

"Who is it?" a male voice said gruffly. "*What* is it?"

"Complimentary fruit basket from the management."

"Go away!"

I kicked the door open.

The lights were off in the little cabin, but enough moonlight came in with me through the doorway to reveal the pair in bed, naked. She was sitting up, her mouth and eyes open in a silent scream, gathering the sheets up protectively over white skin, her dark hair blending with the darkness of the room, making a cameo of her face. He was diving off the bed for the sawed-off shotgun, but I was there to kick it away, wishing I hadn't, wishing I'd let him grab it so I could have had an excuse to put one in his forehead, right where he'd put one in Stanley's.

Boss Rooney wasn't boss of anything now: he was just a naked, balding, forty-four-year-old scam artist, sprawled on the floor. Kicking him would have been easy.

So I did; in the stomach.

He clutched himself and puked. Apparently he'd had the trout too.

I went over and slammed the door shut, or as shut as it could be, half off its hinges. Pointing the gun at her retching, naked boyfriend, I said to the girl, "Turn on the light and put on your clothes."

She nodded and did as she was told. In the glow of a night-stand lamp, I caught glimpses of her white, well-formed body as she stepped into her step-ins; but you know what? She didn't do a thing for me.

"Is Berry here?" I asked Rooney. "Or Arnold?"

"N . . . no," he managed.

"If you're lying," I said, "I'll kill you."

The girl said shrilly, "They aren't here!"

"You can put your clothes on too," I told Rooney. "If you have another gun hidden somewhere, do me a favor. Make a play for it."

His hooded eyes flared. "Who the hell are you?"

"The private cop you *didn't* kill the other night."

He lowered his gaze. "Oh."

The girl was sitting on the bed, weeping; body heaving.

"Take it easy on her, will you?" he said, zipping his fly. "She's just a kid."

I was opening a window to ease the stench of his vomit. "Sure," I said. "I'll say kaddish for her."

I handcuffed the lovebirds to the bed and called the local law; they in turn called the state prosecutor's office in Chicago, and Sergeants Pribyl and Gray made the long drive up the next day to pick up the pair.

It seemed the two cops had already caught Henry Berry—a tipster gave them the West Chicago Avenue address of a second-floor room he was holed up in.

I admitted to Pribyl that I'd been wrong about Tubbo tipping off Rooney and the rest about the raid.

"I figure Rooney lammed out of sheer panic," I said, "the morning after the murder."

Pribyl saw it the same way.

The following March, Pribyl arrested Herbert Arnold running a Northside handbill-distributing agency.

Rooney, Berry, and Rosalie Rizzo were all convicted of murder; the two men got life, and the girl twenty years. Arnold hadn't been part of the kill-happy joyride that took Stanley Gross's young life, and got only one-to-five for conspiracy and extortion.

None of it brought Stanley Gross back, nor did my putting on a beanie and sitting with the Gross family, suffering through a couple of stints at a storefront synagogue on Roosevelt Road.

But it did get Barney off my ass.

Author's Note: While Nathan Heller is a fictional character, this story is based on a real case—names have not been changed, and the events are fundamentally true; source material included an article by John J. McPhaul and information provided by my research associate, George Hagenauer, who I thank for his insights and suggestions.

THE MAN WHO WENT TO CHICAGO (EXCERPT)

BY RICHARD WRIGHT

Illinois Medical District

(Originally published in 1945)

When the work in the post office ended, I was assigned by the relief system as an orderly to a medical research institute in one of the largest and wealthiest hospitals in Chicago. I cleaned operating rooms, dog, rat, mice, cat, and rabbit pans, and fed guinea pigs. Four of us Negroes worked there and we occupied an underworld position, remembering that we must restrict ourselves—when not engaged upon some task—to the basement corridors, so that we would not mingle with white nurses, doctors, or visitors.

The sharp line of racial division drawn by the hospital authorities came to me the first morning when I walked along an underground corridor and saw two long lines of women coming toward me. A line of white girls marched past, clad in starched uniforms that gleamed white; their faces were alert, their step quick, their bodies lean and shapely, their shoulders erect, their faces lit with the light of purpose. And after them came a line of black girls, old, fat, dressed in ragged gingham, walking loosely, carrying tin cans of soap powder, rags, mops, brooms . . . I wondered what law of the universe kept them from being mixed? The sun would not have stopped shining had there been a few black girls in the first line, and the earth would not have stopped whirling on its axis had there been a few white girls in the second line. But the two lines I saw graded social status in purely racial terms.

Of the three Negroes who worked with me, one was a boy about my own age, Bill, who was either sleepy or drunk most of the time. Bill straightened his hair and I suspected that he kept a bottle hidden somewhere in the piles of hay which we fed to the guinea pigs. He did not like me and I did not like him, though I tried harder than he to conceal my dislike. We had nothing in common except that we were both black and lost. While I contained my frustration, he drank to drown his. Often I tried to talk to him, tried in simple words to convey to him some of my ideas, and he would listen in sullen silence. Then one day he came to me with an angry look on his face.

"I got it," he said.

"You've got what?" I asked.

"This old race problem you keep talking about," he said.

"What about it?"

"Well, it's this way," he explained seriously. "Let the government give every man a gun and five bullets, then let us all start over again. Make it just like it was in the beginning. The ones who come out on top, white or black, let them rule."

His simplicity terrified me. I had never met a Negro who was so irredeemably brutalized. I stopped pumping my ideas into Bill's brain for fear that the fumes of alcohol might send him reeling toward some fantastic fate.

The two other Negroes were elderly and had been employed in the institute for fifteen years or more. One was Brand, a short, black, morose bachelor; the other was Cooke, a tall, yellow, spectacled fellow who spent his spare time keeping track of world events through the Chicago *Tribune*. Brand and Cooke hated each other for a reason that I was never able to determine, and they spent a good part of each day quarreling.

When I began working at the institute, I recalled my adolescent dream of wanting to be a medical research worker. Daily I saw young Jewish boys and girls receiving instruction in chemistry and medicine that the average black boy or girl could never receive. When I was alone, I wandered and poked my fingers into strange chemicals, watched intricate machines trace red and black lines on ruled paper. At times I paused and stared at the walls of the rooms, at the floors, at the wide desks at which the white doctors sat; and I realized—with a feeling that I could never quite get used to—that I was looking at the world of another race.

My interest in what was happening in the institute amused the three other Negroes with whom I worked. They had no curiosity about "white folks' things," while I wanted to know if the dogs being treated for diabetes were getting well; if the rats and mice in which cancer had been induced showed any signs of responding to treatment. I wanted to know the principle that lay behind the Aschheim-Zondek tests that were made with rabbits, the Wassermann tests that were made with guinea pigs. But when I asked a timid question I found that even Jewish doctors had learned to imitate the sadistic method of humbling a Negro that the others had cultivated.

"If you know too much, boy, your brains might explode," a doctor said one day.

Each Saturday morning I assisted a young Jewish doctor in slitting the vocal cords of a fresh batch of dogs from the city pound. The object was to devocalize the dogs so that their howls would not disturb the patients in the other parts of the hospital. I held each dog as the doctor injected Nembutal into its veins to make it unconscious; then I held the dog's jaws open as the doctor inserted the scalpel and severed the vocal cords. Later, when the dogs came to, they would lift their heads to the ceiling and gape in a soundless wail. The sight became lodged in my imagination as a symbol of silent suffering.

To me Nembutal was a powerful and mysterious liquid, but when I asked questions about its properties I could not obtain a single intelligent answer. The doctor simply ignored me with: "Come on. Bring me the next dog. I haven't got all day."

One Saturday morning, after I had held the dogs for their vocal cords to be slit, the doctor left the Nembutal on a bench. I picked it up, uncorked it, and smelled it. It was odorless. Suddenly Brand ran to me with a stricken face.

"What're you doing?" he asked.

"I was smelling this stuff to see if it had any odor," I said.

"Did you really smell it?" he asked me.

"Yes."

"Oh, God!" he exclaimed.

"What's the matter?" I asked.

"You shouldn't've done that!" he shouted.

"Why?"

He grabbed my arm and jerked me across the room.

"Come on!" he yelled, snatching open the door.

"What's the matter?" I asked.

"I gotta get you to a doctor 'fore it's too late," he gasped.

Had my foolish curiosity made me inhale something dangerous? "But—is it poisonous?"

"Run, boy!" he said, pulling me. "You'll fall dead."

Filled with fear, with Brand pulling my arm, I rushed out of the room, raced across a rear areaway, into another room, then down a long corridor. I wanted to ask Brand what symptoms I must expect, but we were running too fast. Brand finally stopped, gasping for breath. My heart beat wildly and my blood pounded in my head. Brand then dropped to the concrete floor, stretched out on his back, and yelled with laughter, shaking all over. He beat his fists against the concrete; he moaned, giggled, he kicked.

I tried to master my outrage, wondering if some of the white doctors had told him to play the joke. He rose and wiped tears from his eyes, still laughing. I walked away from him. He knew that I was angry and he followed me.

"Don't get mad," he gasped through his laughter.

"Go to hell," I said.

"I couldn't help it," he giggled. "You looked at me like you'd believe anything I said. Man, you was scared."

He leaned against the wall, laughing again, stomping his feet. I was angry, for I felt that he would spread the story. I knew that Bill and Cooke never ventured beyond the safe bounds of Negro living, and they would never blunder into anything like this. And if they heard about this, they would laugh for months.

"Brand, if you mention this, I'll kill you," I swore.

"You ain't mad?" he asked, laughing, staring at me through tears.

Sniffing, Brand walked ahead of me. I followed him back into the room that housed the dogs. All day, while at some task, he would pause and giggle, then smother the giggling with his hand, looking at me out of the corner of his eyes, shaking his head. He laughed at me for a week. I kept my temper and let him amuse himself. I finally found out the properties of Nembutal by consulting medical books; but I never told Brand.

One summer morning, just as I began work, a young Jewish boy came to me with a stop watch in his hand.

"Dr. ——— wants me to time you when you clean a room," he said. "We're trying to make the institute more efficient."

"I'm doing my work, and getting through on time," I said.

"This is the boss's order," he said.

"Why don't you work for a change?" I blurted, angry.

"Now, look," he said. "*This* is my work. Now *you* work."

I got a mop and pail, sprayed a room with disinfectant, and scrubbed at coagulated blood and hardened dog, rat, and rabbit feces. The normal temperature of a room was ninety, but, as the sun beat down upon the skylights, the temperature rose above a hundred. Stripped to my waist, I slung the mop, moving steadily like a machine, hearing the boy press the button on the stop watch as I finished cleaning a room.

"Well, how is it?" I asked.

"It took you seventeen minutes to clean that last room," he said. "That ought to be the time for each room."

"But that room was not very dirty," I said.

"You have seventeen rooms to clean," he went on as though I had not spoken. "Seventeen times seventeen make four hours and forty-nine minutes." He wrote upon a little pad. "After lunch, clean the five flights of stone stairs. I timed a boy who scrubbed one step and multiplied that time by the number of steps. You ought to be through by six."

"Suppose I want relief?" I asked.

"You'll manage," he said and left.

Never had I felt so much the slave as when I scoured those stone steps each afternoon. Working against time, I would wet five steps, sprinkle soap powder, and then a white doctor or a nurse would come along and, instead of avoiding the soapy steps, would walk on them and track the dirty water onto the steps that I had already cleaned. To obviate this, I cleaned but two steps at a time, a distance over which a ten-year-old child could step. But it did no good. The white people still plopped their feet down into the dirty water and muddied the other clean steps. If I ever really hotly hated unthinking whites, it was then. Not once during my entire stay at the institute did a single white person show enough courtesy to avoid a wet step. I would be on my knees, scrubbing, sweating, pouring out what limited energy my body could wring from my meager diet, and I would hear feet approaching. I would pause and curse with tense lips: "These sonofabitches are going to dirty these steps again, goddamn their souls to hell!"

Sometimes a sadistically observant white man would notice that he had tracked dirty water up the steps, and he would look back down at me and smile and say: "Boy, we sure keep you busy, don't we?"

And I would not be able to answer.

The feud that went on between Brand and Cooke continued. Although they were working daily in a building where scientific history was being made, the light of curiosity was never in their eyes. They were conditioned to their racial "place," had learned to see only a part of the whites and the white world; and the whites, too, had learned to see only a part of the lives of the blacks and their world.

Perhaps Brand and Cooke, lacking interests that could absorb them, fuming like children over trifles, simply invented their hate of each other in order to have something to feel deeply about. Or perhaps there was in them a vague tension stemming from their chronically frustrating way of life, a pain whose cause they did not know; and, like those devocalized dogs, they would whirl and snap at the air when their old pain struck them. Anyway, they argued about the weather, sports, sex, war, race, politics, and religion; neither of them knew much about the subjects they debated, but it seemed that the less they knew the better they could argue.

The tug of war between the two elderly men reached a climax one winter day at noon. It was incredibly cold and an icy gale swept up and down the Chicago streets with blizzard force.

The door of the animal-filled room was locked, for we always insisted that we be allowed one hour in which to eat and rest. Bill and I were sitting on wooden boxes, eating our lunches out of paper bags. Brand was washing his hands at the sink. Cooke was sitting on a rickety stool, munching an apple and reading the Chicago *Tribune*.

Now and then a devocalized dog lifted his nose to the ceiling and howled soundlessly. The room was filled with many rows of high steel tiers. Perched upon each of these tiers were layers of steel cages containing the dogs, rats, mice, rabbits, and guinea pigs. Each cage was labeled in some indecipherable scientific jargon. Along the walls of the room were long charts with zigzagging red and black lines that traced the success or failure of some experiment. The lonely piping of guinea pigs floated unheeded about us. Hay rustled as a rabbit leaped restlessly about in its pen. A rat scampered around in its steel prison. Cooke tapped the newspaper for attention.

"It says here," Cooke mumbled through a mouthful of apple, "that this is the coldest day since 1888."

Bill and I sat unconcerned. Brand chuckled softly.

"What in hell you laughing about?" Cooke demanded of Brand.

"You can't believe what that damn *Tribune* says," Brand said.

"How come I can't?" Cooke demanded. "It's the world's greatest newspaper."

Brand did not reply; he shook his head pityingly and chuckled again.

"Stop that damn laughing at me!" Cooke said angrily.

"I laugh as much as I wanna," Brand said. "You don't know what you talking about. The *Herald-Examiner* says it's the coldest day since 1873."

"But the *Trib* oughta know," Cooke countered. "It's older'n that *Examiner*."

"That damn *Trib* don't know nothing!" Brand drowned out Cooke's voice.

"How in hell you know?" Cooke asked with rising anger.

The argument waxed until Cooke shouted that if Brand did not shut up he was going to "cut his black throat."

Brand whirled from the sink, his hands dripping soapy water, his eyes blazing.

"Take that back," Brand said.

"I take nothing back! What you wanna do about it?" Cooke taunted.

The two elderly Negroes glared at each other. I wondered if the quarrel was really serious, or if it would turn out harmlessly as so many others had done.

Suddenly Cooke dropped the Chicago *Tribune* and pulled a long knife from his pocket; his thumb pressed a button and a gleaming steel blade leaped out. Brand stepped back quickly and seized an ice pick that was stuck in a wooden board above the sink.

"Put that knife down," Brand said.

"Stay 'way from me, or I'll cut your throat," Cooke warned.

Brand lunged with the ice pick. Cooke dodged out of range. They circled each other like fighters in a prize ring. The cancerous and tubercular rats and mice leaped about in their cages. The guinea pigs whistled in fright. The diabetic dogs bared their teeth and barked soundlessly in our direction. The Aschheim-Zondek rabbits flopped their ears and tried to hide in the corners of their pens. Cooke now crouched and sprang forward with the knife. Bill and I jumped to our feet, speechless with surprise. Brand retreated. The eyes of both men were hard and unblinking; they were breathing deeply.

"Say, cut it out!" I called in alarm.

"Them damn fools is really fighting," Bill said in amazement.

Slashing at each other, Brand and Cooke surged up and down the aisles of steel tiers. Suddenly Brand uttered a bellow and charged into Cooke and swept him violently backward. Cooke grasped Brand's hand to keep the ice pick from sinking into his chest. Brand broke free and charged Cooke again, sweeping him into an animal-filled steel tier. The tier balanced itself on its edge for an indecisive moment, then toppled.

Like kingpins, one steel tier slammed into another, then they all crashed to the floor with a sound as of the roof falling. The whole aspect of the room altered quicker than the eye could follow. Brand and Cooke stood stock-still, their eyes fastened upon each other, their pointed weapons raised; but they were dimly aware of the havoc that churned about them.

The steel tiers lay jumbled; the doors of the cages swung open. Rats and mice and dogs and rabbits moved over the floor in wild panic. The Wassermann guinea pigs were squealing as though judgment day had come. Here and there an animal had been crushed beneath a cage.

All four of us looked at one another. We knew what this meant. We might lose our jobs. We were already regarded as black dunces; and if the doctors saw this mess they would take it as final proof. Bill rushed to the door to make sure that it was locked. I glanced at the clock and saw that it was twelve thirty. We had one half-hour of grace.

"Come on," Bill said uneasily. "We got to get this place cleaned."

Brand and Cooke stared at each other, both doubting.

"Give me your knife, Cooke," I said.

"Naw! Take Brand's ice pick *first*," Cooke said.

"The hell you say!" Brand said. "Take his knife *first*!"

A knock sounded at the door.

"Sssssh," Bill said.

We waited. We heard footsteps going away. We'll all lose our jobs, I thought.

Persuading the fighters to surrender their weapons was a difficult task, but at last it was done and we could begin to set things right. Slowly Brand stooped and tugged at one end of a steel tier. Cooke stooped to help him. Both men seemed to be acting in a dream. Soon, however, all four of us were working frantically, watching the clock.

As we labored we conspired to keep the fight a secret; we agreed to tell the doctors—if any should ask—that we had not been in the room during our lunch hour; we felt that that lie would explain why no one had unlocked the door when the knock had come.

We righted the tiers and replaced the cages; then we were faced with the impossible task of sorting the cancerous rats and mice, the diabetic dogs, the Aschheim-Zondek rabbits, and the Wassermann guinea pigs. Whether we kept our jobs or not depended upon how shrewdly we could cover up all evidence of the fight. It was pure guesswork, but we had to try to put the animals back into the correct cages. We knew that certain rats or mice went into certain cages, but we did not know *what* rat or mouse went into *what* cage. We did not know a tubercular mouse from a cancerous mouse—the white doctors had made sure that we would not know. They had never taken time to answer a single question; though we worked in the institute, we were as remote from the meaning of the experiments as if we lived in the moon. The doctors had laughed at what they felt was our childlike interest in the fate of the animals.

First we sorted the dogs; that was fairly easy, for we could remember the size and color of most of them. But the rats and mice and guinea pigs baffled us completely.

We put our heads together and pondered, down in the underworld of the great scientific institute. It was a strange scientific conference; the fate of the entire medical research institute rested in our ignorant, black hands.

We remembered the number of rats, mice, or guinea pigs—we had to handle them several times a day—that went into a given cage, and we supplied the number helter-skelter from those animals that we could catch running loose on the floor. We discovered that many rats, mice, and guinea pigs were missing—they had been killed in the scuffle. We solved that problem by taking healthy stock from other cages and putting them into cages with sick animals. We repeated this process until we were certain that, numerically at least, all the animals with which the doctors were experimenting were accounted for.

The rabbits came last. We broke the rabbits down into two general groups: those that had fur on their bellies and those that did not. We knew that all those rabbits that had shaven bellies—our scientific knowledge adequately covered this point because it was our job to shave the rabbits—were undergoing the Aschheim-Zondek tests. But in what pen did a given rabbit belong? We did not know. I solved the problem very simply. I counted the shaven rabbits: they numbered seventeen. I counted the pens labeled *Aschheim-Zondek*, then proceeded to drop a shaven rabbit into each pen at random. And again we were numerically successful. At least white America had taught us how to count . . .

Lastly we carefully wrapped all the dead animals in newspapers and hid their bodies in a garbage can.

At a few minutes to one the room was in order; that is, the kind of order that we four Negroes could figure out. I unlocked the door and we sat waiting, whispering, vowing secrecy, wondering what the reaction of the doctors would be.

Finally a doctor came, gray-haired, white-coated, spectacled, efficient, serious, taciturn, bearing a tray upon which sat a bottle of mysterious fluid and a hypodermic needle.

"My rats, please."

Cooke shuffled forward to serve him. We held our breath. Cooke got the cage which he knew the doctor always called for at that hour and brought it forward. One by one, Cooke took out the rats and held them as the doctor solemnly injected the mysterious fluid under their skins.

"Thank you, Cooke," the doctor murmured.

"Not at all, sir," Cooke mumbled with a suppressed gasp.

When the doctor had gone we looked at one another, hardly daring to believe that our secret would be kept. We were so anxious that we did not know whether to curse or laugh. Another doctor came.

"Give me A-Z rabbit number 14."

"Yes, sir," I said.

I brought him the rabbit and he took it upstairs to the operating room. We waited for repercussions. None came.

All that afternoon the doctors came and went. I would run into the room—stealing a few seconds from my step-scrubbing—and ask what progress was being made and would learn that the doctors had detected nothing. At quitting time we felt triumphant.

"They won't ever know," Cooke boasted in a whisper.

I saw Brand stiffen. I knew that he was aching to dispute Cooke's optimism, but the memory of the fight he had just had was so fresh in his mind that he could not speak.

Another day went by and nothing happened. Then another day. The doctors examined the animals and wrote in their little black books, in their big black books, and continued to trace red and black lines upon the charts.

A week passed and we felt out of danger. Not one question had been asked.

Of course, we four black men were much too modest to make our contribution known, but we often wondered what went on in the laboratories after that secret disaster. Was some scientific hypothesis, well on its way to validation and ultimate public use, discarded because of unexpected findings on that cold winter day? Was some tested principle given a new and strange refinement because of fresh, remarkable evidence? Did some brooding research worker—those who held stop watches and slopped their feet carelessly in the water of the steps I tried so hard to keep clean—get a wild, if brief, glimpse of a new scientific truth? Well, we never heard . . .

I brooded upon whether I should have gone to the director's office and told him what had happened, but each time I thought of it I remembered that the director had been the man who had ordered the boy to stand over me while I was working and time my movements with a stop watch. He did not regard me as a human being. I did not share his world. I earned thirteen dollars a week and I had to support four people with it, and should I risk that thirteen dollars by acting idealistically? Brand and Cooke would have hated me and would have eventually driven me from the job had I "told" on them. The hospital kept us four Negroes as though we were close kin to the animals we tended, huddled together down in the underworld corridors of the hospital, separated by a vast psychological distance from the significant processes of the rest of the hospital—just as America had kept us locked in the dark underworld of American life for three hundred years—and we had made our own code of ethics, values, loyalty.

PART II

Noir & Neo-Noir

HE SWUNG AND HE MISSED

BY NELSON ALGREN

Lakeview

(Originally published in 1942)

It was Miss Donahue of Public School 24 who finally urged Rocco, in his fifteenth year, out of eighth grade and into the world. She had watched him fighting, at recess times, from his sixth year on. The kindergarten had had no recesses or it would have been from his fifth. She had nurtured him personally through four trying semesters and so it was with something like enthusiasm that she wrote in his autograph book, the afternoon of graduation day, *Trusting that Rocco will make good.*

Ultimately, Rocco did. In his own way. He stepped from the schoolroom into the ring back of the Happy Hour Bar in a catchweight bout with an eight-dollar purse, winner take all. Rocco took it.

Uncle Mike Adler, local promoter, called the boy Young Rocco after that one and the name stuck. He fought through the middleweights and into the light-heavies, while his purses increased to as much as sixty dollars and expenses. In his nineteenth year he stopped growing, and he married a girl called Lili.

He didn't win every one after that, somehow, and by the time he was twenty-two he was losing as often as he won. He fought on. It was all he could do. He never took a dive; he never had a setup or a soft touch. He stayed away from whiskey; he never gambled; he went to bed early before every bout and he loved his wife. He fought in a hundred corners of the city. Under a half-dozen managers, and he fought every man he was asked to, at any hour. He substituted, for better men, on as little as two hours' notice. He never ran out on a fight and he was never put down for a ten-count. He took beatings from the best in the business. But he never stayed down for ten.

He fought a comer from the coast one night and took the worst beating of his career. But he was on his feet at the end. With a jaw broken in three places.

After that one he was hospitalized for three months and Lili went to work in a factory. She wasn't a strong girl and he didn't like it that she had to work. He fought again before his jaw was ready, and lost.

Yet even when he lost, the crowds liked him. They heckled him when he was introduced as Young Rocco, because he looked like thirty-four before he was twenty-six. Most of his hair had gone during his layoff, and scar tissue over the eyes made him look less and less like a young anything. Friends came, friends left, money came in, was lost, was saved; he got the break on an occasional decision, and was occasionally robbed of a duke he'd earned. All things changed but his weight, which was 174, and his wife, who was Lili. And his record of never having been put down for ten. That stood, like his name. Which was forever Young Rocco.

That stuck to him like nothing else in the world but Lili.

At the end, which came when he was twenty-nine, all he had left was his record and his girl. Being twenty-nine, one of that pair had to go. He went six weeks without earning a dime before he came to that realization. When he found her wearing a pair of his old tennis shoes about the house, to save the heels of her only decent pair of shoes, he made up his mind.

Maybe Young Rocco wasn't the smartest pug in town, but

he wasn't the punchiest either. Just because there was a dent in his face and a bigger one in his wallet, it didn't follow that his brain was dented. It wasn't. He knew what the score was. And he loved his girl.

He came into Uncle Mike's office looking for a fight and Mike was good enough not to ask what kind he wanted. He had a twenty-year-old named Solly Classki that he was bringing along under the billing Kid Class. There was money back of the boy, no chances were to be taken. If Rocco was ready to dive, he had the fight. Uncle Mike put no pressure on Rocco. There were two light-heavies out in the gym ready to jump at the chance to dive for Solly Classki. All Rocco had to say was okay. His word was good enough for Uncle Mike. Rocco said it. And left the gym with the biggest purse of his career, and the first he'd gotten in advance, in his pocket: four twenties and two tens.

He gave Lili every dime of that money, and when he handed it over, he knew he was only doing the right thing for her. He had earned the right to sell out as he had sold. The ring owed him more than a C-note, he reflected soundly, and added loudly, for Lili's benefit, "I'll stop the bum dead in his tracks."

They were both happy that night. Rocco had never been happier since Graduation Day.

He had a headache all the way to City Garden that night, but it lessened a little in the shadowed dressing room under the stands. The moment he saw the lights of the ring, as he came down the littered aisle alone, the ache sharpened once more.

Slouched unhappily in his corner for the windup, he watched the lights overhead sway a little, and closed his eyes. When he opened them, a slow dust was rising toward the lights. He saw it sweep suddenly, swift and sidewise, high over the ropes and out across the dark and watchful rows. Below him someone pushed the warning buzzer.

He looked through Kid Class as they touched gloves, and glared sullenly over the boy's head while Ryan, the ref, hurried through the stuff about a clean break in the clinches. He felt the robe being taken from his shoulders, and suddenly, in that one brief moment before the bell, felt more tired than he ever had in a ring before. He went out in a half-crouch and someone called out, "Cut him down, Solly."

He backed to make the boy lead, and then came in long enough to flick his left twice in the teeth and skitter away. The bleachers whooped, sensing blood. He'd give them their money's worth for a couple rounds, anyhow. No use making it look too bad.

In the middle of the second round he began sensing that the boy was telegraphing his right by pulling his left shoulder, and stepped in to trap it. The boy's left came back bloody and Rocco knew he'd been hit by the way the bleachers began again. It didn't occur to him that it was time to dive; he didn't even remember. Instead, he saw the boy telegraphing the right once more and the left protecting the heart slipping loosely down toward the navel, the telltale left shoulder hunching— only it wasn't down, it wasn't a right. It wasn't to the heart. The boy's left snapped like a hurled rock between his eyes and he groped blindly for the other's arms, digging his chin sharply into the shoulder, hating the six-bit bunch out there for thinking he could be hurt so soon. He shoved the boy off, flashed his left twice into the teeth, burned him skillfully against the middle rope, and heeled him sharply as they broke. Then he skittered easily away. And the bell.

Down front, Mike Alder's eyes followed Rocco back to his corner.

Rocco came out for the third, fighting straight up, watching Solly's gloves coming languidly out of the other corner, dangling loosely a moment in the glare, and a flatiron smashed in under his heart so that he remembered, with sagging surprise, that he'd already been paid off. He caught his breath while following indifferent gloves, thinking vaguely of Lili in oversize tennis shoes. The gloves drifted backward and dangled loosely with little to do but catch light idly four feet away. The right broke again beneath his heart and he grunted in spite of himself; the boy's close-cropped head followed in, cockily, no higher than Rocco's chin but coming neckless straight down to the shoulders. And the gloves were gone again. The boy was faster than he looked. And the pain in his head settled down to a steady beating between the eyes.

The great strength of a fighting man is his pride. That was Young Rocco's strength in the rounds that followed. The boy called Kid Class couldn't keep him down. He sat down in the fourth, twice in the fifth, and again in the seventh. In that round he stood with his back against the ropes, standing the boy off with his left in the seconds before the bell. He had the trick of looking impassive when he was hurt, and his face at the bell looked as impassive as a catcher's mitt.

Between that round and the eighth Uncle Mike climbed into the ring beside Young Rocco. He said nothing. Just stood there looking down. He thought Rocco might have forgotten. He'd had four chances to stay down and he hadn't taken one. Rocco looked up. "I'm clear as a bell," he told Uncle Mike. He hadn't forgotten a thing.

Uncle Mike climbed back into his seat, resigned to anything that might happen. He understood better than Young Rocco. Rocco couldn't stay down until his knees would fail to bring him up. Uncle Mike sighed. He decided he liked Young Rocco.

Somehow, he didn't feel as sorry for him as he had in the gym.

I hope he makes it, he found himself hoping. The crowd felt differently. They had seen the lean and scarred Italian drop his man here twenty times before, the way he was trying to keep from being dropped himself now. They felt it was his turn. They were standing up in the rows to see it. The dust came briefly between. A tired moth struggled lamely upward toward the lights. And the bell.

Ryan came over between rounds, hooked Rocco's head back with a crooked forefinger on the chin, after Rocco's Negro handler had stopped the bleeding with collodion, and muttered something about the thing going too far. Rocco spat.

"Awright, Solly, drop it on him," someone called across the ropes.

It sounded, somehow, like money to Rocco. It sounded like somebody was being shortchanged out there.

But Solly stayed away, hands low, until the eighth was half gone. Then he was wide with a right, held and butted as they broke; Rocco felt the blood and got rid of some of it on the boy's left breast. He trapped the boy's left, rapping the kidneys fast before grabbing the arms again, and pressed his nose firmly into the hollow of the other's throat to arrest its bleeding. Felt the blood trickling into the hollow there as into a tiny cup. Rocco put his feet together and a glove on both of Kid Class's shoulders, to shove him sullenly away. And must have looked strong doing it, for he heard the crowd murmur a little. He was in Solly's corner at the bell and moved back to his corner with his head held high, to control the bleeding. When his handler stopped it again, he knew, at last, that his own pride was double-crossing him. And felt glad for that much. Let them worry out there in the rows. He'd been shortchanged since Graduation Day; let them be on the short end tonight. He had the hundred—

he'd get a job in a garage and forget every one of them.

It wasn't until the tenth and final round that Rocco realized he wanted to kayo the boy—because it wasn't until then that he realized he could. Why not do the thing up the right way? He felt the tiredness fall from him like an old cloak at the notion. This was his fight, his round. He'd end it like he'd started, as a fighting man. And saw Solly Kid Class shuffling his shoulders forward uneasily. The boy would be a full-sized heavy in another six months. He bullied him into the ropes and felt the boy fade sidewise. Rocco caught him off balance with his left, hook-fashion, into the short ribs. The boy chopped back with his left uncertainly, as though he might have jammed the knuckles, and held. In a half-rolling clinch along the ropes, he saw Solly's mouthpiece projecting, slipping halfway in and halfway out, and then swallowed in again with a single tortured twist of the lips. He got an arm loose and banged the boy back of the ear with an overhand right that must have looked funny because the crowd laughed a little. Solly smeared his glove across his nose, came halfway in and changed his mind, left himself wide, and was almost steady until Rocco feinted him into a knot and brought the right looping from the floor with even his toes behind it.

Solly stepped in to let it breeze past, and hooked his right hard to the button. Then the left. Rocco's mouthpiece went spinning in an arc into the lights. Then the right.

Rocco spun halfway around and stood looking sheepishly out at the rows. Kid Class saw only his man's back; Rocco was out on his feet. He walked slowly along the ropes, tapping them idly with his glove and smiling vacantly down at the newspapermen, who smiled back. Solly looked at Ryan. Ryan nodded toward Rocco. Kid Class came up fast behind his man and threw the left under the armpit flush onto the point of the chin. Rocco went forward on the ropes and hung there, his chin catching the second strand, and hung on an on, like a man decapitated.

He came to in the locker room under the stands, watching the steam swimming about the pipes directly overhead. Uncle Mike was somewhere near, telling him he had done fine, and then he was alone. They were all gone then, all the six-bit hecklers and the iron-throated boys in the sixty-cent seats. He rose heavily and dressed slowly, feeling a long relief that he'd come to the end. He'd done it the hard way, but he'd done it. Let them all go.

He was fixing his tie, taking more time with it than it required, when she knocked. He called her to come in. She had never seen him fight, but he knew she must have listened on the radio or she wouldn't be down now.

She tested the adhesive over his right eye timidly, fearing to hurt him with her touch, but wanting to be sure it wasn't loose.

"I'm okay," he assured her easily. "We'll celebrate a little 'n forget the whole business." It wasn't until he kissed her that her eyes avoided him; it wasn't till then that he saw she was trying not to cry. He patted her shoulder.

"There's nothin' wrong, Lil'—a couple days' rest 'n I'll be in the pink again."

Then saw it wasn't that after all.

"You told me you'd win," the girl told him. "I got eight-to-one and put the whole damn bankroll on you. I wanted to surprise you, 'n now we ain't got a cryin' dime."

Rocco didn't blow up. He just felt a little sick. Sicker than he had ever felt in his life. He walked away from the girl and sat on a rubbing table, studying the floor. She had sense enough not to bother him until he'd realized what the score was. Then he looked up, studying her from foot to head. His eyes didn't rest on her face: they went back to her feet. To the scarred toes of the only decent shoes; and a shadow passed over his heart. "You got good odds, honey," he told her thoughtfully. "You done just right. We made 'em sweat all night for their money." Then he looked up and grinned. A wide, white grin.

That was all she needed to know it was okay after all. She went to him so he could tell her how okay it really was.

That was like Young Rocco, from Graduation Day. He always did it the hard way; but he did it.

Miss Donahue would have been proud.

I'LL CUT YOUR THROAT AGAIN, KATHLEEN

By Fredric Brown

Magnificent Mile

(Originally published in 1948)

I heard the footsteps coming down the hall and I was watching the door—the door that had no knob on my side of it—when it opened.

I thought I'd recognized the step, and I'd been right. It was the young, nice one, the one whose bright hair made so brilliant a contrast with his white uniform coat.

I said, "Hello, Red," and he said, "Hello, Mr. Marlin. I—I'll take you down to the office. The doctors are there now." He sounded more nervous than I felt.

"How much time have I got, Red?"

"How much—oh, I see what you mean. They're examining a couple of others ahead of you. You've got time."

So I didn't get up off the edge of the bed. I held my hands out in front of me, backs up and the fingers rigid. They didn't tremble anymore. My fingers were steady as those of a statue, and about as useful. Oh, I could move them. I could clench them into fists slowly. But for playing sax and clarinet they were about as good as hands of bananas. I turned them over—and there on my wrists were the two ugly scars where, a little less than a year ago, I'd slashed them with a straight razor. Deeply enough to have cut some of the tendons that moved the fingers.

I moved my fingers now, curling them inward toward the palm, slowly. The interne was watching.

"They'll come back, Mr. Marlin," he said. "Exercise—that's all they need." It wasn't true. He knew that I knew he knew it, for when I didn't bother to answer, he went on, almost defensively, "Anyway, you can still arrange and conduct. You can hold a baton all right. And—I got an idea for you, Mr. Marlin."

"Yes, Red?"

"Trombone. Why don't you take up trombone? You could learn it fast, and you don't need finger action to play trombone."

Slowly I shook my head. I didn't try to explain. It was something you couldn't explain, anyway. It wasn't only the physical ability to play an instrument that was gone. It was more than that.

I looked at my hands once more and then I put them carefully away in my pockets where I wouldn't have to look at them.

I looked up at the interne's face again. There was a look on it that I recognized and remembered—the look I'd seen on thousands of young faces across footlights—hero worship. Out of the past it came to me, that look.

He could still look at me that way, even after—

"Red," I asked him, "don't you think I'm insane?"

"Of course not, Mr. Marlin. I don't think you were ever—" He bogged down on that.

I needled him. Maybe it was cruel, but it was crueler to me. I said, "You don't think I was ever crazy? You think I was sane when I tried to kill my wife?"

"Well—it was just temporary. You had a breakdown. You'd been working too hard—twenty hours a day, about. You were near the top with your band. Me, Mr. Marlin, I think you were *at* the top. You had it on all of them, only most of the public hadn't found out yet. They would have, if—"

"If I hadn't slipped a cog," I said. I thought, what a way to express going crazy, trying to kill your wife, trying to kill yourself, and losing your memory.

Red looked at his wrist watch, then pulled up a chair and sat down facing me. He talked fast.

"We haven't got too long, Mr. Marlin," he said. "And I want you to pass those doctors and get out of here. You'll be all right once you get out of this joint. Your memory will come back, a little at a time—when you're in the right surroundings."

I shrugged. It didn't seem to matter much. I said, "Okay, brief me. It didn't work last time, but—I'll try."

"You're Johnny Marlin," he said. "*The* Johnny Marlin. You play a mean clarinet, but that's sideline. You're the best alto sax in the business, *I* think. You were fourth in the *Down Beat* poll a year ago, but—"

I interrupted him. "You mean I *did* play clarinet and sax. Not anymore, Red. Can't you get that through your head?" I hadn't meant to sound so rough about it, but my voice got out of control.

Red didn't seem to hear me. His eyes went to his wrist watch again and then came back to me. He started talking again.

"We got ten minutes, maybe. I wish I knew what you remember and what you don't about all I've been telling you the last month. What's your right name—I mean, before you took a professional name?"

"John Dettman," I said. "Born June 1, 1920, on the wrong side of the tracks. Orphaned at five. Released from orphanage at sixteen. Worked as bus boy in Cleveland and saved up enough money to buy a clarinet, and took lessons. Bought a sax a year later, and got my first job with a band at eighteen."

"What band?"

"Heinie Wills's—local band in Cleveland, playing at

Danceland there. Played third alto awhile, then first alto. Next worked for a six-man combo called—what was it, Red? I don't remember."

"The Basin Streeters, Mr. Marlin. Look, do you really re-member any of this, or is it just from what I've told you?"

"Mostly from what you've told me, Red. Sometimes I get kind of vague pictures, but it's pretty foggy. Let's get on with it. So the Basin Streeters did a lot of traveling for a while and I left them in Chi for my first stretch with a name band—look, I think I've got that list of bands pretty well memorized. There isn't much time. Let's skip it.

"I joined the army in '42—I'd have been twenty-two then. A year at Fort Billings, and then England. Kayoed by a bomb in London before I ever got to pull a trigger except on rifle range. A month in a hospital there, shipped back, six months in a mental hospital here, and let out on a PN." He knew as well as I did what PN meant, but I translated it for us. "Psycho-neurotic. Nuts. Crazy."

He opened his mouth to argue the point, and then decided there wasn't time.

"So I'd saved my money," I said, "before and during the army, and I started my own band. That would have been—late '44?"

Red nodded. "Remember the list of places you've played, the names of your sidemen, what I told you about them?"

"Pretty well," I said. There wouldn't be time to go into that, anyway. I said, "And early in '47, while I was still getting started, I got married. To Kathy Courteen. *The* Kathy Courteen, who owns a slice of Chicago, who's got more money than sense. She must have, if she married me. We were married June 10, 1947. Why *did* she marry me, Red?"

"Why shouldn't she?" he said. "You're *Johnny Marlin!*"

The funny part of it is he wasn't kidding. I could tell by his voice he meant it. He thought being Johnny Marlin had really been something. I looked down at my hands. They'd got loose out of my pockets again.

I think I knew, suddenly, why I wanted to get out of this gilt-lined nuthouse that was costing Kathy Courteen—Kathy Marlin, I mean—the price of a fur coat every week to keep me in. It wasn't because I wanted *out*, really. It was because I wanted to get away from the hero worship of this redheaded kid who'd gone nuts about Johnny Marlin's band, and Johnny Marlin's saxophone.

"Have you ever seen Kathy, Red?" I asked.

He shook his head. "I've seen pictures of her, newspaper pictures of her. She's beautiful."

"Even with a scar across her throat?" I asked.

His eyes avoided mine. They went to his watch again, and he stood up quickly. "We'd better get down there," he said.

He went to the knobless door, opened it with a key, and politely held it open for me to precede him out into the hallway.

That look in his eyes made me feel foolish, as always. I don't know how he did it, but Red always managed to look *up* at me, from a height a good three inches taller than mine.

Then, side by side, we went down the great stairway of that lush, plush madhouse that had once been a million-dollar mansion and was now a million-dollar sanitarium with more employees than inmates.

We went into the office and the gray-haired nurse behind the desk nodded and said, "They're ready for you."

"Luck, Mr. Marlin," Red said. "I'm pulling for you."

So I went through the door. There were three of them, as last time.

"Sit down please, Mr. Marlin," Dr. Glasspiegel, the head one, said.

They sat each at one side of the square table, leaving the fourth side and the fourth chair for me. I slid into it. I put my hands in my pockets again. I knew if I looked at them or thought about them, I might say something foolish, and then I'd be here awhile again.

Then they were asking me questions, taking turns at it. Some about my past—and Red's coaching had been good. Once or twice, but not often, I had to stall and admit my memory was hazy on a point or two. And some of the questions were about the present, and they were easy. I mean, it was easy to see what answers they wanted to those questions, and to give them.

But it had been like this the last time, I remembered, over a month ago. And I'd missed somewhere. They hadn't let me go. Maybe, I thought, because they got too much money out of keeping me here. I didn't really think that. These men were the best in their profession.

There was a lull in the questioning. They seemed to be waiting for something. For what? I wondered, and it came to me that the last interview had been like this too.

The door behind me opened quietly, but I heard it. And I remembered—that had happened last time too. Just as they told me I could go back to my room and they'd talk it over, someone else had come in. I'd passed him as I'd left the room.

And, suddenly, I knew what I'd missed up on. It had been someone I'd been supposed to recognize, and I hadn't. And here was the same test again. Before I turned, I tried to remember what Red had told me about people I'd known—but there was so little physical description to it. It seemed hopeless.

"You may return to your room now, Mr. Marlin," Dr. Glasspiegel was saying. "We—ah—wish to discuss your case."

"Thanks," I said, and stood up.

I saw that he'd taken off his shell-rimmed glasses and was tapping them nervously on the back of his hand, which lay on the table before him. I thought, okay, so now I know the catch and next time I'll make the grade. I'll have Red get me pictures of my band and other bands I've played with and as many newspaper pictures as he can find of people I knew.

I turned. The man in the doorway, standing there as though waiting for me to leave, was short and fat. There was a tense look in his face, even though his eyes were avoiding mine. He was looking past me, at the doctors. I tried to think fast. Who did I know that was short and—

I took a chance. I'd had a trumpet player named Tubby Hayes.

"Tubby!" I said.

And hit the jackpot. His face lighted up like a neon sign and he grinned a yard wide and stuck out his hand.

"Johnny! Johnny, it's good to see you." He was making like a pump handle with my arm.

"Tubby Hayes!" I said, to let them know I knew his last name too. "Don't tell me you're nuts too. That why you're here?"

He laughed nervously. "I came to get you, Johnny. That is, uh, if—" He looked past me.

Dr. Glasspiegel was clearing his throat. He and the other doctors were standing now.

"Yes," he said, "I believe it will be all right for Mr. Marlin to leave."

He put his hand on my shoulder. They were all standing about me now.

"Your reactions are normal, Mr. Marlin," he said. "Your memory is still a bit impaired but—ah—it will improve gradually. More rapidly, I believe, amid familiar surroundings than here. You—ah—have plans?"

"No," I said frankly.

"Don't overwork again. Take things easy for a while. And . . ."

There was a lot more advice. And then signing things, and getting ready. It was almost an hour before we got into a cab, Tubby and I.

He gave the address, and I recognized it. The Carleton. That was where I'd lived, that last year. Where Kathy still lived.

"How's Kathy?" I asked.

"Fine, Johnny. I guess she is. I mean—"

"You mean what?"

He looked a bit embarrassed. "Well—I mean I haven't seen her. She never liked us boys, Johnny. You know that. But she was square with us. You know we decided we couldn't hold together without you, Johnny, and might as well break up. Well, she paid us what we had coming—the three weeks you were on the cuff, I mean—and doubled it, a three-weeks' bonus to tide us over."

"The boys doing okay, Tubby?"

"Yep, Johnny. All of them. Well—except Harry. He kind of got lost in the snow if you know what I mean."

"That's tough," I said, and didn't elaborate. I didn't know whether I was supposed to know that Harry had been taking cocaine or not. And there had been two Harrys with the band, at that.

So the band was busted up. In a way I was glad. If someone had taken over and held it together maybe there'd have been an argument about trying to get me to come back.

"A month ago, Tubby," I said, "they examined me at the sanitarium, and I flunked. I think it was because I didn't recognize somebody. Was it you? Were you there then?"

"You walked right by me, through the door, Johnny. You never saw me."

"You were there—for that purpose? Both times?"

"Yes, Johnny. That Doc Glasspiegel suggested it. He got to know me, and to think of me, I guess, because I dropped around so often to ask about you. Why wouldn't they let me see you?"

"Rules," I said. "That's Glasspiegel's system, part of it. Complete isolation during the period of cure. I haven't even seen Kathy."

"No!" said Tubby. "They told me you couldn't have visitors, but I didn't know it went that far." He sighed. "She sure must be head over heels for you, Johnny. What I hear, she's carried the torch."

"God knows why," I said. "After I cut—"

"Shut up," Tubby said sharply. "You aren't to think or talk about that. Glasspiegel told me that while you were getting ready."

"Okay," I said. It didn't matter. "Does Kathy know we're coming?"

"We? I'm not going in, Johnny. I'm just riding to the door with you. No, she doesn't know. You asked the doc not to tell her, didn't you?"

"I didn't want a reception. I just want to walk in quietly. Sure, I asked the doctor, but I thought maybe he'd warn her anyway. So she could hide the knives."

"Now, Johnny—"

"Okay," I said.

I looked out of the window of the cab. I knew where we were and just how far from the Carleton. Funny, my topography hadn't gone the way the rest of my memory had. I still knew the streets and their names, even though I couldn't recognize my best friend or my wife. The mind is a funny thing, I thought.

"One worry you won't have," Tubby Hayes said. "That lush

brother of hers, Myron Courteen, the one that was always in your hair."

The redheaded interne had mentioned that Kathy had a brother. Apparently I wasn't supposed to like him.

So I said, "Did someone drop him down a well?"

"Headed west. He's a Los Angeles playboy now. Guess he finally quarreled with Kathy and she settled an allowance on him and let him go."

We were getting close to the Carleton—only a half-dozen blocks to go—and suddenly I realized there was a lot that I didn't know, and should know.

"Let's have a drink, Tubby," I said. "I—I'm not quite ready to go home yet."

"Sure, Johnny," he said, and then spoke to the cab driver.

We swung in to the curb in front of a swanky neon-plated tavern. It didn't look familiar, like the rest of the street did. Tubby saw me looking.

"Yeah, it's new," he said. "Been here only a few months."

We went in and sat at a dimly lighted bar. Tubby ordered two Scotch-and-sodas—without asking me, so I guess that's what I used to drink. I didn't remember. Anyway, it tasted all right, and I hadn't had a drink for eleven months, so even the first sip of it hit me a little.

And when I'd drunk it all, it tasted better than all right. I looked at myself in the blue mirror back of the bar. I thought, there's always this. I can always drink myself to death—on Kathy's money. I knew I didn't have any myself because Tubby had said I was three weeks on the cuff with the band.

We ordered a second round and I asked Tubby, "How come this Myron hasn't money of his own, if he's Kathy's brother?" He looked at me strangely. I'd been doing all right up to now. I said, "Yeah, there are things I'm still hazy about."

"Oh," he said. "Well, that one's easy. Myron is worse than a black sheep for the Courteens. He's a no-good louse and an all-around stinker. He was disinherited, and Kathy got it all. But she takes care of him."

He took a sip of his drink and put it down again. "You know, Johnny," he said, "none of us liked Kathy much because she was against you having the band and wanted you to herself. But we were wrong about her. She's swell. The way she sticks to her menfolk no matter what they do. Even Myron."

"Even me," I said.

"Well—she saved your life, Johnny. With blood—" He stopped abruptly. "Forget it, Johnny."

I finished my second drink. I said, "I'll tell you the truth, Tubby. I can't forget it—because I don't remember it. But I've got to know, before I face her. What did happen that night?"

"Johnny, I—"

"Tell me," I said. "Straight."

He sighed. "Okay, Johnny. You'd been working close to twenty-four hours a day trying to put us over, and we'd tried to get you to slow down and so did Kathy."

"Skip the build-up."

"That night, after we played at the hotel, we rehearsed some new stuff. You acted funny then, Johnny. You forgot stuff, and you had a headache. We made you go home early, in spite of yourself. And when you got home—well, you slipped a cog, Johnny. You picked a quarrel with your wife—I don't know what you accused her of. And you went nuts. You got your razor—you always used to shave with a straight edge—and, well, you tried to kill her. And then yourself."

"You're skipping the details," I said. "How did she save my life?"

"Well, Johnny, you hadn't killed her like you thought. The

cut went deep on one side of her throat but—she must have been pulling away—it went light across the center and didn't get the jugular or anything. But there was a lot of blood and she fainted, and you thought she was dead, I guess, and slashed your own wrists. But she came to, and found you bleeding to death fast. Bleeding like she was, she got tourniquets on both your arms and held 'em and kept yelling until one of the servants woke up and got the Carleton house doctor. That's all, Johnny."

"It's enough, isn't it?" I thought awhile and then I added, "Thanks, Tubby. Look, you run along and leave me. I want to think it out and sweat it out alone, and then I'll walk the rest of the way. Okay?"

"Okay, Johnny," he said. "You'll call me up soon?"

"Sure," I said. "Thanks for everything."

"You'll be all right, Johnny?"

"Sure. I'm all right."

After he left I ordered another drink. My third, and it would have to be my last, because I was really feeling them. I didn't want to go home drunk to face Kathy.

I sat there, sipping it slowly, looking at myself in that blue mirror back of the bar. I wasn't a bad-looking guy, in a blue mirror. Only I should be dead instead of sitting there. I should have died that night eleven months ago. I'd tried to die.

I was almost alone at the bar. There was one couple drinking martinis at the far end of it. The girl was a blonde who looked like a chorus girl. I wondered idly if Kathy was a blonde. I hadn't thought to ask anyone. If Kathy walked in here now, I thought, I wouldn't know her.

The blonde down there picked up some change off the bar and walked over to the jukebox. She put in a coin and punched some buttons, and then swayed her hips back to the bar. The jukebox started playing and it was an old record and a good one—the Harry James version of the "Memphis Blues." Blue and brassy stuff from the days back before Harry went commercial.

I sat there listening, and feeling like the devil. I thought, I've got to get over it. Every time I hear stuff like that I can't go on wanting to kill myself just because I can't play anymore. I'm not the only guy in the world who can't play music. And the others get by.

My hands were lying on the bar in front of me and I tried them again, while I listened, and they wouldn't work. They wouldn't ever work again. My thumbs were okay, but the four fingers on each hand opened and closed together and not separately, as though they were webbed together.

Maybe the Scotch was making me feel better, but—maybe, I decided—maybe it wouldn't be too bad—

Then the Harry James ended and another record slid onto the turntable and started, and it was going to be blue too. "Mood Indigo." I recognized the opening bar of the introduction. I wondered idly if all the records were blues, chosen to match the blue back-bar mirrors.

Deep blue stuff, anyway, and well handled and arranged, whoever was doing it. A few Scotches and a blue mood, and that "Mood Indigo" can take hold of your insides and wring them. And this waxing of it was solid, pretty solid. The brasses tossed it to the reeds and then the piano took it for a moment, backed by wire-brush stuff on the skins, and modulated it into a higher key and built it up and you knew something was coming.

And then something came, and it was an alto sax, a sax with a tone like blue velvet, swinging high, wide and off the beat, and tossing in little arabesques of counterpoint so casually that it never seemed to leave the melody to do it. An alto sax riding high and riding hot, pouring notes like molten gold.

I unwound my fingers from around the Scotch-and-soda glass and got up and walked across the room to the jukebox. I knew already but I looked. The record playing was number 9, and number 9 was "Mood Indigo"—Johnny Marlin.

For a black second I felt that I had to stop it, that I had to smash my fist through the glass and jerk the tone arm off the record. I had to because it was doing things to me. That sound out of the past was making me remember, and I knew suddenly that the only way I could keep on wanting to live at all was *not* to remember.

Maybe I would have smashed the glass. I don't know. But instead I saw the cord and plug where the jukebox plugged into the wall outlet beside it. I jerked on the cord and the box went dark and silent. Then I walked out into the dusk, with the three of them staring at me—the blonde and her escort and the bartender.

The bartender called out, "Hey!" but didn't go on with it when I went on out without turning. I saw them in the mirror on the inside of the door as I opened it, a frozen tableau that slid sidewise off the mirror as the door swung open.

I must have walked the six blocks to the Carleton, through the gathering twilight. I crossed the wide mahogany-paneled lobby to the elevator. The uniformed operator looked familiar to me—more familiar than Tubby had. At least there was an impression that I'd seen him before.

"Good evening, Mr. Marlin," he said, and didn't ask me what floor I wanted. But his voice sounded strange, tense, and he waited a moment, stuck his head out of the elevator and looked around before he closed the door. I got the impression that he was hoping for another passenger, that he hated to shut himself and me in that tiny closed room.

But no one else came into the lobby and he slid the door

shut and moved the handle. The building slid downward past us and came to rest at the eleventh floor. I stepped out into another mahogany-paneled hall and the elevator door slid shut behind me.

It was a short hallway, on this floor, with only four doors leading to what must be quite large suites. I knew which door was mine—or I should say Kathy's. My money never paid for a suite like that.

It wasn't Kathy who opened the door. I knew that because it was a girl wearing a maid's uniform. And she must, I thought, be new. She looked at me blankly.

"Mrs. Marlin in?" I asked.

"No, sir. She'll be back soon, sir."

I went on in. "I'll wait," I said. I followed her until she opened the door of a room that looked like a library.

"In here, please," she said. "And may I have your name?"

"Marlin," I said, as I walked past her. "Johnny Marlin."

She caught her breath a little, audibly. Then she said, "Yes, sir," and hurried away.

Her heels didn't click on the thick carpeting of the hall, but I could tell she was hurrying. Hurrying away from a homicidal maniac, back to the farthest reaches of the apartment, probably to the protective company of a cook who would keep a cleaver handy, once she heard the news that the mad master of the manse was back. And likely there'd be new servants, if any, tomorrow.

I walked up and down awhile, and then decided I wanted to go to my room. I thought, if I don't think about it I can go there. My subconscious will know the way. And it worked; I went to my room.

I sat on the edge of the bed awhile, with my head in my hands, wondering why I'd come here. Then I looked around.

It was a big room, paneled like the rest of the joint, beautifully and tastefully furnished. Little Johnny Dettman of the Cleveland slums had come a long way to have a room like that, all to himself. There was a Capehart radio-phonograph across the room from me, and a big cabinet of albums. Most of the pictures on the walls were framed photographs of bands. In a silver frame on the dresser was the picture of a woman.

That would be Kathy, of course. I crossed over and looked at it. She was beautiful, all right, a big-eyed brunette with pouting, kissable lips. And the fog was getting thinner. I almost knew and remembered her.

I looked a long time at that photograph, and then I put it down and went to the closet door. I opened it and there were a lot of suits in that closet, and a lot of pairs of shoes and a choice of hats. I remembered: John Dettman had worn a sweater to high school one year because he didn't have a suit coat.

But there was something missing in that closet. The instrument cases. On the floor, there at the right, should have been two combination cases for sax and clarinet. Inside them should have been two gold-plated alto saxes and two sleek black Selmer clarinets. At the back of the closet should have been a bigger case that held a baritone sax I sometimes fooled around with at home.

They were all gone, and I was grateful to Kathy for that. She must have understood how it would make me feel to have them around.

I closed the door gently and opened the door next to it, the bathroom. I went in and stood looking at myself in the mirror over the wash bowl. It wasn't a blue mirror. I studied my face, and it was an ordinary face. There wasn't any reason in that mirror why anyone should love me the way my wife must. I wasn't tall and I wasn't handsome. I was just a mug who had played a lot of sax—once.

The mirror was the door of a built-in medicine cabinet sunk into the tile wall and I opened it. Yes, all my toilet stuff was neatly laid out on the shelves of the cabinet, as though I'd never been away, or as though I'd been expected back daily. Even—and I almost took a step backwards—both of my straight razors— the kind of a razor a barber uses—lay there on the bottom shelf beside the shaving mug and brush.

Was Kathy crazy to leave them there, after what I'd used such a thing for? Had it even been one of these very razors? I could, of course, have had three of them, but—no, I remembered, there were only two, a matched pair.

In the sanitarium I'd used an electric razor, naturally. All of them there did, even ones there for less deadly reasons than mine. And I was going to keep on using one. I'd take these and drop them down the incinerator, right now. If my wife was foolhardy enough to leave those things in a madman's room, I wasn't. How could I be sure I'd never go off the beam again?

My hand shook a little as I picked them up and closed the mirrored door. I'd take them right now and get rid of them. I went out of the bathroom and was crossing my own room, out in the middle of it, when there was a soft tap on the door—the connecting door from Kathy's room. "Johnny—" her voice said.

I thrust the razors out of sight into my coat pocket, and answered—I don't remember exactly what. My heart seemed to be in my throat, blocking my voice. And the door opened and Kathy came in—came in like the wind in a headlong rush that brought her into my arms. And with her face buried in my shoulder.

"Johnny, Johnny," she was saying, "I'm so glad you're back."

Then we kissed, and it lasted a long time, that kiss. But it didn't do anything to me. If I'd been in love with Kathy once, I'd have to start all over again, now. Oh, it was nice kissing her, as it would be nice kissing any beautiful woman. It wouldn't be hard to fall again. But so much easier and better, I thought, if I could push away all of the fog, if I could remember.

"I'm glad to be back, Kathy," I said.

Her arms tightened about me, almost convulsively. There was a big lounge chair next to the Capehart. I picked her up bodily, since she didn't want to let go of me, and crossed to the chair. I sat in it with her on my lap. After a minute she straightened up and her eyes met mine, questioningly.

The question was, "Do you love me, Johnny?"

But I couldn't meet it just then. I'd pretend, of course, when I got my bearings, and after a while my memory would come the rest of the way back—or I'd manage to love her again, instead. But just then, I ducked the question and her eyes.

Instead, I looked at her throat and saw the scar. It wasn't as bad as I'd feared. It was a thin, long line that wouldn't have been visible much over a yard away.

"Plastic surgery, Johnny," she said. "It can do wonders. Another year and it won't show at all. It—it doesn't matter." Then, as though to forestall my saying anything more about it, she said quickly, "I gave away your saxophones, Johnny. I—I figured you wouldn't want them around. The doctors said you'll never be able to—to play again."

I nodded. I said, "I guess it's best not to have them around."

"It's going to be so wonderful, Johnny. Maybe you'll hate me for saying it, but I'm—almost—glad. You know that was what came between us, your band and your playing. And it won't now, will it? You won't want to try another band—just directing and not playing—or anything foolish like that, will you, Johnny?"

"No, Kathy," I said.

Nothing, I thought, would mean anything without playing. I'd been trying to forget that. I closed my eyes and tried, for a moment, not to think.

"It'll be so wonderful, Johnny. You can do all the things I wanted you to do, and that you wouldn't. We can travel, spend our winters in Florida, and entertain. We can live on the Riviera part of the time, and we can ski in the Tyrol and play the wheels at Monte Carlo and—and everything I've wanted to do, Johnny."

"It's nice to have a few million," I said.

She pulled back a little and looked at me. "Johnny, you're not going to start *that* again, are you? Oh, Johnny, you can't—now."

No, I thought, I can't. Heaven knows why she wants him to be one, but little Johnny Dettman is a kept man now, a rich girl's darling. He can't make money the only way he knows how now. He couldn't even hold a job as a bus boy or dig ditches. But he'll learn to balance teacups on his knee and smile at dowagers. He'll have to. It was coming back to me now, that endless argument.

But the argument was over now. There wasn't any longer anything to argue about.

"Kiss me, Johnny," Kathy said, and when I had, she said, "Let's have some music, huh? And maybe a dance—you haven't forgotten how to dance, have you, Johnny?"

She jumped up from my lap and went to the record album cabinet.

"Some of mine, will you, Kathy?" I asked. I thought, I might as well get used to it now, all at once. So I won't feel again, ever, as I had when I'd almost put my fist through that jukebox window.

"Of course, Johnny."

She took them from one of the albums, half a dozen of them, and put them on the Capehart. The first one started, and it was a silly gay tune we'd once waxed—"*Chickery chick, cha la, cha la* . . ." And she came back, holding out her hands to me to get up and dance, and I did, and I still knew how to dance.

And we danced over to the French doors that led to the balcony and opened them, and out onto the marble floor of the little railed balcony, into the cool darkness of the evening, with a full moon riding high in the sky overhead.

Chickery chick—a nice tune, if a silly tune. No vocal, of course. We'd never gone for them. Not gut-bucket stuff either, but smooth rhythm, with a beat. And a high-riding alto sax, smooth as silk.

And I was remembering the argument. It had been one, a vicious one. Musician-versus-playboy as my career. I was remembering *Kathy* now, and suddenly tried not to. Maybe it would be better to forget all that bitterness, the quarreling and the overwork and everything that led up to the blankness of the breakdown.

But our feet moved smoothly on the marble. Kathy danced well. And the record ended.

"It's going to be wonderful, Johnny," she whispered, "having you all to myself . . . You're *mine* now, Johnny."

"Yes," I said. I thought, I've *got* to be.

The second record started, and was a contrast. A number as blue as "Mood Indigo," and dirtier. "St. James Infirmary," as waxed by Johnny Marlin and his orchestra. And I remembered the hot day in the studio when we'd waxed it. Again no vocal, but as we started dancing again, the words ran through my mind with the liquid gold of the alto sax I'd once played.

I went down to St. James Infirmary . . . Saw my baby there . . .
Stretched on a long white table . . . so sweet, so cold, so—

I jerked away from her, ran inside, and shut off the phono-graph. I caught sight of my face in the mirror over the dresser as I passed. It was white as a corpse's face. I went back to the balcony. Kathy still stood there—she hadn't moved.

"Johnny, what—?"

"That tune," I said. "Those words. I *remember*, Kathy. I re-member that night. *I didn't do it.*"

I felt weak. I leaned back against the wall behind me. Kathy came closer.

"Johnny—what do you mean?"

"I remember," I said. "I walked in, and you were lying there—with blood all over your throat and your dress—*when I came in the room.* I *don't* remember after that—but that's what must have knocked me off my base, after everything else. That's when I went crazy, not before."

"Johnny—you're wrong—"

The weakness was gone now. I stood straighter.

"Your brother," I said. "He hated you because you ran his life, like you wanted to run mine, because you had the money he thought should be his, and you doled it out to him and *ran* him. Sure, he hated you. I remember him now. Kathy, I remem-ber. That was about the time he got past liquor and was play-ing with dope. Heroin, wasn't it? And that night he must have come in, sky-high and murderous, before I did. And tried to kill you, and must have thought he did, and ran. It must have been just before I came in."

"Johnny, please—you're wrong—"

"You came to, after I keeled over," I said. "It—it sounds in-credible, Kathy, but it had to be that way. And, Kathy, that cold mind of yours saw a way to get everything it wanted. To protect your brother, and to get me, the way you wanted me. It was perfect, Kathy. Fix me so I'd never play again, and at the same time put me in a spot where I'd be tied to you forever because I'd think I tried to kill you."

I said, "You get your way, don't you, Kathy? At any cost. But you didn't want me to die. I'll bet you had those tourniquets ready *before you slashed my wrists*."

She was beautiful, standing there in the moonlight. She stood tall and straight, and she came the step between us and put her soft arms around me.

"I don't see, though," I said, "how you could have known I wouldn't remember what really—wait, I can see how you thought that. I had a drink or two on the way home. You smelled the liquor on me and thought I'd come home drunk, dead drunk. And I always drew a blank when I got drunk. That night I wasn't but the shock and the breakdown did even more to me. Damn you, Kathy."

"But Johnny, don't I win?"

She was beautiful, smiling, leaning back to look up into my face. Yes, she'd won. *So sweet, so cold, so bare*. So bare her throat that in the moonlight I could see the faint scar, the dotted line. And one of my crippled hands, in my pocket, fumbled open one of the razors, brought it out of my pocket, and up and across.

THE PRICE OF SALT (EXCERPT)

BY PATRICIA HIGHSMITH

Gold Coast

(Originally published in 1952)

Carol walked barefoot with little short steps to the shower room in the corner, groaning at the cold. She had red polish on her toenails, and her blue pajamas were too big for her.

"It's your fault for opening the window so high," Therese said.

Carol pulled the curtain across, and Therese heard the shower come on with a rush. "Ah, divinely hot!" Carol said. "Better than last night."

It was a luxurious tourist cabin, with a thick carpet and wood-paneled walls and everything from cellophane-sealed shoe rags to television.

Therese sat on her bed in her robe, looking at a road map, spanning it with her hand. A span and a half was about a day's driving, theoretically, though they probably would not do it. "We might get all the way across Ohio today," Therese said.

"Ohio. Noted for rivers, rubber, and certain railroads. On our left the famous Chillicothe drawbridge, where twenty-eight Hurons once massacred a hundred—morons."

Therese laughed.

"And where Lewis and Clark once camped," Carol added. "I think I'll wear my slacks today. Want to see if they're in that suitcase? If not, I'll have to get into the car. Not the light ones, the navy-blue gaberdines."

Therese went to Carol's big suitcase at the foot of the bed. It was full of sweaters and underwear and shoes, but no slacks. She saw a nickel-plated tube sticking out of a folded sweater. She lifted the sweater out. It was heavy. She unwrapped it, and started so she almost dropped it. It was a gun with a white handle.

"No?" Carol asked.

"No." Therese wrapped the gun up again and put it back as she had found it.

"Darling, I forgot my towel. I think it's on a chair."

Therese got it and took it to her, and in her nervousness as she put the towel into Carol's outstretched hand her eyes dropped from Carol's face to her bare breasts and down, and she saw the quick surprise in Carol's glance as she turned around. Therese closed her eyes tight and walked slowly toward the bed, seeing before her closed lids the image of Carol's naked body.

Therese took a shower, and when she came out, Carol was standing at the mirror, almost dressed.

"What's the matter?" Carol asked.

"Nothing."

Carol turned to her, combing her hair that was darkened a little by the wet of the shower. Her lips were bright with fresh lipstick, a cigarette between them. "Do you realize how many times a day you make me ask you that?" she said. "Don't you think it's a little inconsiderate?"

During breakfast, Therese said, "Why did you bring that gun along, Carol?"

"Oh. So that's what's bothering you. It's Harge's gun, something else he forgot." Carol's voice was casual. "I thought it'd be better to take it than to leave it."

"Is it loaded?"

"Yes, it's loaded. Harge got a permit, because we had a burglar at the house once."

"Can you use it?"

Carol smiled at her. "I'm no Annie Oakley. I can use it. I think it worries you, doesn't it? I don't expect to use it."

Therese said nothing more about it. But it disturbed her whenever she thought of it. She thought of it the next night, when a bellhop set the suitcase down heavily on the sidewalk. She wondered if a gun could ever go off from a jolt like that.

They had taken some snapshots in Ohio, and because they could get them developed early the next morning, they spent a long evening and the night in a town called Defiance. All evening they walked around the streets, looking in store windows, walking through silent residential streets where lights showed in front parlors, and homes looked as comfortable and safe as birds' nests. Therese had been afraid Carol would be bored by aimless walks, but Carol was the one who suggested going one block further, walking all the way up the hill to see what was on the other side. Carol talked about herself and Harge. Therese tried to sum up in one word what had separated Carol and Harge, but she rejected the words almost at once—boredom, resentment, indifference. Carol told her of one time that Harge had taken Rindy away on a fishing trip and not communicated for days. That was a retaliation for Carol's refusing to spend Harge's vacation with him at his family's summer house in Massachusetts. It was a mutual thing. And the incidents were not the start.

Carol put two of the snapshots in her billfold, one of Rindy in jodhpurs and a derby that had been on the first part of the roll, and one of Therese, with a cigarette in her mouth and her hair blowing back in the wind. There was one unflattering picture of Carol standing huddled in her coat that Carol said she was going to send to Abby because it was so bad.

They got to Chicago late one afternoon, crept into its gray, sprawling disorder behind a great truck of a meat-distributing company. Therese sat up close to the windshield. She couldn't remember anything about the city from the trip with her father. Carol seemed to know Chicago as well as she knew Manhattan. Carol showed her the famous Loop, and they stopped for a while to watch the trains and the homeward rush of five thirty in the afternoon. It couldn't compare to the madhouse of New York at five thirty.

At the main post office, Therese found a postcard from Dannie, nothing from Phil, and a letter from Richard. Therese glanced at the letter and saw it began and ended affectionately. She had expected just that, Richard's getting the general delivery address from Phil and writing her an affectionate letter. She put the letter in her pocket before she went back to Carol.

"Anything?" Carol said.

"Just a postcard. From Dannie. He's finished his exams."

Carol drove to the Drake Hotel. It had a black-and-white checked floor, a fountain in the lobby, and Therese thought it magnificent. In their room, Carol took off her coat and flung herself down on one of the twin beds.

"I know a few people here," she said sleepily. "Shall we look somebody up?"

But Carol fell asleep before they quite decided.

Therese looked out the window at the light-bordered lake and at the irregular, unfamiliar line of tall buildings against the still grayish sky. It looked fuzzy and monotonous, like a Pissarro painting. A comparison Carol wouldn't appreciate, she thought. She leaned on the sill, staring at the city, watching a distant car's lights chopped into dots and dashes as it passed behind trees. She was happy.

"Why don't you ring for some cocktails?" Carol's voice said behind her.

"What kind would you like?"

"What kind would you?"

"Martinis."

Carol whistled. "Double Gibsons," Carol interrupted her as she was telephoning. "And a plate of canapés. Might as well get four martinis."

Therese read Richard's letter while Carol was in the shower. The whole letter was affectionate. *You are not like any of the other girls,* he wrote. He had waited and he would keep on waiting, because he was absolutely confident that they could be happy together. He wanted her to write to him every day, send at least a postcard. He told her how he had sat one evening rereading the three letters she had sent him when he had been in Kingston, New York, last summer. There was a sentimentality in the letter that was not like Richard at all, and Therese's first thought was that he was pretending. Perhaps in order to strike at her later. Her second reaction was aversion. She came back to the old decision, that not to write him, not to say anything more, was the shortest way to end it.

The cocktails arrived, and Therese paid for them instead of signing. She could never pay a bill except behind Carol's back.

"Will you wear your black suit?" Therese asked when Carol came in.

Carol gave her a look. "Go all the way to the bottom of that suitcase?" she said, going to the suitcase. "Drag it out, brush it off, steam the wrinkles out of it for half an hour?"

"We'll be a half hour drinking these."

"Your powers of persuasion are irresistible." Carol took the suit into the bathroom and turned the water on in the tub.

It was the suit she had worn the day they had had the first lunch together.

"Do you realize this is the only drink I've had since we left New York?" Carol said. "Of course you don't. Do you know why? I'm happy."

"You're beautiful," Therese said.

And Carol gave her the derogatory smile that Therese loved, and walked to the dressing table. She flung a yellow silk scarf around her neck and tied it loosely, and began to comb her hair. The lamp's light framed her figure like a picture, and Therese had a feeling all this had happened before. She remembered suddenly: the woman in the window brushing up her long hair, remembered the very bricks in the wall, the texture of the misty rain that morning.

"How about some perfume?" Carol asked, moving toward her with the bottle. She touched Therese's forehead with her fingers, at the hairline where she had kissed her that day.

"You remind me of the woman I once saw," Therese said, "somewhere off Lexington. Not you but the light. She was combing her hair up." Therese stopped, but Carol waited for her to go on. Carol always waited, and she could never say exactly what she wanted to say. "Early one morning when I was on the way to work, and I remember it was starting to rain," she floundered on, "I saw her in a window." She really could not go on, about standing there for perhaps three or four minutes, wishing with an intensity that drained her strength that she knew the woman, that she might be welcome if she went to the house and knocked on the door, wishing she could do that instead of going on to her job at the Pelican Press.

"My little orphan," Carol said.

Therese smiled. There was nothing dismal, no sting in the word when Carol said it.

"What does your mother look like?"

"She had black hair," Therese said quickly. "She didn't look anything like me." Therese always found herself talking about her mother in the past tense, though she was alive this minute, somewhere in Connecticut.

"You really don't think she'll ever want to see you again?" Carol was standing at the mirror.

"I don't think so."

"What about your father's family? Didn't you say he had a brother?"

"I never met him. He was a kind of geologist, working for an oil company. I don't know where he is." It was easier talking about the uncle she had never met.

"What's your mother's name now?"

"Esther—Mrs. Nicolas Strully." The name meant as little to her as one she might see in a telephone book. She looked at Carol, suddenly sorry she had said the name. Carol might someday—a shock of loss, of helplessness, came over her. She knew so little about Carol after all.

Carol glanced at her. "I'll never mention it," she said, "never mention it again. If that second drink's going to make you blue, don't drink it. I don't want you to be blue tonight."

The restaurant where they dined overlooked the lake too. They had a banquet of a dinner with champagne and brandy afterward. It was the first time in her life that Therese had been a little drunk, in fact much drunker than she wanted Carol to see. Her impression of Lakeshore Drive was always to be of a broad avenue studded with mansions all resembling the White House in Washington. In the memory there would be Carol's voice, telling her about a house here and there where she had been before, and the disquieting awareness that for a while this had been Carol's world, as Rapallo, Paris, and other places Therese did not know had for a while been the frame of everything Carol did.

That night, Carol sat on the edge of her bed, smoking a cigarette before they turned the light on. Therese lay in her own bed, sleepily watching her, trying to read the meaning of the restless, puzzled look in Carol's eyes that would stare at something in the room for a moment and then move on. Was it of her she thought, or of Harge, or of Rindy? Carol had asked to be called at seven tomorrow, in order to telephone Rindy before she went to school. Therese remembered their telephone conversation in Defiance. Rindy had had a fight with some other little girl, and Carol had spent fifteen minutes going over it, and trying to persuade Rindy she should take the first step and apologize. Therese still felt the effects of what she had drunk, the tingling of the champagne that drew her painfully close to Carol. If she simply asked, she thought, Carol would let her sleep tonight in the same bed with her. She wanted more than that, to kiss her, to feel their bodies next to each other's. Therese thought of the two girls she had seen in the Palermo bar. They did that, she knew, and more. And would Carol suddenly thrust her away in disgust, if she merely wanted to hold her in her arms? And would whatever affection Carol now had for her vanish in that instant? A vision of Carol's cold rebuff swept her courage clean away. It crept back humbly in the question, couldn't she ask simply to sleep in the same bed with her?

"Carol, would you mind—"

"Tomorrow we'll go to the stockyards," Carol said at the same time, and Therese burst out laughing. "What's so damned funny about that?" Carol asked, putting out her cigarette, but she was smiling too.

"It just is. It's terribly funny," Therese said, still laughing,

laughing away all the longing and the intention of the night.

"You're giggly on champagne," Carol said as she pulled the light out.

Late the next afternoon they left Chicago and drove in the direction of Rockford. Carol said she might have a letter from Abby there, but probably not, because Abby was a bad correspondent. Therese went to a shoe-repair shop to get a moccasin stitched, and when she came back, Carol was reading the letter in the car.

"What road do we take out?" Carol's face looked happier.

"Twenty, going west."

Carol turned on the radio and worked the dial until she found some music. "What's a good town for tonight on the way to Minneapolis?"

"Dubuque," Therese said, looking at the map. "Or Waterloo looks fairly big, but it's about two hundred miles away."

"We might make it."

They took Highway 20 toward Freeport and Galena, which was starred on the map as the home of Ulysses S. Grant.

"What did Abby say?"

"Nothing much. Just a very nice letter."

Carol said little to her in the car, or even in the café where they stopped later for coffee. Carol went over and stood in front of a jukebox, dropping nickels slowly.

"You wish Abby'd come along, don't you?" Therese said.

"No," Carol said.

"You're so different since you got the letter from her."

Carol looked at her across the table. "Darling, it's just a silly letter. You can even read it if you want to." Carol reached for her handbag, but she did not get the letter out.

Sometime that evening, Therese fell asleep in the car and

woke up with the lights of a city on her face. Carol was resting both arms tiredly on the top of the wheel. They had stopped for a red light.

"Here's where we stay the night," Carol said.

Therese's sleep still clung to her as she walked across the hotel lobby. She rode up in an elevator and she was acutely conscious of Carol beside her, as if she dreamed a dream in which Carol was the subject and the only figure. In the room, she lifted her suitcase from the floor to a chair, unlatched it and left it, and stood by the writing table, watching Carol. As if her emotions had been in abeyance all the past hours, or days, they flooded her now as she watched Carol opening her suitcase, taking out, as she always did first, the leather kit that contained her toilet articles, dropping it onto the bed. She looked at Carol's hands, at the lock of hair that fell over the scarf tied around her head, at the scratch she had gotten days ago across the toe of her moccasin.

"What're you standing there for?" Carol asked. "Get to bed, sleepyhead."

"Carol, I love you."

Carol straightened up. Therese stared at her with intense, sleepy eyes. Then Carol finished taking her pajamas from the suitcase and pulled the lid down. She came to Therese and put her hands on her shoulders. She squeezed her shoulders hard, as if she were exacting a promise from her, or perhaps searching her to see if what she had said were real. Then she kissed Therese on the lips, as if they had kissed a thousand times before.

"Don't you know I love you?" Carol said.

Carol took her pajamas into the bathroom, and stood for a moment, looking down at the basin.

"I'm going out," Carol said. "But I'll be back right away."

Therese waited by the table while Carol was gone, while time passed indefinitely or maybe not at all, until the door opened and Carol came in again. She set a paper bag on the table, and Therese knew she had only gone to get a container of milk, as Carol or she herself did very often at night.

"Can I sleep with you?" Therese asked.

"Did you see the bed?"

It was a double bed. They sat up in their pajamas, drinking milk and sharing an orange that Carol was too sleepy to finish. Then Therese set the container of milk on the floor and looked at Carol who was sleeping already, on her stomach, with one arm flung up as she always went to sleep. Therese pulled out the light. Then Carol slipped her arm under her neck, and all the length of their bodies touched, fitting as if something had prearranged it. Happiness was like a green vine spreading through her, stretching fine tendrils, bearing flowers through her flesh. She had a vision of a pale white flower, shimmering as if seen in darkness, or through water. Why did people talk of heaven? she wondered.

"Go to sleep," Carol said.

Therese hoped she would not. But when she felt Carol's hand move on her shoulder, she knew she had been asleep. It was dawn now. Carol's fingers tightened in her hair, Carol kissed her on the lips, and pleasure leaped in Therese again as if it were only a continuation of the moment when Carol had slipped her arm under her neck last night. I love you, Therese wanted to say again, and then the words were erased by the tingling and terrifying pleasure that spread in waves from Carol's lips over her neck, her shoulders, that rushed suddenly the length of her body. Her arms were tight around Carol, and she was conscious of Carol and nothing else, of Carol's hand that slid along her ribs, Carol's hair that brushed her bare breasts, and then her body too seemed to vanish in widening circles that leaped farther and farther, beyond where thought could follow. While a thousand memories and moments, words, the first darling, the second time Carol had met her at the store, a thousand memories of Carol's face, her voice, moments of anger and laughter flashed like the tail of a comet across her brain. And now it was pale blue distance and space, an expanding space in which she took flight suddenly like a long arrow. The arrow seemed to cross an impossibly wide abyss with ease, seemed to arc on and on in space, and not quite to stop. Then she realized that she still clung to Carol, that she trembled violently, and the arrow was herself. She saw Carol's pale hair across her eyes, and now Carol's head was close against hers. And she did not have to ask if this was right, no one had to tell her, because this could not have been more right or perfect. She held Carol tighter against her, and felt Carol's mouth on her own smiling mouth. Therese lay still, looking at her, at Carol's face only inches away from her, the gray eyes calm as she had never seen them, as if they retained some of the space she had just emerged from. And it seemed strange that it was still Carol's face, with the freckles, the bending blond eyebrow that she knew, the mouth now as calm as her eyes, as Therese had seen it many times before.

"My angel," Carol said. "Flung out of space."

Therese looked up at the corners of the room, that were much brighter now, at the bureau with the bulging front and the shield-shaped drawer pulls, at the frameless mirror with the beveled edge, at the green-patterned curtains that hung straight at the windows, and the two gray tips of buildings that showed just above the sill. She would remember every detail of this room forever.

"What town is this?" she asked.

Carol laughed. "This? This is Waterloo." She reached for a cigarette. "Isn't that awful."

Smiling, Therese raised up on her elbow. Carol put a cigarette between her lips. "There's a couple of Waterloos in every state," Therese said.

THE STARVING DOGS
OF LITTLE CROATIA

BY BARRY GIFFORD

Wicker Park

(Originally published in 2009)

E very man lives like hunted animal," said Drca Kovic.

"You make this just up?" asked Boro Catolica.

"What is difference," Drca said, "if it is truth?"

The two men, both in their midthirties, were seated next to one another on stools at the bar in Dukes Up Tavern on Anna Ruttar Street drinking shots of Four Sisters backed with Old Style chasers. Brenda Lee was on the jukebox belting out "Rockin' Around the Christmas Tree," just as she did every December. Boro Catolica lit up a Lucky.

"Ten years now Chicago," he said, "and no truth more than Zagreb."

"At least here we drink in peace," said Drca Kovic. "There we drink in war."

"Yes, but probably we end up lying still in alley with cats they are looking at us. Our eyes they are open but not being able see theirs."

It was seven o'clock on a Friday evening two days before Christmas. There were four inches of snow on the ground with more expected. Boro and Drca had been in Dukes Up since ten to five, thirty minutes after dark and twenty minutes following the end of their shift at Widerwille Meatpacking on Pulaski Avenue. The men worked full days Monday through Friday and half days on Saturday.

"You notice old man Widerwille not so often check line now?" said Boro.

"Probably too cold in freezer for him," Drca said. "Blood is thinner."

The front door opened and two boys, both about eleven or twelve years old, entered the tavern, bringing with them a blast of icy air accompanied by a spray of new snow.

Emile Wunsch, the bartender and part owner of Dukes Up, shouted, "No minors allowed! And shut that door!"

"There's a dead guy lyin' out on the sidewalk," said the larger of the two boys.

The smaller boy closed the door.

"How do you know he's dead?" said Emile Wunsch.

"He looks like Arne Pedersen did," said the smaller boy, "after he died from Sterno poisoning last February."

"His body froze overnight," the other boy said, "on the steps of Santa Maria Addolorata."

Boro and Drca went out, followed by the boys. Half a minute later the four of them came back inside.

"It's Bad Lands Bill," said Boro, brushing snow from his head, "the Swede was from North of Dakota."

"The flat-nosed guy used to work at the chicken cannery?" asked Emile.

Drca nodded. "His skin is blue and there is no breathing."

"We saw his eyes were open," said the smaller boy, "so we stopped to look at him."

"He wasn't blinkin'," said the larger boy, "his tongue's stickin' out and it's blue too."

The two Croatian men went back outside, picked up the body, and carried it into Dukes Up, where they set it down on the floor. Boro closed the door.

"I'll call the precinct," said Emile Wunsch, "tell 'em to send a wagon. You boys can stick around to tell the cops how you found him."

Drca and Boro went back to their stools at the bar.

"Boys, you want Coca-Cola?" asked Boro.

"Sure," said the smaller one.

"I am Drca, he is Boro."

"I'm Flip," said the larger boy.

"I'm Roy," said the other.

"Okay they sit at bar?" Boro asked Emile.

Emile was still on the phone to the precinct. He hung up and motioned to Flip and Roy to go ahead. The boys climbed up on stools next to the men.

"You think corpse we should cover?" said Drca.

"Why to bother?" Boro said. "Wagon coming."

"Did Bad Lands Bill drink here?" Roy asked.

Emile came over with Cokes for the boys.

"Not for a while," he said. "He got laid off a few months back. Last time I saw him was in July."

Flip sipped his Coke as he spun around on his stool and looked down at the body. The eyes and mouth were closed.

"Hey," Flip said, "weren't his eyes and mouth open when you carried him in?"

"Yeah," said Roy, "his tongue was hangin' out."

Everyone stared at Bad Lands Bill. His skin was not quite so blue.

"I guess gettin' warmed up changes the body," said Flip. "It's good for him to be inside."

"That's what Midget Fernekes said about himself," said Emile.

"Who's that?" asked Roy.

"A bank robber grew up in Canaryville," the bartender said.

"He was the first person to blow safes usin' nitroglycerin. Midget said he learned more about safecrackin' in the pen than he ever could've on the street."

Drca and Boro drank in silence. Emile poured them each another shot of Four Sisters, then busied himself at the end of the bar. No other customers came in. Roy and Flip finished their Coca-Colas and sat quietly too. For some reason it did not seem right to talk a lot with a dead man lying there.

"The wagon oughta be here by now," said Emile, who came around from behind the bar, walked over to the front door, and looked outside through the small window.

"It's a full-on blizzard out there," he said. "Maybe you kids should go on home now, before it gets any worse. Drca and Boro and I can tell the ambulance boys what happened, if they can even get here."

"Go," said Boro. "Drinks on house. Yes, Emile?"

The bartender nodded.

"Be careful of starving dogs," said Drca. "They are hunting in group when weather is bad."

"This Chicago," said Boro, "not Zagreb. Here dogs eat better than people of half of world."

Roy and Flip got down from their stools and took one more look at Bad Lands Bill. His skin seemed almost normal now and there was a peaceful expression on his face. Emile opened the door a crack.

"Quick, boys," he said, "so the wind don't blow the snow in."

After Flip turned off Anna Ruttar Street to go to his house, Roy bent his head as he trudged forward and thought about packs of hungry wild dogs roaming the streets of Croatian cities and villages attacking kids and old people unable to defend themselves, feasting on stumblebums like Bad Lands Bill, especially if they were already dead. Roy brushed snow from his face. He wondered if Midget Fernekes was really a midget or if he was called that just because he was short. Roy worried that he could end up like Bad Lands Bill or Arne Pedersen, a rummy frozen to death on a sidewalk or in an alley. This was a possibility, he knew, it could happen to any man if enough breaks went against him. Roy tried to keep the snow out of his eyes but it was coming down too fast. He felt as if he were wandering in the clouds only this wasn't heaven. He was where the dogs could get him.

BLUE NOTE

BY STUART M. KAMINSKY

Woodlawn

(Originally published in 1997)

I was sitting in the Blue Note Lounge on Clark Street, just down the street from the Clark Theater. The Clark was the only place in town that had a new double feature every night, sometimes three features. I spent a lot of time in the dark at the Clark Theater, usually waiting for the Blue Note to open.

Maybe it was 1955 or 1957. I know it was winter. I was twenty-four or twenty-six. One of those. I may not remember the year, but I remember that night when I heard Count Basie and Joe Williams and Sonny Payne going wild for a fifteen-minute drum solo.

My name? Pitch Noles. Behind that name was another, the one I was born with, Mitchell Nolowitz. I made my living gambling, but not your ordinary gambling.

I can hear the Count at his piano, lazily running his chubby, delicate fingers over the keys in that tiny, dark room. And that's Joe Williams inside my head belting a baritone, *"Oh well. Oh well. Oh well."* Keeping it up. *"Oh well. Oh well. Oh well. Oh well."*

Audience, most of them white, a few of them black, me in the middle with a Jewish fight-promoter father and a beautiful black mother with a voice that could bring tears. They hadn't lived together since I was fourteen, but Izzy would call her every once in a while just to hear that voice.

Mae would be coming by later. She would touch my face and be waved up on the low platform by the Count and she would sing. She would turn any song into the blues. She did a "Don't Sit Under the Apple Tree," low tempo, deep voice, melancholy voice. Everyone went silent when Mae sang, everybody. Even Joe Williams closed his eyes and smiled when Mae sang. She wasn't Billie, Dinah, Ella, or Sarah. She was Mae. She would be coming.

But now Joe was doing the singing, "Every Day I Have the Blues," and Mae hadn't made her appearance. People were moving their shoulders, dreamy or smiling; maybe both. Sonny Payne was drenched with sweat, his head turned at an angle as if listening to the now almost silent rapping of his own sticks against the taut skin. The blue light of the room quivered with wisps of smoke. I was at home.

I nursed a beer and wondered, with my genes, why I could appreciate music but couldn't carry a tune.

Then Terrance "Dusk" Oliver sat down and placed a book on the table, facedown. He was compact, black, dressed in a $300 blue suit, a white shirt, and a red and blue silk paisley tie. He folded his hands on the table so I could clearly see his heavy silver skull-faced ring. I glanced at him. Dusk Oliver didn't look at me. His eyes were on Joe, but his soul, if he had one, which many doubted, was somewhere else.

When Joe finished and the Count decided on a break, I looked toward the entrance over the heads of the people seated at the tiny round tables.

"She's delayed," said Dusk, his voice high, but don't let that fool you.

I looked at him slow, cool, blue in the Blue Note because Dusk Oliver was not a man to be questioned if you wanted to go through the rest of your life with both your ears and all your fingers.

"She'll be in, in . . ." he looked at his watch, "two minutes."

Terrance's face was round, unblemished, hair cut short, eyes tiny and dark. I wondered, as I had before, what he did for fun. I knew he had studied philosophy and literature at Howard University. He was one of the few people who had turned philosophy and poetry into a practical business asset.

"We sit," he said, "here in the Blue Note, at the epicenter of delusion in the middle of the twentieth century."

Dusk Oliver was always giving out epigrams and books he had read in the hope of finding someone with whom he could talk as an equal. This was a difficult quest since he did not move in the circles of the highly literate and curious. I, with two years at Wright Junior College, was about the best he could do.

A drink appeared in front of him. It dervished with little bubbles. Terrance looked at it and bit his lower lip.

"You know who James Mason is?" he asked.

"The actor, English," I said, not looking at the door but joining Terrance in his fascination with the glass of ginger ale.

"I'd like to meet him. That voice. I'd like to meet him. My bet is he read the fucking *Marble Faun*."

I nodded again. The possibility of James Mason having read Nathaniel Hawthorne opened no new areas of conversation for me.

"You see that movie where he slammed the piano cover down on that skinny blonde's fingers because she couldn't get the song right?"

There was a point to all this. I wasn't sure what it was and I didn't like what it might be.

"Saw it at the Clark," I said. "*The Seventh Veil*."

Dusk Oliver unclasped his fingers and pushed the book he had placed on the table toward me. "*The Fountainhead*," he said. "Read it."

It was said softly, but it was an order. I took the book. It was hard to believe this educated numbers racketeer and supplier of street drugs with little patience for those who owed him money or homage had come to the Blue Note to give me a book.

There was a flurry near the door. Mae appeared. I knew it had been two minutes. I didn't have to look at my watch. If Dusk Oliver said my mother was coming through the door in two minutes, you didn't have to check your watch.

She nodded to a few people, wended her way through the tightly packed tables. She was wearing a black dress and something tight and glittery around her slim brown neck. She was a beauty. No doubt. She came to my table, touched my cheek, and looked briefly into my eyes with eyes like my own. She didn't look at Dusk. There was something soulful in her smile that said all was not well in the smoke-filled demi-darkness.

She turned and made her way around the small, low stage and through a dark curtain to the left.

"Beautiful lady," said Dusk.

I nodded again. Maybe I would spend the night nodding until Terrance decided to ask me a question or simply disappeared.

"She owes me," he said, inching toward the point and leaning toward me. "She is beautiful, misbegotten, a wisp, a waif, Cleopatra, a waft of gardenia freshness when she enters a room. Mae is a piece of work."

This time he paused and looked at me for a response.

"A piece of work," I agreed.

"Elegant."

"Elegant."

"Somewhere about six in the morning, that elegance will be marred by a missing finger," he said.

There was no sign of sympathy and I knew better than to look for one.

"Unless . . ." he went on.

"Unless?"

He looked at his watch again and said, "You go to a house in Hyde Park with ten thousand dollars of my money and sit in on a poker game. You walk out of that poker game with a minimum of forty thousand dollars by five in the morning. You get in a car that will be waiting, hand the driver the money, and get a ride back home or wherever you want to go with half of everything you make over the forty thousand."

"And . . . ?" I asked.

"Mae's debt is repaid," Terrance said.

It wasn't a request or a proposition. I was going to that game. Terrance was counting on my reputation. I was the Prince of the Tell, the Duke of the Giveaway. Some of it was conscious. Some of it was intuition that came from observation, a lot of it from my father. Once I picked twenty-three straight boxing matches correctly, both under- and overcards. I missed twenty-four because the guy I had picked suddenly got a pain in his stomach, doubled over, and took a desperation left uppercut that broke his jaw.

I never bet more than a few hundred dollars on a fight and I never won more than a few thousand max at a poker table. I stayed below the lights. I liked Chicago, day or night. I haunted the Brookfield and Lincoln Park zoos, communing with the gorillas and chimps. Once in a while, I spent a night in a poker game with out-of-towners who saw a kid with a smile and more than ordinary luck. It had little to do with luck. Sometimes, much of the time, it had nothing to do with luck. When I wasn't going to Marigold or Soldier Field or the Coliseum for a fight night, or sitting in a hotel room or the back room of a bar on Elston or Division, I hit the blues bars.

"When?" I asked.

"When Mae finishes," Dusk said.

Basie and the small traveling band came out one at a time and took their places. The audience kept talking.

Joe Williams didn't appear. The band settled itself and Mae entered—serious, beautiful, dark, and smoky. She looked down, moistened her lips. The crowd went quiet.

She looked at me. I knew what she wanted. I couldn't turn her down. I couldn't refuse Dusk Oliver.

We listened to my mother sing "You Don't Know What Love Is," "St. Louis Blues," "Blues for a Lonesome Child," and more. I had the feeling that she didn't want the set to end.

Neither did the audience. Shaharazade in black and glitter putting off the inevitable.

Finally, she stopped and bowed. The audience went well beyond polite. The Count clapped his pudgy fingers and Mae came out for another bow, but no encore.

It was up to me.

"Let's go," Oliver said.

I sat with him in the backseat of a black Chrysler. The driver was alone in the front. I recognized him: Kelly "Two Punch" Jones, heavyweight, great black hope who went from being the man who could put away almost any man with two punches to the man who could be put away by almost anyone with two punches. He never developed even a three-punch combination. He went downhill fast. That was the pros. Now he had another profession and Two Punch was not to be trifled with by civilians.

Dusk took a bundle of bills out of the pocket of his chestnut camel-hair coat, peeled off some of them, tucked them in my jacket pocket, and handed me the rest. "Put them away," he said. "Leave the book in the car."

I put *The Fountainhead* down.

We drove down Lake Shore Drive. The night was winter cold. Ankle-high mounds of dirty snow ran along the curbing. Late-night traffic was light, the windows were closed, Lake Michigan was quiet.

"Three players," Dusk said. "They think you're my nephew."

The family resemblance would best not be questioned.

"You don't know any of them. They don't know you. You walk up to the door by yourself, knock. Don't give your real name. No reason to. The players? Tall, skinny Negro pushing seventy years is Wallace Livingstone. Dapper. He's Elder. Some kind of doctor from Detroit. Been around Wheel City tables longer than double your life. First time in Chicago in twenty years or something. Second guy is younger, maybe fifty, white, bad skin, bad breath, thin hair brushed over. Name is Dunwoody. Nervous little guy. He plays with cash belonging to a New Orleans trucking union local of which he is both treasurer and recording secretary. And that brings us to the Russian. I don't like the guy. He fucking smirks."

Dusk paused as Two Punch made the turn at 53rd and headed west.

"The Russian's no Russian," said Dusk. "He's a Hungarian or something. Maybe not even that. Who cares where he came from. All three of them conned me into a game on Monday and took me for twenty thousand dollars and change. It was rigged. I want it back."

He paused, waiting for an answer to a question that hadn't been asked.

"With interest," I said.

"You know what Hank Sauer said? The only way to prove you're a good sport is to lose. I'm not a good sport."

I could see Dusk Oliver nod in minimal satisfaction as passing streetlights flickered across his face.

"House belongs to a former alderman with bad habits. He gets one percent from every pot and makes himself invisible. The man with the gun who'll open the door for you is a cop. I don't know his name. Don't care. He's there to keep out the unwelcome."

He sat back and said, "You'll like the book. We'll talk about it. We'll pick up some Jew hot dogs at Fluky's and talk about it."

Woodlawn south of 53rd was a line of stone and brick two- and three-story houses. Inside the houses dwelt the dwindling ranks of Hyde Park's old wealthy and the latest wave of University of Chicago administrators and better-paid professors. The wealthy and the educated locked their doors to keep out the poor and the uneducated Negro kids who lived five minutes away across the snow-covered Midway in Woodlawn to the south and the huddled ghetto of Kenwood to the north.

The whites and a few blacks who bolted the doors at night on Woodlawn Avenue honestly proclaimed their oneness with their banished, low-class neighbors. That didn't stop the comfortable but wary of Hyde Park from closing those doors.

Two Punch pulled up in front of a three-story white stone house on the right. There were no lights in the first-floor windows. There was a light behind pulled drapes on the second floor.

Dusk reached past me and opened the door for me to get out.

"Two Punch will be back out here before five. Think about Mae's future, but don't let it get in the way of your play. I want what's due me, kid."

I got out.

Before he closed the door, Dusk added, "Just imagine James Mason's voice telling you to be calm and concentrate and you'll be fine."

The door closed. The car pulled away and I spent no more than two seconds wondering how James Mason's voice was going to help me.

I patted the bills in my jacket pocket and the backup stack in my other pocket. Then I stepped over a knee-high pile of black snow, stepped in front of the door, and used the heavy knocker.

A shadow flickered across the small glass peephole.

The door was opened by the cop, in slacks and a jacket with a tie that didn't come near matching anything either he or I was wearing. The tie was knotted clumsily to the left. It didn't matter. What did matter was his jacket was open enough to make his holstered gun clear.

He led me up a wooden stairway that creaked and, in one or two places, sagged. He didn't ask my name.

The cop with the gun opened a door, let me step in, and then closed the door and stayed outside.

Handshakes and introductions all around. The thin, old doctor introduced as Elder, the jumpy New Orleans union fund thief Dunwoody, and Serge, the Russian. I smiled. The doctor examined my face. The thief wanted to get started. The Russian, who wasn't a Russian, cocked his head to one side slightly to examine me. The Russian was about forty-five, lots of neatly brushed hair with gray sideburns and a salt-and-pepper, neatly trimmed beard.

An antique sideboard against the wall held a variety of alcoholic drinks and sandwiches. I was hungry and dry. I took a Goebel beer, used an opener, put two sandwiches of something that smelled like ham on a plate, and took my seat at the table.

The other three: Wallace Livingtone the Elder on my left, Dunwoody on my right, and Serge the Russian across from me. I took the small stack of cash from my jacket with one hand

and worked on a sandwich with the other. The Elder took my cash and expertly measured out five thousand in chips of red, white, and blue.

The game was five-card stud. Period. One card dealt down and one card turned over for the first bet or fold. Then three more cards, betting on each card.

I started reading the table before the first card was dealt.

The Elder knew his tell. I could see it from the way he stayed erect, not blinking, hands as steady as he could hold them; but they threatened to betray him when the ante went in. The Russian was up for the deal. The Elder was struggling to keep away a tiny tremor. I wasn't sure what it meant. Dunwoody and the Russian hadn't paid any attention.

The Russian didn't say much, but what he did say was open for a tell. Sometimes he dropped his t's. Sometimes he didn't. Sometimes he pronounced his o's as u's. "Long" became "lung." His knowing smile was frozen, less knowing than a truly confident smirk.

The hardest one to read before that first card was dealt was Dunwoody. He kept talking, kept moving his hands, fidgeting; more moves than a third base coach. He didn't have a tell. He had dozens of them.

And then the cards came. We didn't start till almost one in the morning. Four hours wasn't much time.

I started by checking, folding or staying in only when I had a pair. I bet into players knowing I would lose, just to see what they would give away when they were sure to pretty certain they were going to win. Dunwoody always reached eagerly to look at his hole card. Then he would put the card down and tap it. The Elder held the hole card for no more than an instant, not even lifting it from the table, just peeling it back enough for a glimpse. The Russian held his card in front of his eyes, touched his nose, smiled, turned his card in a circle, and placed it facedown on the table.

By the time I was down by almost four thousand dollars, I could see how they were trying to hide every read. The tells took awhile to spot. All three of them were good. I wasn't about to make any mistakes. I couldn't afford to. The clock was ticking toward Mae's fingers.

By the time it was almost three I had a good idea of what kinds of hands each man played, how and when they bluffed. That left only luck of the draw, but even that could be overcome with smart bluffing.

The problem was that it can take time to wear down a player you could read who was drawing lucky and betting recklessly.

Dunwoody sometimes bet with no chance of winning on the table. The Elder came in hard when he had something, but came in just as hard about one hand in six when he had nothing. Sometimes he did it twice in a row. Sometimes he didn't do it for a dozen bad hands.

The Russian always bet to kill.

I was down to four hundred of the five thousand I'd put on the table, when I pulled out the backup stack of five thousand at three thirty.

I knew now that when he had something, the Elder let his hands rest lightly on the table, so lightly that they were almost not touching. When he had nothing, the hands came down just a touch heavier, maybe the width of a butterfly wing, but I saw it.

Dunwoody was down even more than I was. It wasn't his money any more than it was my money at stake. He had nothing to lose but other people's money and his arms if he got caught. He didn't go out till all was hopeless. If he had a good hand, that was the big tell. He ran his tongue gently along his upper teeth with his mouth almost closed. It was hard to spot, but it was there.

The Russian held his chips about half an inch higher when he bet with good cards.

My father had taught me that everybody has a tell—boxers, betters, bankers, every blind man and Catholic bishop. Even if you cover your head and eyes, keep a stone face, keep your hands flat on the table and always count to exactly thirty-two before you bet or folded, something would give you away.

I started to win. Slow at first. I would have won less and a lot slower if I didn't know Dusk Oliver was probably sitting across a table from my mother somewhere, with a small but sharp garden pruning shears in his hand. By four fifteen I was almost fifteen thousand over the stake Dusk had given me. I passed the deal and gave up position so I wouldn't be accused of manipulating the cards.

"Lucky fuckin' . . ." Dunwoody said.

Larry the Elder shrugged.

The Russian allowed himself a serviceable frown.

I was going to make it. Table rule was you could not quit when you were ahead until the last hand of any hour.

Then something went wrong. I started to lose and the Russian started to smile and I started to worry. I ate sandwiches. Nobody else did. I ate an egg salad, a ham salad, and two shrimp salads, all on white, no crusts.

Dunwoody went bust at four thirty. The Elder bowed out a few minutes later, though he was almost even. I met the Russian's eyes and didn't like what I was seeing. Confidence.

I was still five thousand short of Dusk's demand with twenty minutes till five.

And then I knew. The Russian was reading me. He saw a tell. I thought mine were covered. They weren't.

Then it got even worse. The tells the Russian had been flashing for almost three hours disappeared. He had played me, probably the way he had played Dusk.

I lost four more hands going over my movements, finding nothing. Dunwoody and the Elder watched with interest. I was sure I hadn't been doing something I'd done before.

Then I got it. Big pot. Figured it out. Asked myself the question: why did he wait so long to nail me? Answer: I was doing something now I hadn't done earlier in the game.

"Bet two thousand," the Russian said.

He had a jack in the hole and a pair of jacks. I had a pair of fours. It was almost five o'clock. Two Punch was parked in front of the house. *The Fountainhead* was lying on the backseat. In an hour, Mae would lose a finger. She wouldn't scream, wouldn't let herself make a sound, not Mae. It wouldn't kill her, but she would never be the same.

My right eye stung.

I didn't reach up to wipe perspiration away.

That's what was telling the Russian all he needed to know.

I bet a bad hand. He raised me.

It was a few minutes to five. I went to the drink table for a last sandwich and came back. I wasn't hungry but I ate.

I looked at my watch and the Russian said, "You half somewhere to go to?"

"Yes," I said. "To see my mother."

"At this hour?" asked the Russian.

"She works nights."

The cards were dealt. I had a nine in the hole. I bet it. The Russian raised. I stayed with him. He turned two spades, one a queen, one a king, and then a third spade. I turned a second nine to match the hole nine I'd been dealt.

"Last hand?" the Russian asked.

"Looks that way," I said.

"Make this interestin' perhaps?"

I wiped my upper lip with the back of my hand and said, "Why not?"

"How much you wanting to bet?"

"Ten thousand," I said.

Dunwoody paused, a glass of watery Scotch almost to his lips. The Elder shook his head at the folly of the much younger generation.

"Ten thousand," the Russian agreed, stacking his chips in the center of the table.

"Cash?" I asked.

The Russian opened his palms to show he was a sporting man. I put in ten thousand dollars and the last card was turned over.

"Two nines," said the Russian, showing his hole card.

"Two tens," I said, showing mine.

I'll give the Russian this. He didn't break. I was sure he didn't understand, not yet. I had let him read my last tell, but it had been a sham. When I was getting my sandwich, I had palmed a small chunk of ice and brought it to the table. When the last game started, I touched my upper lip. It was moist when I had made my final bet. The Russian, meanwhile, overconfident, had inadvertently touched his thumb to his finger.

I pushed all the chips toward the Elder, who was the banker.

I didn't meet anyone's eyes. I half expected the door to open and the cop with the badly knotted tie to come in and say I wasn't leaving. Or maybe the Russian was going to reach into his jacket and come up with a sharp or explosive surprise.

But nothing happened. The Elder counted his remaining chips and handed me the cash. Dunwoody looked at the draped window and shook his head. The Russian waited for me to look up and nodded at me.

I forced myself to calmly gather and fold the bills before I said my good-nights, thanked them all, and escaped.

The car was waiting. It was ten minutes after five.

I got in the seat next to Two Punch and handed him the money. He turned on the dashboard light and slowly counted.

"Forty thousand, six hundred and ten," he said looking at me.

"If you say so," I agreed. "Let's go."

We got to Dusk Oliver's current headquarters, the Rib Emporium on 82nd Street, at ten minutes to six. The sweet smell of barbecue sauce made me wish I hadn't eaten all those sandwiches. The place was dark. Two Punch had a key. I followed him in, trying not to stumble in the dark as we went through a door in the rear of the restaurant.

Dusk was seated at a table in the small kitchen, an iced tea clinking in front of him. Two Punch handed him the money. Dusk stacked it neatly in front of him.

"It's a good feeling to get back at those who cheat you," he said.

I nodded.

No one had cheated Dusk Oliver; not the Elder, not Dunwoody, not the Russian. No one had cheated at the table for the four hours I had played. I had seen Dusk play poker. The Russian in an all-night game could have taken Dusk without cheating. No contest. Dusk's high opinion of his skill was not merited.

I said nothing.

He pushed a pile of bills in my direction. I took them.

"You think I'd really cut off one of Mae's fingers?"

"Yes," I said.

"Yes," he said. "You're right. I would have. Consider her debts canceled."

I knew Mae's debts would start up again in a day or two. Not owing money to a dealer didn't get you to suddenly quit taking. If anything, it gave the taker a breather and the feeling he or she could start over, that they had bought time. Dusk Oliver was a lousy poker player but a smart drug dealer. He understood.

"Don't forget the book," he said.

"I won't."

"Two Punch has a big bucket of ribs and chicken for you. Julius doesn't sell day-old."

"Is it Christmas?" I asked.

"Don't be a smart-ass. You look into the mouth of a gift horse and you're liable to get your dick bitten off."

The metaphor was mixed but it could turn into a reality if I didn't shut up.

"We'll do more business now," he said.

Nothing to say.

The Blue Note was closed for the morning. The sun was coming out. Two Punch dropped me at Stella's on Diversey Avenue just off of Western. I recognized all four of the musicians playing. Three were black, one was a redheaded white kid with a cigarette dangling from the side of his mouth and burning his eyes. The redheaded kid was a music student at Northwestern. He was coaxing the guitar on his lap. They were playing "Blue and Sentimental."

Five people, all male except for my mother, were seated on folding chairs, listening, smoking, wandering into a back room to take something for the edge, something to bring on the dreams and hold back the nightmares. I laid out my tribute, a bucket of chicken.

Mae's legs were crossed. She looked up at me. I nodded. She understood. Her fingers were safe for a while. Why didn't she look tired? Bored maybe, but not tired. I sat next to her and listened to the music. She touched my hand.

"Thanks," she said.

And then the song stopped and without being told or invited, Mae walked forward and started to sing. I had never figured it out. I wasn't a musician. If there was a tell, I never spotted it. Musicians like my mother and the Count didn't need words. They knew what to play, what to sing. Two notes, just two notes from Mae, were enough for the musicians to start.

"*I'll never smile again,*" Mae sang, almost just spoke, looking at her hands. Then she looked at me and the sad voice of my mother sang, "*Until I smile at you.*"

I felt rather than saw someone sit in the chair Mae had vacated. I didn't look but I sensed and then was sure.

"She is good," the Russian whispered.

"She's the best," I answered.

"Dunwoody knew someone who knew where I'd find you. He knew who you were when you sat down at the table with us."

Nothing to say, at least not on my part.

"You gave it all to Oliver?"

"All," I said, which was true though he had given some of it back to me.

"I couldn't leave this dark and glorious city without letting you know."

"Part of the game," I said. "Sometimes when it's over, going over the game is the best part."

We both looked at and listened to Mae. Before she started "Love for Sale," the Russian stood.

"Ice on the upper lip," he said. "You must have been desperate."

"Lady singing is my mother. Dusk said he was going to be unkind to her at six if I didn't win."

"I know. We knew it when you sat down."

"You let me win," I said.

It wasn't a question.

"Leaving the game ahead of Mr. Oliver seemed like a bad bet," said the Russian. "He is obviously a very bad loser. We didn't know how bad a loser he could be until after we took him for the twenty thousand and people let us know. Letting him have his money back with a little interest seemed like a good idea. Letting him think he had taken us seemed like an even better idea. Never again sitting down with him is the best idea of all."

The Russian reached over and offered his hand. I took it.

"If you're ever in Dallas, look me up. Marty O'Brien. Leave a message at the Texas Independence Restaurant."

"I will," I said.

"I look forward to playing you Even Steven across the table, Pitch Noles."

"Me too, Marty O'Brien."

Then he was gone and I settled back. I should have been in bed sleeping, but I was young and Mae was singing and this moment would be gone. I wanted to hold onto it for a while, at least till the sun came up.

I'd get around to reading *The Fountainhead*, but not for a while.

THE WHOLE WORLD IS WATCHING

BY LIBBY FISCHER HELLMANN

Gramt Park

(Originally published in 2007)

T*he whole world is watching.*" Bernie Pollak snorted and slammed his locker door. "You wanna know what they're watching? They're watching these long-hair commie pinkos tear our country apart. That's what they're watching!"

Officer Kevin Dougherty strapped on his gun belt, grabbed his hat, and followed his partner into the squad room. Bernie was a former Marine who'd seen action in Korea. When he moved to Beverly, he bought a flagpole for his front lawn and raised Old Glory every morning.

Captain Greer stood behind the lectern, scanning the front page of the *Chicago Daily News*. Tall, with a fringe of gray hair around his head, Greer was usually a man of few words and fewer expressions. He reminded Kevin of his late father, who'd been a cop too. Now Greer made a show of folding the paper and looked up. "Okay, men. You all know what happened last night, right?"

A few of the twenty-odd officers shook their heads. It was Monday, August 26, 1968.

"Where you been? On Mars? Well, about five thousand of them—agitators—showed up in Lincoln Park yesterday after-noon. Festival of Life, they called it." Kevin noted the slight curl of Greer's lip. "When we wouldn't allow 'em to bring in a flatbed truck, it got ugly. By curfew, half of 'em were still in the park, so we moved in again. They swarmed into Old Town. We went after them and arrested a bunch. But there were injuries all around. Civilians too."

"Who was arrested?" an officer asked.

Greer frowned. "Don't know 'em all. But another wing of 'em was trying to surround us down at headquarters. We cut them off and headed them back up to Grant Park. We got—what's his name—Hayden."

"Tom Hayden?" Kevin said.

Greer gazed at Kevin. "That's him."

"He's the leader of SDS," Kevin whispered to Bernie.

"Let's get one thing straight." Greer's eyes locked on Kevin, as if he'd heard his telltale whisper. "No matter what they call themselves—Students for a Democratic Society, Yippies, MOBE—they are the enemy. They want to paralyze our city. Hizzoner made it clear that isn't going to happen."

Kevin kept his mouth shut.

"All days off and furloughs have been suspended," Greer went on. "You'll be working overtime too. Maybe a double shift." He picked up a sheet of paper. "I'm gonna read your assignments. Some of you will be deployed to Grant Park, some to Lincoln Park. And some of you to the Amphitheater and the convention."

Bernie and Kevin pulled the evening shift at the Amphitheater, and were shown their gas masks, helmets, riot sticks, and tear gas canisters. Kevin hadn't done riot control since the Academy, but Bernie had worked the riots after Martin Luther King's death.

"I'm gonna get some shut-eye," Bernie said, shuffling out of the room after inspecting his gear. "I have a feeling this is gonna be a long night."

"Mom wanted to talk to me. I guess I'll head home."

Bernie harrumphed. "Just remember, kid, there's more to life than the Sears catalog."

Kevin smiled weakly. Bernie'd been saying that for years, and Kevin still didn't know what it meant. But Bernie was the patrolman who broke in the rookies, and the rumor was he'd make sergeant soon. No need to tick him off.

"Kev . . ." Bernie laid a hand on his shoulder. "You're still a young kid, and I know you got—what—mixed feelings about this thing. But these . . . these *agitators*—they're all liars. Wilkerson was there last night." He yanked a thumb toward another officer. "He says they got this fake blood, you know? They holler over loudspeakers, rile up the crowd, then pour the stuff all over themselves and tell everyone they were hit on the head. Now they're threatening to pour LSD into the water supply." He faced Kevin straight on. "They're bad news, Kev."

Kevin hoisted his gear over his shoulder. "I thought they were here just to demonstrate against the war."

"These people want to destroy what we have. What do you think all that flag burning is about?" Bernie shook his head. "Our boys are over there saving a country, and all these brats do is whine and complain and get high. They don't know what war is. Not like us."

Kevin drove down to 31st and Halstead, part of a lace-curtain Irish neighborhood with a tavern on one corner and a church on the other. When he was little, Kevin thought the church's bell tower was a castle, and he fought imaginary battles on the sidewalk in front with his friends. One day the priest came out and explained how it was God's tower and should never be confused with a place of war. Kevin still felt a twinge when he passed by.

His parents' home, a two-story frame house with a covered

porch, was showing its age. He opened the door. Inside the air was heavy with a mouth-watering aroma.

"That you, sweetheart?" a woman's voice called.

"Is that pot roast?"

"It's not ready yet."

He went down the hall, wondering if his mother would ever get rid of the faded wallpaper with little blue flowers. He walked into the kitchen. Between the sultry air outside and the heat from the oven, he felt like he was entering the mouth of hell. "It's frigging hot in here."

"The AC's on." She turned from the stove and pointed to a window unit that was coughing and straining and failing to cool. Kevin loosened his collar. His mother was tall, almost six feet. Her thick auburn hair, still long and free of gray, was swept back into a ponytail. Her eyes—as blue as an Irish summer sky, his father used to say in one of his rare good moods—looked him over. "Are you all right?"

"Great." He gave her a kiss. "Why wouldn't I be?"

"I've been listening to the radio. It's crazy what's happening downtown."

"Don't you worry, Ma." He flashed her a cheerful smile. "We got it under control."

Her face was grave. "I love you, son, but don't try to con me. I was a cop's wife." She waved him into a chair. "I'm worried about Maggie," she said softly.

Kevin straddled the chair backward. "What's going on?"

"She hasn't come out of her room for three days. Just keeps listening to all that whiny music. And the smell—haven't you noticed that heavy sweet scent seeping under her door?"

Kevin shook his head.

His mother exhaled noisily. "I think she's using marijuana."

Kevin nodded. "Okay. Don't worry, Ma. I'll talk to her."

* * *

As he climbed the stairs, strains of *Surrealistic Pillow* by the Airplane drifted into the hall. He knocked on his sister's door, which was firmly shut.

"It's me, Mags. Kev."

"Hey. Come on in."

He opened the door. The window air conditioner rumbled, providing a noisy underbeat to the music, but it was still August hot inside the room. Kevin wiped a hand across his brow. Her shades were drawn, and the only light streamed out from a tiny desk lamp. Long shadows played across posters taped on the wall: the Beatles in Sgt. Pepper uniforms, Jim Morrison and the Doors, and a yellow and black sunflower with *WAR IS NOT HEALTHY FOR CHILDREN AND OTHER LIVING THINGS.*

Maggie sprawled on her bed reading the *Chicago Seed.* What was she doing with that underground garbage? The dicks read it down at the station. Said they got good intelligence from it. But his sister? He wanted to snatch it away.

"What's happening?"

Maggie looked up. She had the same blue eyes and features as her mother, but her hair was brown, not auburn, and it reached halfway down her back. Today it was held back by a red paisley bandanna. She was wearing jeans and a puffy white peasant blouse. She held up the newspaper. "You want to know, read this."

She slid off her bed and struck a match over a skinny black stick on the windowsill. A wisp of smoke twirled up from the stick. Within a few seconds, a sickly sweet odor floated through the air.

The music ended. The arm of the record player clicked, swung back, and a new LP dropped on the turntable. As Maggie flounced back on the bed, another smell, more potent than the incense, swam toward him. Kevin covered his nose. "What is that awful smell?"

"Patchouli oil."

"Pa—who oil?"

"Pa-chu-lee. It's a Hindu thing. Supposed to balance the emotions and calm you when you're upset."

Kevin took the opening. "Mom's worried about you."

"She ought to be worried. The country is falling apart."

Bernie had said the same thing, he recalled. But for different reasons. "How do you mean?"

"Idiots are running things. And anytime someone makes sense, they get assassinated."

"Does that mean you should just stay in your room and listen to music?"

"You'd rather see me in the streets?"

"Is that where you want to be?"

"Maybe." Then, "You remember my friend Jimmy?"

"The guy you were dating . . ."

She nodded. "He was going to work for Bobby."

"Who?"

"Bobby Kennedy. They asked him to be the youth coordinator for Bobby's campaign. He was going to drop out of college for a semester. I was too. It would have been amazing. But now . . ." She shrugged.

"Hey . . ." Kevin tried to think of a way to reach her. "Don't give up. What would Dad say?"

"He'd understand. He might have been a cop, but he hated what was happening. Especially to Michael."

Kevin winced. Two years ago their older brother Michael had been drafted. Twenty-Fifth Infantry. Third Brigade. Pleiku. A year ago they got word he was MIA. Their father died three months after that, ostensibly from a stroke. His mother still wasn't the same.

"Dad would have told you that Michael died doing his job," he said slowly.

"Launching an unprovoked, unlawful invasion into a quiet little country was Michael's job?"

"That sounds like something you read in that—in that." Kevin pointed a finger at the *Seed*.

Maggie's face lit with anger. "Kevin, what rock have you been hiding under? First Martin Luther King, then Bobby. And now we're trying to annihilate an entire culture because of some outdated concept of geopolitical power. This country is screwed up!"

Kevin felt himself get hot. "Damn it, Mags. It's not that complicated. We're over there trying to save the country, not destroy it. It's only these—these agitators who are trying to convince you it's wrong."

"These 'agitators,' as you call them, are the sanest people around."

"Throwing rocks, nominating pigs for president?"

"That's just to get attention. It got yours." Maggie glared. "Did you know Father Connor came out against the war?"

Kevin was taken aback.

She nodded. "He said it's become the single greatest threat to our country. And that any American who acquiesces to it, actively or passively, ought to be ashamed before God."

Kevin ran his tongue around his lips. "He's just a priest," he said finally.

She spread her hands. "Maybe you should have gone into the army instead of the police. What good is a deferment if you don't understand why you got it?"

"I'm the oldest son. The primary support of the family."

"Well then, start supporting us."

He stared at his sister. "Dad would be ashamed of you, Maggie."

"How do you know? Mother came out against the war."

"What are you talking about?"

"You should have seen her talking to Father Connor after church last week. Why don't you ask her how she feels?"

"I don't need to. I already know."

Maggie shook her head. "You're wrong. It's different now, Kevin. You're gonna have to choose."

He averted his eyes and gazed at an old photo on the windowsill. Himself, Mike, and Maggie. He remembered when it was taken. He and Mike were eleven and twelve, Maggie seven. Mike had been wearing mismatched argyle socks. He was scared his father would notice, and he begged Kevin not to tell. Kevin never did. It was their secret forever.

Monday night Mayor Daley formally opened the 1968 Democratic National Convention. Marchers set up a picket line near the Amphitheater, and thirty demonstrators were arrested. But there was no violence, and it was a relatively quiet shift. Kevin didn't need his riot gear.

It was a different story at Lincoln Park, he learned the next morning, as he and Bernie huddled with other cops in the precinct's parking lot.

"They beat the crap out of us," Wilkerson said. "See this?" He pointed to a shiner around his left eye. "But don't worry." He nodded at the sympathetic noises from the men. "I gave it back." He went on to describe how hundreds of protestors had barricaded themselves inside the park after the eleven o'clock curfew. Patrol cars were pelted by rocks. Demonstrators tried to set cars on fire. When that didn't work, they lobbed baseballs embedded with nails. The police moved in with tear gas, the crowd spilled into Old Town, and there were hundreds of injuries and arrests. Wilkerson said the mayor was calling in the guard.

"What did I tell you?" Bernie punched Kevin's shoulder. "No respect. For anything." When Kevin didn't answer, Bernie spat on the asphalt. "Well, I'm ready for some breakfast."

They drove to a place in the Loop that served breakfast all day and headed to an empty booth, still wearing their uniforms. Two men at a nearby table traded glances. Kevin slouched in his seat.

One of the men cleared his throat. "Look . . ." He folded the newspaper and showed it to his companion. Even from a distance, Kevin could see photos of police bashing in heads. "Listen to this," the man recited in a voice loud enough to carry over to them. "'*The savage beatings of protestors were unprecedented. And widespread. Police attacked without reason, even targeting reporters and photographers.* For example, one reporter saw a young man shouting at a policeman, *Hey, I work for the Associated Press!* The police officer responded, *Is that right, creep?* and proceeded to crack the reporter's skull with his nightstick.'"

Bernie drummed his fingers on the table and pretended not to hear. When their food came, Kevin pushed his eggs around the plate. "My parish priest came out against the war," he said.

Bernie chewed his bacon. "I'm sure the Father is a sincere man. But has he ever seen any action?"

"Not in 'Nam."

"What about Lincoln Park? Has he ever dealt with these—these *demonstrators*?" Bernie lowered his voice when he spoke the word, as if it was profane.

Kevin shrugged.

"Well, then." Bernie dipped his head, as if he'd made a significant point.

I'll call your shiner and raise you an MIA? How could you compare Vietnam to Lincoln Park? "Maybe they have a point," Kevin said wearily.

"What point comes out of violence?"

"Couldn't they say the same about us?"

"We're soldiers, son." Bernie scowled. "We have a job to do. You can bet if I was on the front line . . ." He threw a glance at the two men at the next table, then looked back at Kevin. "Hey, are you sure you're up for this?"

"What do you mean?"

"You seem, well, I dunno." He gazed at him. "I got this feeling."

Kevin tightened his lips. "I'm fine, Bernie. Really."

The cemetery hugged the rear of the parish church. It was a small place, with only one or two mausoleums. Unlike the Doughertys, most Bridgeport dignitaries chose Rosehill, the huge cemetery on the North Side, as their final resting place. Kevin avoided going inside the church; he didn't want to run into Father Connor.

Despite the blanket of heat, birds twittered, and a slight breeze stirred an elm that somehow escaped Dutch elm disease. He strolled among the headstones until he reached the third row, second from the left. The epitaph read: *HERE LIES A GOOD MAN, FATHER, AND GUARDIAN OF THE LAW.*

Life with Owen Dougherty hadn't been easy. He was strict, and he rarely smiled, especially after he gave up drinking. But he'd been a fair man. Kevin remembered when he and his buddy Frank smashed their neighbor's window with a fly ball. Frank got a beating from his father, but Kevin didn't. His father forked over the money for the window, then made Kevin deliver groceries for six months to pay him back.

He sat beside his father's grave, clasped his hands together, and bowed his head. "What would you do, Dad?" Kevin asked. "This war may be wrong. It took Michael. But I'm a cop. I have a job to do. What should I do?"

The birds seemed to stop chirping. Even the traffic along Archer Avenue grew muted as Kevin waited for an answer.

Tuesday night Kevin and Bernie were assigned to the Amphitheater again. The convention site was quiet, but the rest of the city wasn't. On Wednesday morning Kevin heard how a group of clergymen showed up at Lincoln Park to pray with the protestors. Despite that, there was violence and tear gas and club-swinging, and police cleared the park twice. Afterward, the demonstrators headed south to the Loop and Grant Park. At three a.m. the National Guard came in to relieve the police.

Greer transferred Bernie and Kevin to Michigan Avenue for the noon-to-midnight. Tension had been mounting since the Democrats defeated their own peace plank. When the protestors in Grant Park heard the news, the American flag near the band shell was lowered to half-mast, which triggered a push by police. When someone raised a red shirt on the flagpole, the police moved in again. A group of youth marshals lined up to try and hold back the two sides, but the police broke through, attacking with clubs, Mace, and tear gas.

As darkness fell, demonstration leaders put out an order to gather at the downtown Hilton. Protestors poured out of Grant Park onto Lake Shore Drive, trying to cross one of the bridges back to Michigan. The Balbo and Congress bridges were sealed off by guardsmen with machine guns and grenades, but the Jackson Street Bridge was passable. The crowd surged across.

The heat had lost its edge, and it was a beautiful summer night, the kind of night that begged for a ride in a convertible.

When they were teenagers, Kevin's brother had yearned for their neighbor's yellow T-Bird. He'd made Kevin walk past their neighbor's driveway ten times a day with him to ogle it. He never recovered when it was sold to someone from Wisconsin.

"Hey, Dougherty. Look alive!" Kevin jerked his head up. Bernie's scowl was so fierce his bushy eyebrows had merged into a straight line. About thirty cops, including Kevin and Bernie, were forming a barricade. Behind the police line were guardsmen with bayonets on their rifles. A wave of kids broke toward them. When the kids reached the cops, they kept pushing. The cops pushed back. Kevin heard pops as canisters of tear gas were released. The kids covered their noses and mouths.

"Don't let them through!" Bernie yelled. Kevin could barely hear him above the din. He twisted around. Bernie's riot stick was poised high above his head. He watched as Bernie swung, heard the *thwack* as it connected with a solid mass. A young boy in front of them dropped. Bernie raised his club again. Another *thwack*. The boy fell over sideways, shielding his head with his arms.

The police line wobbled and broke into knots of cops and kids, each side trying to advance. Kevin caught a whiff of cordite. Had some guardsman fired a rifle? The peppery smell of tear gas thickened the air. His throat was parched, and he could barely catch his breath. He threw on his gas mask, but it felt like a brick. He tore it off and let it dangle by the strap around his neck. Around him were screams, grunts, curses. An ambulance wailed as it raced down Congress. Its flashing lights punctuated the dark with theatrical, strobe-like bursts.

Somehow Kevin and Bernie became separated, and a young girl suddenly appeared in front of Kevin. She was wearing a white fluffy blouse and jeans, and her hair was tied back with a bandanna. She looked like Maggie. Young people streamed past, but she lingered as if she had all the time in the world. She stared at him, challenging him with her eyes. Then she slowly held up two fingers in a V sign.

Kevin swallowed. A copper he didn't know jabbed her with his club. "You! Get back! Go back home to your parents!"

She stumbled forward and lost her balance. Kevin caught her and helped her up. She wiped her hands on her jeans, her eyes darting from the other cop to Kevin. She didn't seem to be hurt. She disappeared back into the crowd. Kevin was relieved.

A few yards away a group of cops and kids were shoving and shouting at each other. Rocks flew through the air.

"Traitors!" An angry voice that sounded like Bernie rose above the melee. His outburst was followed by more pops. As the tear gas canisters burst, a chorus of screams rose. The protestors tried to scatter, but they were surrounded by cops and guardsmen, and there was nowhere to go. The cops closed in and began making arrests.

Coughing from the gas, Kevin moved in. He was only a few feet away when the girl with the long hair and peasant blouse appeared again. This time she was accompanied by a slender boy with glasses. He was wearing a black T-shirt and jeans. The girl's bandanna was wet and was tied around her nose and mouth. She was carrying a poster of a yellow sunflower with the words, *WAR IS NOT HEALTHY FOR CHILDREN AND OTHER LIVING THINGS.*

The boy looked Kevin over. He and the girl exchanged nods. "What are you doing, copper man?" His eyes looked glassy.

Kevin kept his mouth shut.

"You don't want this blood on your hands. She told me how you helped her up. Come with us. You can, you know." The boy held out his hand as if he expected Kevin to take it.

Wisps of tear gas hovered over the sidewalk. Kevin tightened his grip on his club. He stared at the kids. The girl looked more and more like Maggie.

Suddenly, Bernie's voice came at them from behind: "Kevin, no! Don't even look at 'em!"

Kevin looked away.

"Don't listen to him, man!" The boy's voice rose above Bernie's. "You're not one of the pigs. You don't agree with this war, I can tell. Come with us."

Kevin looked down.

"Get back, you little creep!" Bernie moved to Kevin's side and hoisted his club.

The boy stood his ground. "You know you don't belong with"—he waved a hand—"him."

A commander in a white shirt at the edge of the barricade yelled through a megaphone, "Clear the streets! Do you hear me, men? Clear the streets! Now!"

Someone else shouted, "All right, grab your gear! Let's go!"

A line of police pressed forward, but the boy and girl remained where they were. Everything fell away except the sound of the boy's voice. In an odd way it felt as silent as the cemetery behind the church.

"Time's running out, man," the boy said, his hand half covering his mouth. "How can you defend the law when you know it's wrong?"

Bernie's voice slammed into them like a hard fist: "Kev, don't let him talk to you like that!"

Kevin spun around. Bernie's face was purple with rage. Brandishing his riot stick, he swung it down at the boy's head. The boy jumped, but the club dealt a glancing blow to his temple. The boy collapsed.

"Bernie, no!" Kevin seized Bernie's arm.

Bernie snatched his arm away. "Do your job, Dougherty."

He pointed to the kids with his club. "They are the enemy!"

The girl turned to Kevin with a desperate cry. "Make him stop!"

Kevin strained to see her face in the semidark. "Go. Now. Get lost!"

"No! Help me get him up!" She knelt beside the boy.

"What are you waiting for, Dougherty?" Bernie's voice shot out, raw and brutal. He clubbed the boy again. The boy lay curled on his side on the ground, moaning. Blood gushed from his head. His glasses were smashed.

"Do something!" the girl screamed at Kevin. "Please!"

Her anguish seemed to throw Bernie into a frenzy. His eyes were slits of fury. He raised his stick over his head.

Kevin froze. Everything slowed down. Images of Maggie floated through his mind. She could be in the crowd. Maybe Father Connor. Even his mother. He thought about Mike. And his father. What Bernie was doing. What *his* duty was. His duty was to serve and protect.

The moment of clarity came so sharply it hurt. His chest tightened, and his hands clenched into fists. For the first time—maybe in his entire twenty-three years—he knew what that duty meant.

"Dougherty," Bernie kept at him, his voice raspy. "Either you do it, or I will!"

Kevin stared at his partner. Then he dropped his club and threw himself over the girl. She groaned as his weight knocked the wind out of her. Her body folded up beneath him, but it didn't matter: she was safe. Kevin twisted around and caught a glimpse of Bernie. His riot stick was still raised high above his head.

Kevin wondered what his partner would do now. He hoped the whole world was watching.

PART III

MODERN CRIME

PART III

SKIN DEEP

BY SARA PARETSKY

Michigan Avenue

(Originally published in 1987)

I

The warning bell clangs angrily and the submarine dives sharply. Everyone to battle stations. The Nazis pursuing closely, the bell keeps up its insistent clamor, loud, urgent, filling my head. My hands are wet: I can't remember what my job is in this cramped, tiny boat. If only someone would turn off the alarm bell. I fumble with some switches, pick up an intercom. The noise mercifully stops.

"Vic! Vic, is that you?"

"What?"

"I know it's late. I'm sorry to call so late, but I just got home from work. It's Sal, Sal Barthele."

"Oh, Sal. Sure." I looked at the orange clock readout. It was four thirty. Sal owns the Golden Glow, a bar in the south Loop I patronize.

"It's my sister, Vic. They've arrested her. She didn't do it. I know she didn't do it."

"Of course not, Sal—didn't do what?"

"They're trying to frame her. Maybe the manager . . . I don't know."

I swung my legs over the side of the bed. "Where are you?"

She was at her mother's house, 95th and Vincennes. Her

sister had been arrested three hours earlier. They needed a law-yer, a good lawyer. And they needed a detective, a good detec-tive. Whatever my fee was, she wanted me to know they could pay my fee.

"I'm sure you can pay the fee, but I don't know what you want me to do," I said as patiently as I could.

"She—they think she murdered that man. She didn't even know him. She was just giving him a facial. And he dies on her."

"Sal, give me your mother's address. I'll be there in forty minutes."

The little house on Vincennes was filled with neighbors and relatives murmuring encouragement to Mrs. Barthele. Sal is very black, and statuesque. Close to six feet tall, with a ma-jestic carriage, she can break up a crowd in her bar with a look and a gesture. Mrs. Barthele was slight, frail, and light-skinned. It was hard to picture her as Sal's mother.

Sal dispersed the gathering with characteristic firmness, telling the group that I was here to save Evangeline and that I needed to see her mother alone.

Mrs. Barthele sniffed over every sentence. "Why did they do that to my baby?" she demanded of me. "You know the po-lice, you know their ways. Why did they come and take my baby, who never did a wrong thing in her life?"

As a white woman, I could be expected to understand the machinations of the white man's law. And to share responsibil-ity for it. After more of this meandering, Sal took the narrative firmly in hand.

Evangeline worked at La Cygnette, a high-prestige beauty salon on North Michigan. In addition to providing facials and their own brand-name cosmetics at an exorbitant cost, they massaged the bodies and feet of their wealthy clients, stuffed them into steam cabinets, ran them through a Bataan-inspired exercise routine, and fed them herbal teas. Signor Giuseppe would style their hair for an additional charge.

Evangeline gave facials. The previous day she had one client booked after lunch, a Mr. Darnell.

"Men go there a lot?" I interrupted.

Sal made a face. "That's what I asked Evangeline. I guess it's part of being a yuppie—go spend a lot of money getting cream rubbed into your face."

Anyway, Darnell was to have had his hair styled before his facial, but the hairdresser fell behind schedule and asked Evangeline to do the guy's face first.

Sal struggled to describe how a La Cygnette facial worked—neither of us had ever checked out her sister's job. You sit in something like a dentist's chair, lean back, relax—you're naked from the waist up, lying under a big down comforter. The facial expert—cosmetician was Evangeline's official title—puts cream on your hands and sticks them into little electrically heated mitts, so your hands are out of commission if you need to protect yourself. Then she puts stuff on your face, covers your eyes with heavy pads, and goes away for twenty minutes while the face goo sinks into your hidden pores.

Apparently while this Darnell lay back deeply relaxed, someone had rubbed some kind of poison into his skin. "When Evangeline came back in to clean his face, he was sick—heaving, throwing up, it was awful. She screamed for help and started trying to clean his face—it was terrible, he kept vomiting on her. They took him to the hospital, but he died around ten tonight.

"They came to get Baby at midnight—you've got to help her, V.I.—even if the guy tried something on her, she never did a thing like that—she'd haul off and slug him, maybe, but rubbing poison into his face? You go help her."

II

Evangeline Barthele was a younger, darker edition of her mother. At most times, she probably had Sal's energy—sparks of it flared now and then during our talk—but a night in the holding cells had worn her down.

I brought a clean suit and makeup for her: justice may be blind but her administrators aren't. We talked while she changed.

"This Darnell—you sure of the name?—had he ever been to the salon before?"

She shook her head. "I never saw him. And I don't think the other girls knew him either. You know, if a client's a good tipper or a bad one they'll comment on it, be glad or whatever that he's come in. Nobody said anything about this man."

"Where did he live?"

She shook her head. "I never talked to the guy, V.I."

"What about the PestFree?" I'd read the arrest report and talked briefly to an old friend in the M.E.'s office. To keep roaches and other vermin out of their posh Michigan Avenue offices, La Cygnette used a potent product containing a wonder chemical called chorpyrifos. My informant had been awestruck—"Only an operation that didn't know shit about chemicals would leave chorpyrifos lying around. It's got a toxicity rating of five—it gets you through the skin—you only need a couple of tablespoons to kill a big man if you know where to put it."

Whoever killed Darnell had either known a lot of chemistry or been lucky—into his nostrils and mouth, with some rubbed into the face for good measure, the pesticide had made him convulsive so quickly that even if he knew who killed him he'd have been unable to talk, or even reason.

Evangeline said she knew where the poison was kept—everyone who worked there knew, knew it was lethal and not to touch it, but it was easy to get at. Just in a little supply room that wasn't kept locked.

"So why you? They have to have more of a reason than just that you were there."

She shrugged bitterly. "I'm the only black professional at La Cygnette—the other blacks working there sweep rooms and haul trash. I'm trying hard not to be paranoid, but I gotta wonder."

She insisted Darnell hadn't made a pass at her, or done anything to provoke an attack—she hadn't hurt the guy. As for anyone else who might have had opportunity, salon employees were always passing through the halls, going in and out of the little cubicles where they treated clients—she'd seen any number of people, all with legitimate business in the halls, but she hadn't seen anyone emerging from the room where Darnell was sitting.

When we finally got to bond court later that morning, I tried to argue circumstantial evidence—any of La Cygnette's fifty or so employees could have committed the crime, since all had access and no one had motive. The prosecutor hit me with a very unpleasant surprise: the police had uncovered evidence linking my client to the dead man. He was a furniture buyer from Kansas City who came to Chicago six times a year, and the doorman and the maids at his hotel had identified Evangeline without any trouble as the woman who accompanied him on his visits.

Bail was denied. I had a furious talk with Evangeline in one of the interrogation rooms before she went back to the holding cells.

"Why the hell didn't you tell me? I walked into the courtroom and got blindsided."

"They're lying," she insisted.

"Three people identified you. If you don't start with the truth right now, you're going to have to find a new lawyer and a new detective. Your mother may not understand, but for sure Sal will."

"You can't tell my mother. You can't tell Sal!"

"I'm going to have to give them some reason for dropping your case, and knowing Sal it's going to have to be the truth."

For the first time she looked really upset. "You're my lawyer. You should believe my story before you believe a bunch of strangers you never saw before."

"I'm telling you, Evangeline, I'm going to drop your case. I can't represent you when I know you're lying. If you killed Darnell we can work out a defense. Or if you didn't kill him and knew him we can work something out, and I can try to find the real killer. But when I know you've been seen with the guy any number of times, I can't go into court telling people you never met him before."

Tears appeared on the ends of her lashes. "The whole reason I didn't say anything was so Mama wouldn't know. If I tell you the truth, you've got to promise me you aren't running back to Vincennes Avenue talking to her."

I agreed. Whatever the story was, I couldn't believe Mrs. Barthele hadn't heard hundreds like it before. But we each make our own separate peace with our mothers.

Evangeline met Darnell at a party two years earlier. She liked him, he liked her—not the romance of the century, but they enjoyed spending time together. She'd gone on a two-week trip to Europe with him last year, telling her mother she was going with a girlfriend.

"First of all, she has very strict morals. No sex outside marriage. I'm thirty, mind you, but that doesn't count with her. Second, he's white, and she'd murder me. She really would. I think that's why I never fell in love with him—if we wanted to get married I'd never be able to explain it to Mama."

This latest trip to Chicago, Darnell thought it would be fun to see what Evangeline did for a living, so he booked an appointment at La Cygnette. She hadn't told anyone there she knew him. And when she found him sick and dying she'd panicked and lied.

"And if you tell my mother of this, V.I.—I'll put a curse on you. My father was from Haiti and he knew a lot of good ones."

"I won't tell your mother. But unless they nuked Lebanon this morning or murdered the mayor, you're going to get a lot of lines in the paper. It's bound to be in print."

She wept at that, wringing her hands. So after watching her go off with the sheriff's deputies, I called Murray Ryerson at the *Herald-Star* to plead with him not to put Evangeline's liaison in the paper. "If you do she'll wither your testicles. Honest."

"I don't know, Vic. You know the *Sun-Times* is bound to have some kind of screamer headline like, *DEAD MAN FOUND IN FACE-LICKING SEX ORGY.* I can't sit on a story like this when all the other papers are running it."

I knew he was right, so I didn't push my case very hard.

He surprised me by saying, "Tell you what: you find the real killer before my deadline for tomorrow's morning edition and I'll keep your client's personal life out of it. The sex scoop came in too late for today's paper. The *Trib* prints on our schedule and they don't have it, and the *Sun-Times* runs older, slower presses, so they have to print earlier."

I reckoned I had about eighteen hours. Sherlock Holmes had solved tougher problems in less time.

III

Roland Darnell had been the chief buyer of living-room furnishings for Alexander Dumas, a high-class Kansas City department store. He used to own his own furniture store in the nearby town of Lawrence, but lost both it and his wife when he was arrested for drug smuggling ten years earlier. Because of some confusion about his guilt—he claimed his partner, who disappeared the night he was arrested, was really responsible—he'd only served two years. When he got out, he moved to Kansas City to start a new life.

I learned this much from my friends at the Chicago police. At least, my acquaintances. I wondered how much of the story Evangeline had known. Or her mother. If her mother didn't want her child having a white lover, how about a white ex-con, ex- (presumably) drug-smuggling lover?

I sat biting my knuckles for a minute. It was eleven now. Say they started printing the morning edition at two the next morning, I'd have to have my story by one at the latest. I could follow one line, and one line only—I couldn't afford to speculate about Mrs. Barthele—and anyway, doing so would only get me killed. By Sal. So I looked up the area code for Lawrence, Kansas, and found their daily newspaper.

The *Lawrence Daily Journal-World* had set up a special number for handling press inquiries. A friendly woman with a strong drawl told me Darnell's age (forty-four); place of birth (Eudora, Kansas); ex-wife's name (Ronna Perkins); and ex-partner's name (John Crenshaw). Ronna Perkins was living elsewhere in the country and the *Journal-World* was protecting her privacy. John Crenshaw had disappeared when the police arrested Darnell.

Crenshaw had done an army stint in Southeast Asia in the late '60s. Since much of the bamboo furniture the store specialized in came from the Far East, some people speculated that Crenshaw had set up the smuggling route when he was out there in the service. Especially since Kansas City immigration officials discovered heroin in the hollow tubes making up chair backs. If Darnell knew anything about the smuggling, he had never revealed it.

"That's all we know here, honey. Of course, you could come on down and try to talk to some people. And we can wire you photos if you want."

I thanked her politely—my paper didn't run too many photographs. Or even have wire equipment to accept them. A pity—I could have used a look at Crenshaw and Ronna Perkins.

La Cygnette was on an upper floor of one of the new marble skyscrapers at the top end of the Magnificent Mile. Tall white doors opened onto a hushed waiting room reminiscent of a high-class funeral parlor. The undertaker, a middle-aged highly made-up woman seated at a table that was supposed to be French provincial, smiled at me condescendingly.

"What can we do for you?"

"I'd like to see Angela Carlson. I'm a detective."

She looked nervously at two clients seated in a far corner.

I lowered my voice. "I've come about the murder."

"But—but they made an arrest."

I smiled enigmatically. At least I hoped it looked enigmatic. "The police never close the door on all options until after the trial." If she knew anything about the police she'd know that was a lie—once they've made an arrest you have to get a presidential order to get them to look at new evidence.

The undertaker nodded nervously and called Angela Carlson in a whisper on the house phone. Evangeline had given me the names of the key players at La Cygnette; Carlson was the manager.

She met me in the doorway leading from the reception area into the main body of the salon. We walked on thick, silver pile through a white maze with little doors opening onto it. Every now and then we'd pass a white-coated attendant who gave the manager a subdued hello. When we went by a door with a police order slapped to it, Carlson winced nervously.

"When can we take that off? Everybody's on edge and that sealed door doesn't help. Our bookings are down as it is."

"I'm not on the evidence team, Ms. Carlson. You'll have to ask the lieutenant in charge when they've got what they need."

I poked into a neighboring cubicle. It contained a large white dentist's chair and a tray covered with crimson pots and bottles, all with the cutaway swans which were the salon's trademark. While the manager fidgeted angrily I looked into a tiny closet where clients changed—it held a tiny sink and a few coat hangers.

Finally she burst out, "Didn't your people get enough of this yesterday? Don't you read your own reports?"

"I like to form my own impressions, Ms. Carlson. Sorry to have to take your time, but the sooner we get everything cleared up, the faster your customers will forget this ugly episode."

She sighed audibly and led me on angry heels to her office, although the thick carpeting took the intended ferocity out of her stride. The office was another of the small treatment rooms with a desk and a menacing phone console. Photographs of a youthful Mme. de Leon, founder of La Cygnette, covered the walls.

Ms. Carlson looked through a stack of pink phone messages. "I have an incredibly busy schedule, officer. So if you could get to the point . . ."

"I want to talk to everyone with whom Darnell had an appointment yesterday. Also the receptionist on duty. And before I do that I want to see their personnel files."

"Really! All these people were interviewed yesterday." Her eyes narrowed suddenly. "Are you really with the police? You're not, are you? You're a reporter. I want you out of here now. Or I'll call the real police."

I took my license photostat from my wallet. "I'm a detective. That's what I told your receptionist. I've been retained by the Barthele family. Ms. Barthele is not the murderer and I want to find out who the real culprit is as fast as possible."

She didn't bother to look at the license. "I can barely tolerate answering police questions. I'm certainly not letting some snoop for hire take up my time. The police have made an arrest on extremely good evidence. I suppose you think you can drum up a fee by getting Evangeline's family excited about her innocence, but you'll have to look elsewhere for your money."

I tried an appeal to her compassionate side, using half-forgotten arguments from my court appearances as a public defender. Outstanding employee, widowed mother, sole support, intense family pride, no prior arrests, no motive. No sale.

"Ms. Carlson, you the owner or the manager here?"

"Why do you want to know?"

"Just curious about your stake in the success of the place and your responsibility for decisions. It's like this: you've got a lot of foreigners working here. The immigration people will want to come by and check out their papers.

"You've got lots and lots of tiny little rooms. Are they sprinklered? Do you have emergency exits? The fire department can make a decision on that.

"And how come your only black professional employee was just arrested and you're not moving an inch to help her out? There are lots of lawyers around who'd be glad to look at a discrimination suit against La Cygnette.

"Now if we could clear up Evangeline's involvement fast,

we could avoid having all these regulatory people trampling around upsetting your staff and your customers. How about it?"

She sat in indecisive rage for several minutes: how much authority did I have, really? Could I offset the munificent fees the salon and the building owners paid to various public officials just to avoid such investigations? Should she call headquarters for instruction? Or her lawyer? She finally decided that even if I didn't have a lot of power I could be enough of a nuisance to affect business. Her expression compounded of rage and defeat, she gave me the files I wanted.

Darnell had been scheduled with a masseuse, the hair expert Signor Giuseppe, and with Evangeline. I read their personnel files, along with that of the receptionist who had welcomed him to La Cygnette, to see if any of them might have hailed from Kansas City or had any unusual traits, such as an arrest record for heroin smuggling. The files were very sparse. Signor Giuseppe Fruttero hailed from Milan. He had no next-of-kin to be notified in the event of an accident. Not even a good friend. Bruna, the masseuse, was Lithuanian, unmarried, living with her mother. Other than the fact that the receptionist had been born as Jean Evans in Hammond but referred to herself as Monique from New Orleans, I saw no evidence of any kind of cover-up.

Angela Carlson denied knowing either Ronna Perkins or John Crenshaw or having any employees by either of those names. She had never been near Lawrence herself. She grew up in Evansville, Indiana, came to Chicago to be a model in 1978, couldn't cut it, and got into the beauty business. Angrily she gave me the names of her parents in Evansville and summoned the receptionist.

Monique was clearly close to sixty, much too old to be Roland Darnell's ex-wife. Nor had she heard of Ronna or Crenshaw.

"How many people knew that Darnell was going to be in the salon yesterday?"

"Nobody knew." She laughed nervously. "I mean, of course I knew—I made the appointment with him. And Signor Giuseppe knew when I gave him his schedule yesterday. And Bruna, the masseuse, of course, and Evangeline."

"Well, who else could have seen their schedules?"

She thought frantically, her heavily mascaraed eyes rolling in agitation. With another nervous giggle she finally said, "I suppose anyone could have known. I mean, the other cosmeticians and the makeup artists all come out for their appointments at the same time. I mean, if anyone was curious they could have looked at the other people's lists."

Carlson was frowning. So was I. "I'm trying to find a woman who'd be forty now, who doesn't talk much about her past. She's been divorced and she won't have been in the business long. Any candidates?"

Carlson did another mental search, then went to the file cabinets. Her mood was shifting from anger to curiosity and she flipped through the files quickly, pulling five in the end.

"How long has Signor Giuseppe been here?"

"When we opened our Chicago branch in 1980 he came to us from Miranda's—I guess he'd been there for two years. He says he came to the States from Milan in 1970."

"He a citizen? Has he got a green card?"

"Oh, yes. His papers are in good shape. We are very careful about that at La Cygnette." My earlier remark about the immigration department had clearly stung. "And now I really need to get back to my own business. You can look at those files in one of the consulting rooms—Monique, find one that won't be used today."

It didn't take me long to scan the five files, all uninformative. Before returning them to Monique I wandered on through the back of the salon. In the rear a small staircase led to an upper story. At the top was another narrow hall lined with small offices and storerooms. A large mirrored room at the back filled with hanging plants and bright lights housed Signor Giuseppe. A dark-haired man with a pointed beard and a bright smile, he was ministering gaily to a thin, middle-aged woman, talking and laughing while he deftly teased her hair into loose curls.

He looked at me in the mirror when I entered. "You are here for the hair, signora? You have the appointment?"

"*No, Signor Giuseppe. Sono qui perchè la sua fama se è sparsa di fronte a lei. Milano è una bella città, non è vero?*"

He stopped his work for a moment and held up a deprecating hand. "Signora, it is my policy to speak only English in my adopted country."

"*Una vera stupida e ignorante usanza io direi.*" I beamed sympathetically and sat down on a high stool next to an empty customer chair. There were seats for two clients. Since Signor Giuseppe reigned alone, I pictured him spinning at high speed between customers, snipping here, pinning there.

"Signora, if you do not have the appointment, will you please leave? Signora Dotson here, she does not prefer the audience."

"Sorry, Mrs. Dotson," I said to the lady's chin. "I'm a detective. I need to talk to Signor Giuseppe, but I'll wait."

I strolled back down the hall and entertained myself by going into one of the storerooms and opening little pots of La Cygnette creams and rubbing them into my skin. I looked in a mirror and could already see an improvement. If I got Evangeline sprung maybe she'd treat me to a facial.

Signor Giuseppe appeared with a plastically groomed Mrs. Dotson. He had shed his barber's costume and was dressed for the street. I followed them down the stairs. When we got to the bottom I said, "In case you're thinking of going back to Milan— or even to Kansas—I have a few questions."

Mrs. Dotson clung to the hairdresser, ready to protect him.

"I need to speak to him alone, Mrs. Dotson. I have to talk to him about bamboo."

"I'll get Miss Carlson, Signor Giuseppe," his guardian offered.

"No, no, Signora. I will deal with this crazed woman myself. A million thanks. *Grazie, grazie.*"

"Remember, no Italian in your adopted America," I said nastily.

Mrs. Dotson looked at us uncertainly.

"I think you should get Ms. Carlson," I said. "Also a police escort. Fast."

She made up her mind to do something, whether to get help or flee I wasn't sure, but she scurried down the corridor. As soon as she had disappeared, he took me by the arm and led me into one of the consulting rooms.

"Now, who are you and what is this?" His accent had improved substantially.

"I'm V.I. Warshawski. Roland Darnell told me you were quite an expert on fitting drugs into bamboo furniture."

I wasn't quite prepared for the speed of his attack. His hands were around my throat. He was squeezing and spots began dancing in front of me. I didn't try to fight his arms, just kicked sharply at his shin, following with my knee to his stomach. The pressure at my neck eased. I turned in a half circle and jammed my left elbow into his rib cage. He let go.

I backed to the door, keeping my arms up in front of my face, and backed into Angela Carlson.

"What on earth are you doing with Signor Giuseppe?" she asked.

"Talking to him about furniture." I was out of breath. "Get the police and don't let him leave the salon."

A small crowd of white-coated cosmeticians had come to the door of the tiny treatment room. I said to them, "This isn't Giuseppe Fruttero. It's John Crenshaw. If you don't believe me, try speaking Italian to him—he doesn't understand it. He's probably never been to Milan. But he's certainly been to Thailand, and he knows an awful lot about heroin."

IV

Sal handed me the bottle of Black Label. "It's yours, Vic. Kill it tonight or save it for some other time. How did you know he was Roland Darnell's ex-partner?"

"I didn't. At least not when I went to La Cygnette. I just knew it had to be someone in the salon who killed him, and it was most likely someone who knew him in Kansas. And that meant either Darnell's ex-wife or his partner. And Giuseppe was the only man on the professional staff. And then I saw he didn't know Italian—after praising Milan and telling him he was stupid in the same tone of voice and getting no response, it made me wonder."

"We owe you a lot, Vic. The police would never have dug down to find that. You gotta thank the lady, Mama."

Mrs. Barthele grudgingly gave me her thin hand. "But how come those police said Evangeline knew that Darnell man? My baby wouldn't know some convict, some drug smuggler."

"He wasn't a drug smuggler, Mama. It was his partner. The police have proved all that now. Roland Darnell never did anything wrong." Evangeline, chic in red with long earrings that bounced as she spoke, made the point hotly.

Sal gave her sister a measuring look. "All I can say, Evangeline, is it's a good thing you never had to put your hand on a Bible in court about Mr. Darnell."

I hastily poured a drink and changed the subject.

DEATH AND THE POINT SPREAD

BY PERCY SPURLARK PARKER

Lawndale

(Originally published in 1995)

Big Bull Benson had the coffee waiting when Rod Felton came into the office. Rod took his with cream and sugar, Bull with a shot of Grand-Dad.

Rod's old man had been Lucky Felton. The big newspapers had their nationally syndicated sports writers. *The Daily Challenger*, the rag that carried the news to the black communities of the city, had Lucky Felton. Back in '78, Lucky had gone with Affirmed as a Triple Crown cinch, when most had picked Alydar to upset things. He'd had the '85 Bears all along, and had correctly predicted the '94 baseball season would be a short one.

Bull had attended Lucky's funeral earlier in the week. Hit-and-run. It had happened on the West Side, Lucky had just left a bar and was struck down as he crossed the street. He had never been a heavy drinker but he barhopped a lot. He said it helped him keep his finger on the pulse of the city's betting spirit.

The car involved was found the next day, stripped and dumped in a vacant lot. It had been stolen, the usual hot-wire job. So far the cops hadn't come up with anyone to pin it on. And from what Bull had heard it didn't look too likely that they would.

Rod didn't waste much time, taking out a small spiral scratch pad and handing it to him. He'd called earlier telling Bull he'd found something he wanted Bull to see.

"It was Dad's and it's his handwriting."

The spiral notepad was folded open to one of the back pages. There were only three words on the page, scrawled in pencil, *pharaohs, fix, wizzy*.

It was clear enough to Bull. The Pharaohs were the City-South College football team. They were conference champs and the favorites heading into a bowl game in two weeks. Bets are placed on football games not so much on who wins or loses, but how much they win or lose by. The point spread. The fix was in, somebody or bodies on the Pharaohs were being paid to control the spread. And Lucky had gotten or was getting his information from Wizzy Lee.

"Well?" Rod looked a lot like his father then, the way his thin eyebrows wrinkled as he sat leaning slightly forward, his broad face at a tilt. Bull couldn't guess the number of times Lucky had occupied the same chair, debating the merits of some upcoming sporting event.

"Looks like Lucky got hold of something." He tried his coffee, the Grand-Dad giving it an edge that mildly scratched his throat.

Rod nodded. "It looked that way to me too, but I wasn't sure if I was just making up something that wasn't there. Know who or what Wizzy is?"

"Nickel-and-dimer. Used to be in tight with the Phil Breeden crowd. They've been splits for a while now. But if a fix was in, Wizzy would stand a damn good chance of knowing about it."

"Breeden plays kind of rough, doesn't he?"

"The man has got a temper," Bull said. "Probably the only

reason Wizzy's still walking around is he and Breeden are second or third cousins or something."

Rod straightened somewhat in the chair, several lines playing across his forehead. "Do you think maybe it wasn't an accident, Bull? Was my dad murdered?"

Bull had toyed with the idea long before Rod showed up with the scratch pad. He had no more to go on than the fact that Lucky was dead, a hit-and-run, but had it been intentional? Maybe a part of him wanted it to be that way, more than a simple accident. Maybe he wanted someone to hate for having killed Lucky and not pity some poor slob for having no business behind the wheel of a car.

"I don't know, Rod, it's something for the police to handle."

"I know you, Bull, don't hand me that. If my dad was murdered, you'd want the bastard as much as I do. Only difference is you know your way around these things. I don't."

Bull didn't argue. He had a rep, more true than false. Whether it was more good than bad depended on who was doing the judging. He'd gotten involved with murder before, helped point the cops in the right direction a few times. Some liked him for it, some wanted to push him in front of a bus. He took a good swig of his coffee, sweetened it with a splash of Grand-Dad, then put the bottle back in the bottom desk drawer.

"Okay, so what do you want me to do?"

"Find out which it is, Bull. Please."

Sam Devlin came into the office after Rod left. He'd been working the bar out front in the Bull Pen Lounge, which took up most of the first floor of the Benson Hotel. Bull had won the deed to the hotel in an all-night poker game some years back. Sam had installed himself as bartender from day one. He was old and bald, and he talked around the wooden match in the corner of his mouth.

"Well, what'd the kid have to show ya that was so important?"

Sam had been a part of Bull's life for so long, there wasn't much Bull could keep from him, or tried.

"The fix is in on the Pharaohs' game?" Sam said, after Bull explained.

"I could be wrong, but it looks that way. Seems Lucky got caught up in it."

Sam worked on his matchstick. "I don't much like the idea of someone gettin' away with bumpin' off Lucky, but you best be careful. Phil Breeden has always been a hard ass, and he ain't had too much in the finesse department either. Piss him off and he'll go for ya quick."

Bull caught up with Sergeant Vern Wonler at the Moore Street Precinct.

"Marge was expecting you for dinner last Saturday," Vern said.

"Yeah, she got on my case when I called to see if you were home. I tried to make it but something came up."

"Female or a deck of cards?"

"A little of both."

Vern grinned, shaking his long dark face. "You'll never change."

"I hope not."

They had grown up together. Two black kids running the streets. Now one was a cop, married with twin boys. And Bull, thanks to Sam's tutoring, had done his nine-to-five with a deck of cards, a pair of dice, and a scratch sheet in his back pocket.

Vern sat down at his desk pushing papers and folders aside. "Murders, burglaries, muggings, another fun week at Moore Street. What can I do for you, Bull? Don't tell me you're selling tickets to the Gamblers' Ball?"

"It's about Lucky."

Vern sobered, his wide grin straightening, then turning into a frown. "I see this crap every day, but it's still hard to believe he's gone. I keep picking up the *Challenger* expecting to see his column."

"Me too. Rod came by to see me today. He found this with some of Lucky's things."

Vern studied the scratch pad for a long time. "Wizzy Lee?"

"That's my guess. If we can get hold of him, maybe we can find out for sure."

"I think we're a little late," Vern said, shifting through the papers on his desk.

He handed Bull a police report. Hit-and-run. It had occurred at 2:13 a.m. that morning outside Wizzy's apartment building on West 17th Street. Witnesses described the vehicle as a four- or five-year-old Ford sedan. No one was able to tell how many people were in the car or who was driving. The victim, Leonard "Wizzy" Lee, twenty-five, was dead at the scene when the ambulance arrived.

Bull tossed the report back on the desk. "Looks like we've got an epidemic."

Bull was six-six and working on two eighty-five. Most men he came in contact with were smaller in stature. Phil Breeden was a runt, five-one at the most, and maybe 120 pounds when he strapped on his shoulder holster. But he was as mean as he was short. Word was he'd never been in a fair fight, at least not from his end. He ran the biggest book on the West Side, and dealt in a little juice action as well.

For extra muscle there was Guy Woodley or Pedro Barnes. One or the other was usually with him, and a good part of their job was holding Breeden off some jerk who was dumb enough to be late with a payment. Retribution was best handled without witnesses, but Breeden's temper rarely took that precaution into consideration.

"Tired of dealin' with the folks on the South Side, Bull?" Phil asked. He was sitting in a booth at the back of the greasy spoon he used as a front, a pad and pen on the table before him. He was sporting a box cut these days, probably an attempt to make himself look taller. A dapper dresser, his tailored dark brown jacket was a shade or two lighter than his complexion. Pedro stood next to the booth, arms folded across his thick chest, watching.

"Everything's cool on my home turf, Phil. I was close by, so I stopped to see where the heavy money's going these days," Bull said, squeezing himself in the booth across from Breeden.

"Three-to-five, Pharaohs by eight."

They were interesting odds. It would take three dollars to win two, if the Pharaohs won by nine or more points. But the Pharaohs had averaged twenty-four points a game their last four outings, while holding their opponents to thirteen or under. Going with the Pharaohs was still a pretty good bet.

Bull dug out a cigar and fired it up. "I guess if the Pharaohs don't make the point spread you're going to clean up."

Breeden shrugged his small shoulders. "It's the nature of the business. You can always bet against them."

"And you've got places around the country where you can do the same."

"Yeah, so? What are you trying to say, Bull?"

"I think you know, Phil. You got the fix in on the Pharaohs' game."

"Talk like that can get somebody dead."

"Yeah, I know. Lucky Felton and your cousin Wizzy so far."

"Wizzy's dead? Damn, it's about time."

"I'm supposed to believe you didn't know?"

"I don't care what you believe."

"Maybe I ought to stick with what I know."

"It's usually advisable."

"I know you've got a lot of money riding on that game. I know with the fix in you're going to clean up big time. I know that if you haven't informed certain members of the betting community of the fix, and they get wind of it, your little ass better find a good place to hide."

Bull was fishing more than anything else but it got a reaction. Breeden began breathing heavier, a slight snarl to the set of his lips, and his eyes tightened into dark little beads.

"The one thing I don't know is how many lives all this is worth to you."

"There's always room for one more," Breeden said, reaching inside of his jacket.

Pedro grabbed him. "Boss, cool it."

"Get your hands off me, Pedro, this son of a bitch got it coming," Breeden said, struggling against Pedro's grip.

"Bull," Pedro said, motioning with his head for him to leave.

Bull took a big drag on his cigar, blowing the smoke across the table as he rose. He felt more amused than threatened. It hadn't taken much to get Breeden going but if it'd come down to it, he would've knocked the runt into next week. Pedro would've taken a little more effort, but he could be handled as well. A fight wouldn't have proven anything, however, or helped him learn more than he already knew.

The City-South Pharaohs were having closed practice sessions. Bull parked at the curb by the team exit gate. He spent the better part of an hour listening to an old Motown tape of Gladys Knight and the Pips. Gladys had always been his favorite. There were a number of good women singers around, but in his estimation none of them came close. The only thing that spoiled the tape was the thought of Lucky's murder. It stayed with him, dancing out of step with each song that played.

The fix was in. Lucky and Wizzy were killed because of it. These were the obvious conclusions. Not so clear was Breeden's involvement. He was the money man all right, the one who stood to make the most out of the setup. Lucky would've been murdered to keep him quiet, but why Wizzy? And Bull couldn't say for sure Breeden had known about Wizzy's death.

A fire engine–red Dodge Neon pulled up to the curb a couple car lengths in front of Bull's Caddy. The babe that got out wore a pair of tight-fitting jeans and a gold and green City-South school jacket. Winter had been taking over the city for the past two weeks, no real snow but a lot of wind and low temperatures. The weather didn't seem to bother her as she went around to the passenger side and rested her plump rump on the Neon's fender. She was the color of strong coffee, her hair a wealth of long, tight braids. Young, late teen, early twenties. She'd never been a wallflower; it was evident in her walk as she got out of the car and perched herself on the fender. He silently congratulated whoever she was waiting for.

The second and third stringers started filing through the exit gate, some still wearing their numberless practice jerseys. There wasn't one of them who passed by her that didn't look back. She was definitely worth a second look.

Bull started out of his car when he recognized Rye Kirkland, the Pharaohs' quarterback. He was tall and rangy, and his throwing arm was one of the prime reasons the Pharaohs were heading for a bowl game. Ms. Tight Jeans got to Kirkland first, throwing her arms around his neck and smothering his lips with hers. Then they piled into the Neon, and she kicked the car to life. From the deep growl of the engine there was more under the hood than what the factory had put there. She sped off with tires screeching, exhaust vapors billowing from shiny twin chrome pipes.

"Who's the little lady?" Bull asked Mike Justin. He was offensive coach for the Pharaohs, and had been walking behind Kirkland.

"That, Bull, is Miss Takisha James. Let's see, this year's homecoming queen, captain and choreographer of our cheerleading squad, she carries a B average and she's on the student council. Word is she did the work on the Neon herself."

"I'm impressed. All that and a mechanic too."

"You must know her old man, Paul James? He owns Reliable Auto Wreckers."

Reliable was the largest black-owned auto-scavenging outfit in the state, but Bull couldn't recall ever meeting its owner. "How long has she had Kirkland wrapped up?"

Justin grinned and the gray previously hidden in his stubbled beard seemed to peek through. "Right after our second game, when we buried Nohambar Central thirty-seven to nothing. She latched on to him and hasn't let go."

"Wouldn't think he'd be able to keep his mind on the game."

A bigger grin this time. "She's a hot little number all right. I had some concerns along those lines myself. But actually, Rye's been working harder since they hooked up. My hat's off to the kid. You know his story, he was in that street gang on the West Side. The gang was known for ripping off cars, keeping the chop shops supplied. Then his high school gym teacher noticed the raw talent, talked him into going out for the football team his sophomore year. Now, I've got me one of the top three quarterbacks in college ball."

Bull had heard the story a number of times from Lucky. Kirkland never admitted stealing any cars and the police never collected any hard evidence to charge against him. Football had been the turning point for Kirkland, and he had never had to look back.

There were only a few stragglers leaving the practice field now. The chill in the air was becoming more persistent, urged on by an increasing wind. Bull gathered his coat about his neck. "Mike?" He tried to pick his words carefully. "Think it's possible someone on the team might shave a few points?"

"Hell no. Not on my team."

"Think about it. It could be the reason Lucky Felton is dead."

"No way, Bull. That would mean it would have to be one of my key people. Rye, my running back Shaw, or Peters or Dubrow, my receivers."

"I don't like the idea myself, but it's the only way it adds up."

"Get a new adding machine, Bull. Somebody's lying to you."

"That's what you're going to tell the cops? They'll be coming around. Better start giving it some thought. Any of your key people acting different lately?"

"My guys are innocent, Bull. I'll tell you and I'll tell the cops. Now"—his eyes narrowed—"we got nothing else to say to each other."

With that Mike walked off mumbling something Bull couldn't make out, but he was sure it wasn't pleasant.

Smitty's was the local hangout of the City-South students. It wasn't much more than a hamburger and hot dog joint, but it was near campus so the students had made it their own. Bull swung by there, deciding to stop only when he spotted the Neon in the side lot.

The noise level in the place was definitely for younger ears. It was a combination of R. Kelly blasting through the speakers which hung from the ceiling in each corner and the occupants themselves, who had to shout to be heard across the small tables. The counter and grill took up the back wall, flanked by worn-looking booths. Kirkland and Takisha were hugged up in one of the booths on his right.

He made his way through the maze of tables and students that filled the floor. "That was some exit you made from the practice field." They both looked up at him, puzzlement registering in their knotted brows. "You parked in front of my Caddy. I was waiting to have a word with Rye but you were too fast."

"Sorry, mister, you should've shouted or something."

"That's all right, it gave me a chance to talk to Justin."

"You know the coach?"

"Yeah, we've run into each other off and on for a couple of years now," he said, sitting across from them. "I'm Bull Benson, Rye. I was a good friend of Lucky Fenton's."

Kirkland smiled. It was the same wide, dimple-cheeked melter that got plastered over the sport pages. "Lucky was my main man, ya know? He was the first one ta put me in the papers, back when I was in high school."

Lucky had often boasted the same.

"What can I do for ya, Mr. Benson? Ya taking over Lucky's place at the *Challenger?*"

"Naw, I'm just trying to clear up a couple of things for the family." It was as close to the truth as he wanted to get just now.

"Hey, man, I'm here for ya if I can help."

"Do you know a guy named Wizzy Lee?"

"Wizzy?" Takisha laughed. "Sounds like a cold. I'd remember if I'd ever met someone like that." Close up she was even cuter, her skin clear and smooth, her eyeliner faintly accenting her big brown eyes.

Kirkland grinned along with her, his arm slung over her shoulders. "Sorry, I've never met him. Was he a friend of Lucky's too?"

"They knew each other. Maybe you saw him around here." It had been a year or so since Bull had last seen Wizzy and he knew it didn't take that much for a person's appearance to change, but he gave them what he remembered. "Skinny, about your height, few years older, dark, used to clear his throat a lot when he talked."

He waited as they looked at each other, shrugged. "Oh, yeah," he added, as something else came to mind. "The bottom tip of his left ear was missing." Hell, it had been Wizzy's most noticeable feature, funny how it had slipped his mind.

"God, I hope I don't see him," Takisha said. "Anybody that ugly would probably mark any baby I'll ever think about having."

They both got a good laugh out of that one, and when they settled down, Kirkland said, "I still can't help ya, man. We don't know him."

He spoke to several other people in the place, asking them straight out if they knew a Wizzy Lee. No one admitted recognizing the name or the description.

As he was leaving he ran into Tom Dubrow and Chuck Shaw. He got pretty much the same response except Dubrow thought he'd seen someone who looked like Wizzy around a time or two, either at Smitty's or at the practice field.

"I can't be positive but it sounds right." He was a little short for a wide receiver, but he had the credentials, burning speed and a pair of sure hands.

"We haven't seen anyone like that," Shaw said forcefully. He was taller than Dubrow, slower, but a clutch player.

"Which way is it, guys? You can't remember seeing him or you can?"

Dubrow started to say something, looked over to Shaw.

"We haven't seen him," Shaw said.

Dubrow shrugged, cleared his throat. "Look, mister, lately we've been getting as many strangers in here as we have students. Hell, the mayor even paraded his ass down here right after we got the bowl bid."

It was a valid point, yet it didn't explain Shaw's behavior. Prebowl jitters? Just plain tired of talking to people? Maybe. Or maybe he had something to hide.

Out in the parking lot, Bull mulled over the whole mess on his way to his car. The fix was in for the Pharaohs' bowl game. Lucky and Wizzy were killed because of it. Phil Breeden was the money man behind the fix. These things he knew. Any way he looked at it, it came out the same way. He was just lacking a little something called proof. And he hadn't learned anything so far that gave him any real hope of gaining any. Plus, he hadn't gotten any closer to who had actually committed the murders. Right now he couldn't even make a good guess.

Police work should be left for the police, they have the patience for it. Hell, he was a gambler. A deck of cards, a pair of dice, these were the things he knew the ins and outs about. Sure, he'd gotten backed into corners before, or tried to do a favor for a friend. The situations had gotten a little hairy at times but he had managed.

Still, this was different. If there was someone to grab hold of and shake the truth out of, he would. But who? It might be Kirkland, or Dubrow, or both. Maybe it was Shaw or Peters. Who for sure was involved? Breeden. Yeah, that would be the right answer, Bull knew, but roughing him up wouldn't work.

Breeden would go down for the count before he gave up any info on himself or anybody else.

He pulled his cellular phone out as he walked toward his Caddy. The little flip phone always felt like a toy in his big mitt, but he'd had it for about a year now and wouldn't be without it. He tried Vern's beeper when he couldn't reach him at the precinct, climbed into the car out of the early evening chill, and waited.

A good third of his cigar was gone by the time Vern returned his call. "Yeah, Bull?"

"Just got tired of banging my head against the wall. I'm heading back to my place, thought I'd give you what little I had."

"Go ahead, but I think I got a good leg up on closing this one out."

"How'd you do that?"

"First off, we found the car that did Wizzy. Stolen, another hot-wire job."

"Who needs a gun when a car is just as effective?"

"Something like that. Dumped in another vacant lot on the West Side. It hadn't been stripped but the report said it was wiped clean." Vern paused, as though waiting for a reply. When none was forthcoming, he continued, "I paid a visit to Breeden. What the hell did you say to him anyway? He was still boiling when I got there."

"It doesn't take much for him."

"True. Anyway, he didn't confess to any wrongdoing."

"Naturally."

"He's just a misunderstood restaurant owner who's trying to get out from under the bad label placed on him for some past indiscretions."

"I almost feel sorry for him."

"Then I tried the bar where Lucky was the night he got run down. The only question the bartender had been asked when it appeared to be a simple hit-and-run was if he'd seen anything. I asked a few more."

Bull took a pull on his cigar and waited.

"The bar is right in the heart of Wizzy's old neighborhood, and Lucky had been there twice before with Wizzy. The bartender couldn't say what they were talking about, both times they kept to themselves at a back table. Lucky was by himself that last night, he even commented on his way out that he'd been stood up."

"Setup sounds more like it."

"Exactly. But the kicker is, it's Rye Kirkland's old neighborhood too. He and Wizzy used to live in the same building. It was just something that slipped out during our conversation. Bartender used to have a lady friend who lived across the street."

"You sure of this?"

"Yeah, and that's not all. I had Wizzy's file pulled. He was in the same car-theft ring Kirkland was rumored to belong to. He was doing eighteen months in our downstate correctional facility when Kirkland started shining on the football field."

"Kirkland is the one Breeden's got in his pocket," Bull said. Most of the guesswork was out of it now. A few facts and the answers were lining up like his hotel patrons on a Saturday night. But there was still no answer to the big question. Who killed Lucky and Wizzy?

"I'm heading over to Kirkland's now, I think a trip down to the station is in order."

"You won't find him at home, he's here at Smitty's, the burger joint on 55th. I just got through talking to him."

"Good, let's leave it at that. You said you were going back to your place, do it. I'll handle it from here."

"Sure thing, Vern."

"Bull, damn you. That was a little too easy. I'm warning you, just stay—"

He switched his cellular off. The connection between Kirkland, Wizzy, and Breeden was too strong to doubt Kirkland's guilt. It made sense; the one person who had the opportunity to affect the scoring most was the quarterback. The team had mainly gotten to where they were because of Kirkland. Anybody could have an off day. If Kirkland's off day happened to be bowl day, then so be it, the coaches weren't going to bench him. He'd miss a pass here, a bad handoff there, the Pharaohs could still win as long as Kirkland saw to it that it wasn't by more than eight points. The team would have the national praise, the glory of a bowl win, yet everybody who bet on them would get screwed.

He was wrestling with himself on whether to go back to his place like Vern wanted him to, or back into Smitty's and confront Kirkland, when Kirkland and Takisha came out and turned into the parking lot.

They were too wrapped up in each other to notice him. Takisha had her arm looped through Kirkland's, talking and laughing as they walked. He didn't get their attention until he stepped in front of them. Takisha was in midsentence when she stopped abruptly and the sparkle seemed to leave her face.

"Mr. Benson," Kirkland said, still the confident young gladiator. "Thought you'd left."

"Almost, but I'm going to be waiting around a bit. You are too."

Kirkland shook his head. "Naw, I don't think so, man." He smiled down at Takisha. "Me and my baby got some other plans."

"I'm making some changes." Bull took the last drag off his cigar and flipped the butt to the ground. "You lied to me about Wizzy, you two used to run together. Cops know all about it. Fact is they're on their way over here now to talk to you. So, you won't be going anywhere until they get here."

Bull could see the confidence drain from Kirkland, in the tilt of his head, the square set of his shoulders. There wasn't even a trace of the smile left on his face. "Okay, okay. Maybe I know Wizzy, so what? What'd the cops want to see me for?"

"Taking money to fix the bowl game for starters. How much did Breeden pay you?"

There wasn't a lot of traffic on the adjacent street but Kirkland's eyes darted to the sound of each passing vehicle. "Naw, man, you're wrong. And I ain't talking to no cops."

Kirkland made a sudden move to his right, spun, reversing himself, and took off in high gear. The kid was good; by the time Bull reacted Kirkland was nearing the end of the parking lot. Bull kept himself in pretty good shape, hitting the gym at least twice a week, but chasing down quarterbacks wasn't part of his regular routine.

He took a couple of steps and Takisha latched on to his arm, trying to hold him back. He easily shook her loose, leaving her behind yelling for him to stop. He rounded the corner of the parking lot to find Kirkland halfway down the block. He was somewhat surprised Kirkland hadn't gotten any farther. Kirkland crossed the street, running behind a lumbering van, and just missed being hit by a taxi. Bull continued on his side of the block, keeping Kirkland in sight and actually gaining. He didn't cross over until he was sure he wasn't going to be playing tag with any oncoming traffic.

Kirkland kept looking back, which might have interfered with his gait. He broke stride a couple of times and Bull gained a little more. Another street, no traffic this time, then midway down the block Kirkland turned into an alley. Bull had done some of his best work in alleys, from crap games to fistfights. He considered the concrete canyons his home turf.

Bull hit the mouth of the alley as fast as he could, jumping to one side. It's a rarity to get a well-lit alley, most offer more shadows than anything else. Thanks to a lamppost on the street corner at the other end, he had a clear view of the center of the alley. But the path along the way was clouded with shadows. Kirkland hadn't had the chance to clear the alley. If he'd still been running Bull would've seen him, which meant he was hiding somewhere along the way with probably a brick in his hand or a broken bottle.

Bull took his time, looking from one side of the alley to the other as he proceeded. The chill night air did little to keep the stench of the garbage in check. Something scurried by, a cat or a rat, he couldn't tell. In this neighborhood they came pretty much the same size.

He was nearing the end of the alley when Kirkland sprang up swinging from behind a garbage dumpster. Bull blocked the blow with his left arm, the impact flinging the bottle Kirkland was holding against the side of the building. Bull jammed a couple of rights to Kirkland's midsection that took the wind out, and a chopping left that sent him to the pavement.

He reached down, grabbing Kirkland by his collar and hauling him to his feet. "You should've just stuck to football," Bull said.

He thought of Lucky, of the hopes Lucky had expressed for Kirkland's career, and how Kirkland had repaid him. He was about to swing again, one parting shot for Lucky, when he heard the roar of the car behind him.

He looked back into a pair of bright headlights that blinded him as they grew larger, coming closer and closer, the roar of the engine louder, nearer. He dragged Kirkland with him, flattening them both against the side of the building as a Geo Tracker sped by, the shadowy figure of the driver hunched over the wheel like an Indy pro. The Tracker's brakes screamed like hell as it roared out onto the street trying a 360, but the Tracker was too top-heavy to hold the maneuver. It flipped, bounced just once, and wrapped itself around the lamppost at the mouth of the opposite alley.

Bull poured himself a shot of Grand-Dad, put the bottle back in his desk drawer. A week had passed since the Tracker had tried to run him down. There was a *Challenger* on his desk, turned to the sports page. Rod Felton had been offered his father's old job and his first column dealt with the scheme to fix the bowl game. He did a credible job, sticking to reporting and managing to control the sentiment. But he promised his readers he'd be there when the guilty parties were brought to trial.

There were a lot of conflicting stories for the police to filter through. But they had gone with Takisha's version, mainly because she had given her statement when she thought she was going to die. It had taken the fire department a half hour to free her from the wreckage of the Tracker. It had also taken eight hours of surgery and another two days in intensive care before the doctors had given her any hope of surviving.

The whole deal had been Wizzy's idea. He took it to Breeden for backing with the promise of getting Kirkland to go along with the deal. Wizzy had started out by threatening to tie Kirkland to the old car-theft ring. But it wasn't necessary, Takisha liked the idea and that was all Kirkland needed to know. Takisha had even gotten Breeden to up Kirkland's end of the take. The plan was to win the game, just control the point spread.

It had all blown up when Breeden decided to cut Wizzy out of the deal. Wizzy got mad and went to Lucky. Lucky went to Kirkland to verify the story. Kirkland denied the whole thing and Lucky took his word for it but said he would be checking into Wizzy's motive for trying to start trouble. Takisha didn't want to take the chance Lucky would discover the truth, especially her involvement in the whole thing. Working around her father's business, she'd learned how to hot-wire a car by the time she was twelve. She'd contacted Lucky to set up a meeting; he had chosen the location. Then fearing Wizzy would take his story to someone else she treated him to the same fate. When Bull ran after Kirkland, Takisha turned to her murder weapon of choice. She'd hot-wired the Tracker and followed.

Kirkland and Breeden weren't involved in the murders, but there were a half-dozen other charges they were going to be facing.

Bull folded the *Challenger*, leaning back in his chair. Rod had ended his column by predicting even with Kirkland out of the lineup, and with all the adverse publicity, the Pharaohs were going to win their bowl appearance handily.

It's the way Lucky would have done it, no sitting on the fence. Bull realized he was smiling, and figured somewhere Lucky was smiling too. He raised his glass, saying goodbye to an old friend and welcoming a new.

ONE HOLY NIGHT

BY SANDRA CISNEROS

Pilsen

(Originally published in 1988)

About the truth, if you give it to a person, then he has power over
you. And if someone gives it to you, then they have made them-
selves your slave. It is a strong magic. You can never take it back.

—Chaq Uxmal Paloquín

He said his name was Chaq. Chaq Uxmal Paloquín.
That's what he told me. He was of an ancient line of
Mayan kings. Here, he said, making a map with the
heel of his boot, this is where I come from, the Yucatán, the
ancient cities. This is what Boy Baby said.

It's been eighteen weeks since Abuelita chased him away
with the broom, and what I'm telling you I never told nobody,
except Rachel and Lourdes, who know everything. He said
he would love me like a revolution, like a religion. Abuelita
burned the pushcart and sent me here, miles from home, in
this town of dust, with one wrinkled witch woman who rubs my
belly with jade, and sixteen nosy cousins.

I don't know how many girls have gone bad from selling cu-
cumbers. I know I'm not the first. My mother took the crooked
walk too, I'm told, and I'm sure my Abuelita has her own story,
but it's not my place to ask.

Abuelita says it's Uncle Lalo's fault because he's the man
of the family and if he had come home on time like he was sup-

posed to and worked the pushcart on the days he was told to and watched over his goddaughter, who is too foolish to look after herself, nothing would've happened, and I wouldn't have to be sent to Mexico. But Uncle Lalo says if they had never left Mexico in the first place, shame enough would have kept a girl from doing devil things.

I'm not saying I'm not bad. I'm not saying I'm special. But I'm not like the Allport Street girls, who stand in doorways and go with men into alleys.

All I know is I didn't want it like that. Not against the bricks or hunkering in somebody's car. I wanted it come undone like gold thread, like a tent full of birds. The way it's supposed to be, the way I knew it would be when I met Boy Baby.

But you must know, I was no girl back then. And Boy Baby was no boy. Chaq Uxmal Paloquín. Boy Baby was a man. When I asked him how old he was he said he didn't know. The past and the future are the same thing. So he seemed boy and baby and man all at once, and the way he looked at me, how do I explain?

I'd park the pushcart in front of the Jewel food store Saturdays. He bought a mango on a stick the first time. Paid for it with a new twenty. Next Saturday he was back. Two mangoes, lime juice, and chili powder, keep the change. The third Saturday he asked for a cucumber spear and ate it slow. I didn't see him after that till the day he brought me Kool-Aid in a plastic cup. Then I knew what I felt for him.

Maybe you wouldn't like him. To you he might be a bum. Maybe he looked it. Maybe. He had broken thumbs and burnt fingers. He had thick greasy fingernails he never cut and dusty hair. And all his bones were strong ones like a man's. I waited every Saturday in my same blue dress. I sold all the mango and cucumber, and then Boy Baby would come finally.

What I knew of Chaq was only what he told me, because nobody seemed to know where he came from. Only that he could speak a strange language that no one could understand, said his name translated into boy, or boy-child, and so it was the street people nicknamed him Boy Baby.

I never asked about his past. He said it was all the same and didn't matter, past and the future all the same to his people. But the truth has a strange way of following you, of coming up to you and making you listen to what it has to say.

Nighttime. Boy Baby brushes my hair and talks to me in his strange language because I like to hear it. What I like to hear him tell is how he is Chaq, Chaq of the people of the sun, Chaq of the temples, and what he says sounds sometimes like broken clay, and at other times like hollow sticks, or like the swish of old feathers crumbling into dust.

He lived behind Esparza & Sons Auto Repair in a little room that used to be a closet—pink plastic curtains on a narrow window, a dirty cot covered with newspapers, and a cardboard box filled with socks and rusty tools. It was there, under one bald bulb, in the back room of the Esparza garage, in the single room with pink curtains, that he showed me the guns—twenty-four in all. Rifles and pistols, one rusty musket, a machine gun, and several tiny weapons with mother-of-pearl handles that looked like toys. So you'll see who I am, he said, laying them all out on the bed of newspapers. So you'll understand. But I didn't want to know.

The stars foretell everything, he said. My birth. My son's. The boy-child who will bring back the grandeur of my people from those who have broken the arrows, from those who have pushed the ancient stones off their pedestals.

Then he told how he had prayed in the Temple of the Magician years ago as a child when his father had made him promise to bring back the ancient ways. Boy Baby had cried in the temple dark that only the bats made holy. Boy Baby who was man and child among the great and dusty guns lay down on the newspaper bed and wept for a thousand years. When I touched him, he looked at me with the sadness of stone.

You must not tell anyone what I am going to do, he said. And what I remember next is how the moon, the pale moon with its one yellow eye, the moon of Tikal, and Tulum, and Chichén, stared through the pink plastic curtains. Then something inside bit me, and I gave out a cry as if the other, the one I wouldn't be anymore, leapt out.

So I was initiated beneath an ancient sky by a great and mighty heir—Chaq Uxmal Paloquín. I, Ixchel, his queen.

The truth is, it wasn't a big deal. It wasn't any deal at all. I put my bloody panties inside my T-shirt and ran home hugging myself. I thought about a lot of things on the way home. I thought about all the world and how suddenly I became a part of history and wondered if everyone on the street, the sewing machine lady and the *panadería* saleswomen and the woman with two kids sitting on the bus bench, didn't all know. *Did I look any different? Could they tell?* We were all the same somehow, laughing behind our hands, waiting the way all women wait, and when we find out, we wonder why the world and a million years made such a big deal over nothing.

I know I was supposed to feel ashamed, but I wasn't ashamed. I wanted to stand on top of the highest building, the top-top floor, and yell, *I know!*

Then I understood why Abuelita didn't let me sleep over at Lourdes's house full of too many brothers, and why the Roman girl in the movies always runs away from the soldier, and what happens when the scenes in love stories begin to fade, and why brides blush, and how it is that sex isn't simply a box you check M or F on in the test we get at school.

I was wise. The corner girls were still jumping into their stupid little hopscotch squares. I laughed inside and climbed the wooden stairs two by two to the second floor rear where me and Abuelita and Uncle Lalo live. I was still laughing when I opened the door and Abuelita asked, Where's the pushcart?

And then I didn't know what to do.

It's a good thing we live in a bad neighborhood. There are always plenty of bums to blame for your sins. If it didn't happen the way I told it, it really could've. We looked and looked all over for the kids who stole my pushcart. The story wasn't the best, but since I had to make it up right then and there with Abuelita staring a hole through my heart, it wasn't too bad.

For two weeks I had to stay home. Abuelita was afraid the street kids who had stolen the cart would be after me again. Then I thought I might go over to the Esparza garage and take the pushcart out and leave it in some alley for the police to find, but I was never allowed to leave the house alone. Bit by bit the truth started to seep out like a dangerous gasoline.

First the nosy woman who lives upstairs from the laundromat told my Abuelita she thought something was fishy, the pushcart wheeled into Esparza & Sons every Saturday after dark, how a man, the same dark Indian one, the one who never talks to anybody, walked with me when the sun went down and pushed the cart into the garage, that one there, and yes we went inside, there where the fat lady named Concha, whose hair is dyed a hard black, pointed a fat finger.

I prayed that we would not meet Boy Baby, and since the gods listen and are mostly good, Esparza said yes, a man like that had lived there but was gone, had packed a few things and left the pushcart in a corner to pay for his last week's rent.

We had to pay twenty dollars before he would give us our pushcart back. Then Abuelita made me tell the real story of how the cart had disappeared, all of which I told this time, except for that one night, which I would have to tell anyway, weeks later, when I prayed for the moon of my cycle to come back, but it would not.

When Abuelita found out I was going to *dar a luz*, she cried until her eyes were little, and blamed Uncle Lalo, and Uncle Lalo blamed this country, and Abuelita blamed the infamy of men. That is when she burned the cucumber pushcart and called me a *sinvergüenza* because I *am* without shame.

Then I cried too—Boy Baby was lost from me—until my head was hot with headaches and I fell asleep. When I woke up, the cucumber pushcart was dust and Abuelita was sprinkling holy water on my head.

Abuelita woke up early every day and went to the Esparza garage to see if news about that *demonio* had been found, had Chaq Uxmal Paloquín sent any letters, any, and when the other mechanics heard that name they laughed, and asked if we had made it up, that we could have some letters that had come for Boy Baby, no forwarding address, since he had gone in such a hurry.

There were three. The first, addressed *Occupant*, demanded immediate payment for a four-month-old electric bill. The second was one I recognized right away—a brown envelope fat with cake-mix coupons and fabric-softener samples—because we'd gotten one just like it. The third was addressed in a spidery Spanish to a Señor C. Cruz, on paper so thin you could read it unopened by the light of the sky. The return address a convent in Tampico.

This was to whom my Abuelita wrote in hopes of finding

the man who could correct my ruined life, to ask if the good nuns might know the whereabouts of a certain Boy Baby—and if they were hiding him it would be of no use because God's eyes see through all souls.

We heard nothing for a long time. Abuelita took me out of school when my uniform got tight around the belly and said it was a shame I wouldn't be able to graduate with the other eighth graders.

Except for Lourdes and Rachel, my grandma and Uncle Lalo, nobody knew about my past. I would sleep in the big bed I share with Abuelita same as always. I could hear Abuelita and Uncle Lalo talking in low voices in the kitchen as if they were praying the rosary, how they were going to send me to Mexico, to San Dionisio de Tlaltepango, where I have cousins and where I was conceived and would've been born had my grandma not thought it wise to send my mother here to the United States so that neighbors in San Dionisio de Tlaltepango wouldn't ask why her belly was suddenly big.

I was happy. I liked staying home. Abuelita was teaching me to crochet the way she had learned in Mexico. And just when I had mastered the tricky rosette stitch, the letter came from the convent which gave the truth about Boy Baby—however much we didn't want to hear.

He was born on a street with no name in a town called Miseria. His father, Eusebio, is a knife sharpener. His mother, Refugia, stacks apricots into pyramids and sells them on a cloth in the market. There are brothers. Sisters too of which I know little. The youngest, a Carmelite, writes me all this and prays for my soul, which is why I know it's all true.

Boy Baby is thirty-seven years old. His name is Chato which means fat-face. There is no Mayan blood.

* * *

I don't think they understand how it is to be a girl. I don't think they know how it is to have to wait your whole life. I count the months for the baby to be born, and it's like a ring of water inside me reaching out and out until one day it will tear from me with its own teeth.

Already I can feel the animal inside me stirring in his own uneven sleep. The witch woman says it's the dreams of weasels that make my child sleep the way he sleeps. She makes me eat white bread blessed by the priest, but I know it's the ghost of him inside me that circles and circles, and will not let me rest.

Abuelita said they sent me here just in time, because a little later Boy Baby came back to our house looking for me, and she had to chase him away with the broom. The next thing we hear, he's in the newspaper clippings his sister sends. A picture of him looking very much like stone, police hooked on either arm . . . *on the road to Las Grutas de Xtacumbilxuna, the Caves of the Hidden Girl . . . eleven female bodies . . . the last seven years . . .*

Then I couldn't read but only stare at the little black-and-white dots that make up the face I am in love with.

All my girl cousins here either don't talk to me, or those who do ask questions they're too young to know *not* to ask. What they want to know really is how it is to have a man, because they're too ashamed to ask their married sisters.

They don't know what it is to lay so still until his sleep breathing is heavy, for the eyes in the dim dark to look and look without worry at the man-bones and the neck, the man-wrist and man-jaw thick and strong, all the salty dips and hollows, the stiff hair of the brow and sour swirl of sideburns, to lick the fat earlobes that taste of smoke, and stare at how perfect is a man.

I tell them, "It's a bad joke. When you find out you'll be sorry."

I'm going to have five children. Five. Two girls. Two boys. And one baby.

The girls will be called Lisette and Maritza. The boys I'll name Pablo and Sandro.

And my baby. My baby will be named Alegre, because life will always be hard.

Rachel says that love is like a big black piano being pushed off the top of a three-story building and you're waiting on the bottom to catch it. But Lourdes says it's not that way at all. It's like a top, like all the colors in the world are spinning so fast they're not colors anymore and all that's left is a white hum.

There was a man, a crazy who lived upstairs from us when we lived on South Loomis. He couldn't talk, just walked around all day with this harmonica in his mouth. Didn't play it. Just sort of breathed through it, all day long, wheezing, in and out, in and out.

This is how it is with me. Love I mean.

THE THIRTIETH AMENDMENT

BY HUGH HOLTON

Bridgeport

(Originally published in 1995)

The Future

Congress repealed the Bill of Rights with the Thirtieth Amendment. Instead of playing games with idealistic crap about search and seizure, rights against self-incrimination and protection from double jeopardy, the Gingrich White House took aim at the criminal element which was turning America into a wasteland. The Tri-X Law, as it was called, made the death penalty not only legal but mandatory for the maggots, drug dealers, child molesters, and social undesirables who murdered, kidnapped, and played treasonous games with scum like the Iraqi dictator Saddam Hussein.

Mr. Law and Order himself, President Newt Gingrich, supported a broader interpretation of the Tri-X Law at the state level. So in California bikers who engaged in violent acts on public highways were added to the list. In New York and Chicago punks engaged in illegal acts on rapid transit lines were added to the list. In Texas, which I always thought was a pretty progressive state, corrupt politicians were added to the list. The other sixty-three states, with the exception of Old Mexico, soon followed suit.

This caused a remarkable increase in executions, which became the growth industry in the USA for the twenty-first century. My name is Jules Freitag and I managed to get in on the ground floor, so to speak. I majored in Public Executions and Human Terminations at Harvard. The course took six years to complete at a cost of $600,000. The first three years were spent on Law and Sociology, as these subjects relate to the Tri-X Law. The last three years were devoted exclusively to an intricate study of Physiology, not from a medical standpoint, but rather from the termination end. Efficiency was our aim and by efficiency I don't mean just speed, as at times it is decreed that pain must be as much an integral part of the sentence as the death itself.

I am a master of my art.

Randolph Nimrod, the Deputy Commissioner of the National Bureau of Executions and Public Terminations in Miami, called me into his office. He was an intense man of sixty who had given his all to our profession and was considered a living legend. A man with no family or friends, he had risen within the Bureau to the rank of deputy because of his supreme devotion to the field and his administrative skill. For some reason, though, he didn't like me, which made what he had to say that much harder to understand.

"I've selected you for a special assignment, Freitag."

I am usually not a very demonstrative fellow. My vocation demands this. But Nimrod did get my eyes to widen a bit. "Me?"

"Yes, you!" He frowned, grimacing as if he had just been administered a Xyclon cube, which tastes like a sugar cookie and kills in eight seconds.

I stood at attention and waited, as there was nothing else I could do.

"There's an inmate in Chicago named Darka Paris. A vicious convicted murderess. Cut off her lover's head with a butcher knife. I want you to size her."

I stared at him. As a Bureau Deputy Commissioner, he had

a staff of over a thousand professional executioners to choose from. There were any number of them beholden to him for their positions who would be eager to do as he asked. My pride told me I was selected because I was the best. But I knew Nimrod would never admit it.

The Jetstar got me from Miami to Chicago in twenty minutes. The state prison was in the inner city. The walls stretched from 35th Street on the north near the old ball park, down what had once been an expressway for ground vehicles called the Dan Ryan, to 53rd Street on the south, and west over to State Street. The surrounding area had become an urban desert.

I was admitted through the seven normal security gates leading into the prison. The buildings had originally been highrise, low-income housing which social neglect had transformed into human zoos. So, during the final year of the Quayle presidency, remaining residents were ordered out and the maximum-security penitentiary was established in the sixteen-story monstrosities near the center of what had once been the second largest city in the United States.

The Tri-X inmates were held at the center of the complex in the 4444 Building. As I stood in the shadow of the imposing edifice, surrounded by machine guns, electrified barbed wire, and guards recruited primarily for their ability to inflict violence on their fellow man rather than for their intellect, I recalled a phrase from a high school literature class: *Abandon hope all ye who enter here.* Very appropriate, I thought, as I was admitted inside. But then I was a professional who had no time for poetry.

Inside the Tri-X section it was bright, clean, and terrifying, especially if one were an inmate forced to spend the last moments of one's life on Earth here. The thick-foreheaded guard escorted me to a private room where I could check my equipment and put on my work clothing. There was a surliness in his manner initially which was quickly erased when I exited wearing the black hood which displayed only my eyes and mouth.

It was the same everywhere I went. The hood generated a fear so intense it tended to manifest itself as a separate physical entity. This made my work much easier.

"The girl is in Block L," he said, staunchly refusing to look at me. "She's a real looker. Keeps saying she's innocent, but they all say that." He laughed, glancing sideways at me to see if I had enjoyed his little joke. All he could see was the outside of the hood, which revealed no more emotion than my face beneath it.

We came to her cell and he started to open the door.

"Stop!" I ordered so abruptly he jumped. "You must properly prepare the inmate before I enter."

He caught on quick enough and took the garments I gave him before slipping inside the cell. I waited in the corridor studying the cracked plaster on the walls of the high-rise gallery until he came out.

"She's ready," he said, still refusing to look at me.

I entered to find the inmate securely chained to a chair. Her head was covered with a hood, very much like my own, and her body was shrouded in a black full-length robe. The only flesh exposed was that of her hands, arms, and neck, which I would need to work with directly.

I prided myself on the efficiency of my sizings, which involved the taking of vital statistics about the inmate to aid in the selection of the method I would choose for her death. I could generally do an accurate, very thorough sizing in less than two hours. With her it would take longer because she violated the regulations by talking continuously.

"I know you're here to kill me and that you're trained to ignore what I say but, for the love of God, you must listen!"

It was strictly forbidden by the Executioner's Code of Conduct for me to speak to her. We wore the hoods to maintain mutual anonymity and to prevent any buildup of sympathies between inmate and executioner. Talking could engender some degree of sympathy, but in Executioner Psychology 412, it was plainly established that condemned inmates were liars. It was simple self-preservation to try to maintain one's existence as long as possible by whatever means necessary. So they lied.

"I *am* innocent!"

Of course you are, my thoughts mocked her. How many times had I heard that before. I could have her gagged, but then she had a nice voice. One that could even be called sexy. I scolded myself for my lack of professionalism and concentrated on my work.

"I would never kill Arthur! I loved him! Someone followed us and executed him! It happened so quickly only one of you people could have done it!"

The last statement got through to me. She was making me angry by impugning the integrity of one of the last truly noble professions on Earth. My job was to kill her and her crime limited the means by which I could do it. But then there were always certain tricks of the trade that could be used to make my method of dispatch pure agony for a very long time.

"It had to be an executioner!" Her anger bubbled on the edge of hysteria. "Who else has the knowledge and ability to kill like that?"

Like what? But I forced the question out of my mind. I didn't care.

"What kind of people kill without warning? Would kill Arthur without giving him a chance to defend himself?"

I wanted to ask how it happened but I figured she'd tell me soon enough at the rate she was going.

"You people are cowards! You hide behind your black masks and slaughter people like animals! You're nothing but murderers!"

Look who was talking. I could do the sizing procedure in the order I chose. Now I felt it was time to slow her down a bit. I'd heard all of this before.

Judging by her size, a pint should do the trick. I started drawing blood from her jugular vein.

"His head was . . . severed . . . from . . . his . . . body."

The food in this place wasn't that bad, as prisons go, but then those on death row seldom had much of an appetite. So she was weak and the way I drew blood was just a tad slower than a speed that would induce shock. She was coming down a bit too fast, so I cut the flow slightly.

She hit a plateau, which she managed to maintain for a time. "They said . . . that I . . . did it . . . with a . . ." She was starting to ramble.

Butcher knife, darling! You did it with a butcher knife. Deputy Commissioner Nimrod told me.

As a professional, educated practitioner of the fine art of Executioning, I knew such an act as severing a head cleanly to be impossible except by guillotine or at the hands of a master craftsman of the highest caliber. I studied my inmate and the stats of her sizing. If her victim were asleep . . . ?

"One stroke . . ."

I removed the tube from her neck and cleaned her up. I would have to leave word with the stupid guard to make sure she was given a proper supper with plenty of liquids to replace the blood. I was putting my needles away when something she just said intrigued me.

"One stroke . . ." she repeated in a weak, dazed voice.

One stroke? At Harvard we had studied World History of Executions I, II, III, IV, and Advanced. Crucifixion, drawing and quartering, and boiling in oil were all methods we had been forced to review and write extensive research papers about. My paper had been on beheadings, and during the first year after Tri-X passed this method was quite popular.

There had been few skilled practitioners of the art of severing a head cleanly from the body. When accidents started occurring with some frequency there was a public outcry and the method was outlawed in the States, although France kept it for historical reasons.

"One stroke," she mumbled again.

As I recalled from the research I had done for my paper, to do the job cleanly, it took several things to carry one off with precision: either a guillotine or a sharp, heavy blade; a strong steady hand; and the eye of a sharpshooter. Outside of the lucky amateur, there was maybe one executioner who had really been good at it . . .

"One stroke."

She was beginning to bore me. Enough of this nonsense! I had work to do.

My sizing completed, I decided that this inmate would die in exactly twenty-four hours by being burned alive.

Back in my quarters I kept thinking about beheadings. I used my pocket 1,000 K computer to call up historical data, most of which I already knew. I'd always wanted to do a beheading myself, but by the time I completed my studies at Harvard, the law had changed. But Nimrod had said she used a butcher knife. Of course the inmate was lying, but in the Day Before Death Seminar IV it was taught that there was always motivation behind any lie. I decided to check out her story.

* * *

The Illinois Division of the two million–strong National Police Force had taken over the Merchandise Mart on the Chicago River. Although Illinois had a relatively small contingent compared to the New York and California divisions, they were crammed into what was once the largest office building in the world and were constantly searching for more space. It was rumored the NPF would soon be taking over the old Sears Tower, which could be confiscated from its current owners under Section V, 3, C. sub. para. f. (1), 2. of the Tri-X Law, which states: *No property or possessions will be held secure from seizure by the NPF established by this Amendment, where such seizure relates to the safety, security, and peace of the United States of America.*

Under Section V, the NPF could confiscate yachts, summer homes, bank accounts, and anything else they desired in the name of law and order. This was an excellent system for the NPF to utilize as a peacekeeping tool, as it was unnecessary to make many arrests. All they had to do was confiscate everything the recalcitrant owned. The only vocal critics of this section of the Tri-X Law were currently penniless, stateless street people. This was another twenty-first-century advance of the Gingrich White House.

The captain I was directed to see had an I'm-too-busy-for-this-shit attitude until he found out who I was. He might be able to confiscate property, but I could simultaneously confiscate his life. Isn't this a great country?

"This is an unusual request coming from Executions," the captain said when the Darka Paris file was delivered to his office by a clerk.

"Oh?" I found it best to speak in soft monosyllables when I was trying to scare the red corpuscles out of someone. Especially a pompous ass from the NPF.

He coughed, stuttered, and handed over the file. "Take it with you. Don't worry about getting it back to me. In fact, you can keep it." He ushered me out the door with more than a small sigh of relief.

The photographs were beautiful. They revealed a work of art the likes of which I had never seen before. The head had been lopped off with a precision that would make a heart surgeon look like a beef boner. I was so excited I studied them for hours. Aside from my admiration for the work, I realized instantly that Darka Paris could not have killed this man. Not with a butcher knife, a chain saw, or a hyperbolic laser. There was no doubt in my mind that a razor-sharp blade had been used. A blade in the hands of a master executioner.

I read the NPF report. The assigned detective had done a slipshod investigation. The evidence was sketchy, contradictory, or circumstantial. A butcher knife with the inmate's fingerprints all over it was listed and cataloged as the murder weapon.

Putting the file down and examining the artwork in the photos once more I made a decision. I would have to find whoever did this. Just to talk briefly with such a craftsman would be a supreme honor indeed.

The same guard who had escorted me into the inmate's cell at 4444 was on duty again. He was considerably more attentive than during our first meeting and I was glad he was there because I was going to need him.

After I changed, he went into the cell to prepare the inmate. While I waited outside I thought about the girl. She was innocent but that was a secondary consideration. She would lead me to the master, then . . .

"She's ready," the guard said, stepping from the cell.

"I'll need your assistance."

"Me?" He took a step backward. "I don't know nothing about no executions."

"It's a good thing to learn, friend." I had a very difficult time talking to him like this. Especially since he wasn't wearing an inmate's hood. "Executions is the growth industry of the twenty-first century."

He seemed barely convinced, so I didn't give him a chance to think it over. "Inside—now!"

He jumped and followed me. He stood awkwardly in the corner of the cell not knowing what to do. The inmate was again hooded, robed, and chained in her chair. She trembled violently.

"This is a simple procedure," I said for the guard's benefit. "Efficient and self-contained with very little mess to clean up later." I pulled a pint spray bottle containing nitroholic acid from my bag.

"It's easy. You just spray it on . . ." I pointed the nozzle first at the inmate before turning it on the guard. He screamed and went for his electric truncheon but he was far too slow. ". . . and ignite." I held the mini-torch in my gloved hand. The flame licked across the confined space and enveloped him. He ignited, flared, and burned away as fast as tissue paper. Only a few ashes remained, which would be enough to temporarily convince prison officials the execution had been carried out. It had gone off quick and efficient, the way I liked it.

"Now, my dear," I said, undoing her chains, "you and I are going to get out of here."

Hooded executioners can go anywhere without question. Together we walked out of Chicago State Prison and were given a limousine ride to the jet port on the lake. It was not until we were in my private compartment aboard the Jetstar that I permitted her to remove her hood.

"Thank you," she said, embracing me. "I could sense when you walked in the cell that you were a decent man. I knew you'd help me."

She was an attractive woman, as looks go, with soft features and a petite body. Under different circumstances I might have liked to spend some of my yearly ninety-five-day vacation time with her, but I had more important things to think about now. On top of that she was a condemned prisoner whom I had already sized and I would have to terminate anyway. After all, it was still my job. I had merely postponed implementation of sentence temporarily.

"I want you to tell me everything about Arthur's murder that you can remember. Leave nothing out. It's the only way I can help you." The lie came off my lips easily, as I had been taught by the best liars in the country in Political Terminations 343. It suddenly occurred to me that all of my instructors in the course had either been politicians or bureaucrats like Nimrod.

She was so willing to help me she made me sick. She told me everything. She and Arthur Hickey—the deceased victim—were engaged. They had taken a prenuptial vacation, as was the current custom, to Atlantis (formerly Australia). While there, Hickey began complaining that someone was following them. He became moody and withdrawn from her, constantly looking over his shoulder. He became to obsessed with the belief they were being watched, he cut short their vacation and returned to the States. A day later he was dead.

"It happened so fast I can barely recall it now," she said. "There was a knock at the door of our cubicle. Arthur opened it and . . ."

I let her cry. I knew the rest anyway. The NPF detective had probably made the erroneous connection that she murdered him with the knife simply because it was in the kitchen section of the ten-foot by ten-foot cubicle they rented for $1,000 a week, and she was the only suspect because the detective didn't look for any other.

I went back to my computer. I concentrated on prenuptial vacations, divorce honeymoons, funeral excursions, and terminal illness jaunts. I matched all the names on these lists against anyone who had been beheaded under any circumstances in the past twenty years. I came up with 568 hits.

Amazing! And everything pointed in one direction. I had all the answers before we set down in Miami.

Deputy Commissioner Nimrod looked up from his desk when we walked in. When he saw Darka he stiffened. Then his eyes flared angrily at me.

"What are you doing, Freitag?" he said in a choked voice. "Are you insane? I sent you to do a simple execution. Why did you bring her back here?"

I was sorry he was taking it this way. I really had hoped we could be friends now. The reason I'd brought the girl here was to give her to Nimrod so he could work his artistic execution style on her. The computer had revealed that my esteemed leader had been at or near each of the 568 locations where the bodies with severed heads had been found. That kind of coincidence was too much for even the NPF to swallow. I could only presume that he had been doing a little practice freelancing, which I could understand. After all, he was just a deskbound executioner trying to keep his hand in.

I was starting to explain when he leaped from behind his desk swinging a very formidable-looking sixteenth-century battle ax with an edge that gleamed with terrifying sharpness. I knew that in his hands it was as lethal as a nuclear suppository.

Darka screamed and backed away into a corner, as Nimrod

advanced on me. With nothing else I could do, I fumbled in my bag and came up with the spray bottle and torch I had used in the Chicago prison. I was merely going to use them to ward Nimrod off, but he feinted toward me and then drew back to hurl the ax.

In the instant he threw that blade, I knew I was being terminated with no chance of escape, but I admired his artistry to the last. I managed to spray a liberal amount of nitroholic acid on him before my head was sliced off my shoulders to drop to the floor.

I was dying at light speed, but still able to see and think. It happened so fast my headless body was still standing a few feet away with the spray bottle and mini-torch in my hands. I could see Darka over in the corner cringing in fear and Nimrod looking at me with supreme triumph etched on his face.

My last act in life was willing my hand to ignite the torch. As I blinked off into eternity I was certain I had failed because mind and body were no longer part of the same mechanism.

But the fates were kind to me, at least as far as Nimrod went. When I arrived at the Gates of Hell, he was waiting for me. It seems his being instantly cremated succeeded in making his trip to the Netherworld faster. There we found ourselves in the company of some of history's greatest killers. For the rest of time we sat around talking methodology, practice, and execution. It wasn't Heaven, but what the hell.

WE DIDN'T

BY STUART DYBEK

Old Street Beach

(Originally published in 1993)

> *We did it in front of the mirror*
> *And in the light. We did it in darkness,*
> *In water, and in the high grass.*
>
> —Yehuda Amichai, "We Did It"

We didn't in the light; we didn't in darkness. We didn't in the fresh-cut summer grass or in the mounds of autumn leaves or on the snow where moonlight threw down our shadows. We didn't in your room on the canopy bed you slept in, the bed you'd slept in as a child, or in the backseat of my father's rusted Rambler, which smelled of the smoked chubs and kielbasa he delivered on weekends from my uncle Vincent's meat market. We didn't in your mother's Buick Eight, where a rosary twined the rearview mirror like a beaded black snake with silver cruciform fangs.

At the dead end of our lovers' lane—a side street of abandoned factories—where I perfected the pinch that springs open a bra; behind the lilac bushes in Marquette Park, where you first touched me through my jeans and your nipples, swollen against transparent cotton, seemed the shade of lilacs; in the balcony of the now defunct Clark Theater, where I wiped popcorn salt from my palms and slid them up your thighs and you whispered, "I feel like Doris Day is watching us," we didn't.

How adept we were at fumbling, how perfectly mistimed our timing, how utterly we confused energy with ecstasy.

Remember that night becalmed by heat, and the two of us, fused by sweat, trembling as if a wind from outer space that only we could feel was gusting across Oak Street Beach? Entwined in your faded Navajo blanket, we lay soul-kissing until you wept with wanting.

We'd been kissing all day—all summer—kisses tasting of different shades of lip gloss and too many Cokes. The lake had turned hot pink, rose rapture, pearl amethyst with dusk, then washed in night black with a ruff of silver foam. Beyond a momentary horizon, silent bolts of heat lightning throbbed, perhaps setting barns on fire somewhere in Indiana. The beach that had been so crowded was deserted as if there was a curfew. Only the bodies of lovers remained, visible in lightning flashes, scattered like the fallen on a battlefield, a few of them moaning, waiting for the gulls to pick them clean.

On my fingers your slick scent mixed with the coconut musk of the suntan lotion we'd repeatedly smeared over each other's bodies. When your bikini top fell away, my hands caught your breasts, memorizing their delicate weight, my palms cupped as if bringing water to parched lips.

Along the Gold Coast, high-rises began to glow, window added to window, against the dark. In every lighted bedroom, couples home from work were stripping off their business suits, falling to the bed, and doing it. They did it before mirrors and pressed against the glass in streaming shower stalls; they did it against walls and on the furniture in ways that required previously unimagined gymnastics, which they invented on the spot. They did it in honor of man and woman, in honor of beast, in honor of God. They did it because they'd been released, because they were home free, alive, and private, because they couldn't wait any longer, couldn't wait for the appointed hour, for the right time or temperature, couldn't wait for the future, for Messiahs, for peace on earth and justice for all. They did it because of the Bomb, because of pollution, because of the Four Horsemen of the Apocalypse, because extinction might be just a blink away. They did it because it was Friday night. It was Friday night and somewhere delirious music was playing—flutter-tongued flutes, muted trumpets meowing like cats in heat, feverish plucking and twanging, tom-toms, congas, and gongs all pounding the same pulsebeat.

I stripped your bikini bottom down the skinny rails of your legs, and you tugged my swimsuit past my tan. Swimsuits at our ankles, we kicked like swimmers to free our legs, almost expecting a tide to wash over us the way the tide rushes in on Burt Lancaster and Deborah Kerr in *From Here to Eternity*—a love scene so famous that although neither of us had seen the movie, our bodies assumed the exact position of movie stars on the sand and you whispered to me softly, "I'm afraid of getting pregnant," and I whispered back, "Don't worry, I have protection," then, still kissing you, felt for my discarded cutoffs and the wallet in which for the last several months I had carried a Trojan as if it was a talisman. Still kissing, I tore its flattened, dried-out wrapper, and it sprang through my fingers like a spring from a clock and dropped to the sand between our legs. My hands were shaking. In a panic, I groped for it, found it, tried to dust it off, tried as Burt Lancaster never had to, to slip it on without breaking the mood, felt the grains of sand inside it, a throb of lightning, and the Great Lake behind us became, for all practical purposes, the Pacific, and your skin tasted of salt and to the insistent question that my hips were asking your body answered yes, your thighs opened like wings from my waist as we surfaced panting from a kiss that left you pleading *Oh, Christ yes*, a *yes* gasped sharply as a cry of pain so that for a moment I thought that we *were* already doing it and that somehow I had missed the instant when I entered you, entered you in the bloodless way in which a young man discards his own virginity, entered you as if passing through a gateway into the rest of my life, into a life as I wanted it to be lived *yes* but Oh then I realized that we were still floundering unconnected in the slick between us and there was sand in the Trojan as we slammed together still feeling for that perfect fit, still in the *Here* groping for an *Eternity* that was only a fine adjustment away, just a millimeter to the left or a fraction of an inch farther south though with all the adjusting the sandy Trojan was slipping off and then it was gone but *yes* you kept repeating although your head was shaking *no-not-quite-almost* and our hearts were going like mad and you said, *Yes. Yes, wait . . . Stop!*

"What?" I asked, still futilely thrusting as if I hadn't quite heard you.

"Oh. God!" You gasped, pushing yourself up. "What's coming?"

"Gin, what's the matter?" I asked, confused, and then the beam of a spotlight swept over us and I glanced into its blinding eye.

All around us lights were coming, speeding across the sand. Blinking blindness away, I rolled from your body to my knees, feeling utterly defenseless in the way that only nakedness can leave one feeling. Headlights bounded toward us, spotlights crisscrossing, blue dome lights revolving as squad cars converged. I could see other lovers, caught in the beams, fleeing bare-assed through the litter of garbage that daytime hordes had left behind and that night had deceptively concealed. You were crying, clutching the Navajo blanket to your breasts with one hand and clawing for your bikini with the other, and I was trying to calm your terror with reassuring phrases such as "Holy shit! I don't fucking believe this!"

Swerving and fishtailing in the sand, police calls pouring from their radios, the squad cars were on us, and then they were by us while we struggled to pull on our clothes.

They braked at the water's edge, and cops slammed out, brandishing huge flashlights, their beams deflecting over the dark water. Beyond the darting of those beams, the far-off throbs of lightning seemed faint by comparison.

"Over there, goddamn it!" one of them hollered, and two cops sloshed out into the shallow water without even pausing to kick off their shoes, huffing aloud for breath, their leather cartridge belts creaking against their bellies.

"Grab the son of a bitch! It ain't gonna bite!" one of them yelled, then they came sloshing back to shore with a body slung between them.

It was a woman—young, naked, her body limp and bluish beneath the play of flashlight beams. They set her on the sand just past the ring of drying, washed-up alewives. Her face was almost totally concealed by her hair. Her hair was brown and tangled in a way that even wind or sleep can't tangle hair, tangled as if it had absorbed the ripples of water—thick strands, slimy looking like dead seaweed.

"She's been in there awhile, that's for sure," a cop with a beer belly said to a younger, crew-cut cop, who had knelt beside the body and removed his hat as if he might be considering the kiss of life.

The crew-cut officer brushed the hair away from her face, and the flashlight beams settled there. Her eyes were closed. A bruise or a birthmark stained the side of one eye. Her features appeared swollen, her lower lip protruding as if she was pouting.

An ambulance siren echoed across the sand, its revolving red light rapidly approaching.

"Might as well take their sweet-ass time," the beer-bellied cop said.

We had joined the circle of police surrounding the drowned woman almost without realizing that we had. You were back in your bikini, robed in the Navajo blanket, and I had slipped on my cutoffs, my underwear dangling out of a back pocket.

Their flashlight beams explored her body, causing its whiteness to gleam. Her breasts were floppy; her nipples looked shriveled. Her belly appeared inflated by gallons of water. For a moment, a beam focused on her mound of pubic hair, which was overlapped by the swell of her belly, and then moved almost shyly away down her legs, and the cops all glanced at us—at you, especially—above their lights, and you hugged your blanket closer as if they might confiscate it as evidence or to use as a shroud.

When the ambulance pulled up, one of the black attendants immediately put a stethoscope to the drowned woman's swollen belly and announced, "Drowned the baby too."

Without saying anything, we turned from the group, as unconsciously as we'd joined them, and walked off across the sand, stopping only long enough at the spot where we had lain together like lovers, in order to stuff the rest of our gear into a beach bag, to gather our shoes, and for me to find my wallet and kick sand over the forlorn, deflated Trojan that you pretended not to notice. I was grateful for that.

Behind us, the police were snapping photos, flashbulbs throbbing like lightning flashes, and the lightning itself, still distant but moving in closer, rumbling audibly now, driving a lake wind before it so that gusts of sand tingled against the metal sides of the ambulance.

Squinting, we walked toward the lighted windows of the Gold Coast, while the shadows of gapers attracted by the whirling emergency lights hurried past us toward the shore.

"What happened? What's going on?" they asked without waiting for an answer, and we didn't offer one, just continued walking silently in the dark.

It was only later that we talked about it, and once we began talking about the drowned woman it seemed we couldn't stop.

"She was pregnant," you said. "I mean, I don't want to sound morbid, but I can't help thinking how the whole time we were, we almost—you know—there was this poor, dead woman and her unborn child washing in and out behind us."

"It's not like we could have done anything for her even if we had known she was there."

"But what if we *had* found her? What if after we had—you know," you said, your eyes glancing away from mine and your voice tailing into a whisper, "what if after we did it, we went for a night swim and found her in the water?"

"But Gin, we didn't," I tried to reason, though it was no more a matter of reason than anything else between us had ever been.

It began to seem as if each time we went somewhere to make out—on the back porch of your half-deaf, whiskery Italian grandmother, who sat in the front of the apartment cackling at *I Love Lucy* reruns; or in your girlfriend Tina's basement rec room when her parents were away on bowling league nights and Tina was upstairs with her current crush, Brad; or way off in the burbs, at the Giant Twin Drive-In during the weekend they called Elvis Fest—the drowned woman was with us.

We would kiss, your mouth would open, and when your tongue flicked repeatedly after mine, I would unbutton the first button of your blouse, revealing the beauty spot at the base of your throat, which matched a smaller spot I loved above a corner of your lips, and then the second button, which opened on a delicate gold cross—which I had always tried to regard as merely a fashion statement—dangling above the cleft of your breasts. The third button exposed the lacy swell of your bra, and I would slide my hand over the patterned mesh, feeling for the firmness of your nipple rising to my fingertip, but you would pull slightly away, and behind your rapid breath your kiss would grow distant, and I would kiss harder, trying to lure you back from wherever you had gone, and finally, holding you as if only consoling a friend, I'd ask, "What are you thinking?" although of course I knew.

"I don't want to think about her but I can't help it. I mean, it seems like some kind of weird omen or something, you know?"

"No, I don't know," I said. "It was just a coincidence."

"Maybe if she'd been farther away down the beach, but she was so close to us. A good wave could have washed her up right beside us."

"Great, then we could have had a ménage à trois."

"Gross! I don't believe you just said that! Just because you said it in French doesn't make it less disgusting."

"You're driving me to it. Come on, Gin, I'm sorry," I said. "I was just making a dumb joke to get a little different perspective on things."

"What's so goddamn funny about a woman who drowned herself and her baby?"

"We don't even know for sure she did."

"Yeah, right, it was just an accident. Like she just happened to be going for a walk pregnant and naked, and she fell in."

"She could have been on a sailboat or something. Accidents happen; so do murders."

"Oh, like murder makes it less horrible? Don't think that hasn't occurred to me. Maybe the bastard who knocked her up killed her, huh?"

"How should I know? You're the one who says you don't want to talk about it and then gets obsessed with all kinds of theories and scenarios. Why are we arguing about a woman we don't even know, who doesn't have the slightest thing to do with us?"

"I *do* know about her," you said. "I dream about her."

"You dream about her?" I repeated, surprised. "Dreams you remember?"

"Sometimes they wake me up. In one I'm at my *nonna*'s cottage in Michigan, swimming for a raft that keeps drifting farther away, until I'm too tired to turn back. Then I notice there's a naked person sunning on the raft and start yelling, *Help!* and she looks up and offers me a hand, but I'm too afraid to take it even though I'm drowning because it's her."

"God! Gin, that's creepy."

"I dreamed you and I are at the beach and you bring us a couple hot dogs but forget the mustard, so you have to go all the way back to the stand for it."

"Hot dogs, no mustard—a little too Freudian, isn't it?"

"Honest to God, I dreamed it. You go back for mustard and I'm wondering why you're gone so long, then a woman screams that a kid has drowned and everyone stampedes for the water. I'm swept in by the mob and forced under, and I think, *This is it, I'm going to drown,* but I'm able to hold my breath longer than could ever be possible. It feels like a flying dream—flying under water—and then I see this baby down there flying too, and realize it's the kid everyone thinks has drowned, but he's no more drowned than I am. He looks like Cupid or one of those baby angels that cluster around the face of God."

"Pretty weird. What do you think all the symbols mean?—hot dogs, water, drowning . . ."

"It means the baby who drowned inside her that night was a love child—a boy—and his soul was released there to wander through the water."

"You don't really believe that?"

We argued about the interpretation of dreams, about whether dreams are symbolic or psychic, prophetic or just plain nonsense, until you said, "Look, Dr. Freud, you can believe what you want about your dreams, but keep your nose out of mine, okay?"

We argued about the drowned woman, about whether her death was a suicide or a murder, about whether her appearance that night was an omen or a coincidence, which, you argued, is what an omen is anyway: a coincidence that means something. By the end of summer, even if we were no longer arguing about the woman, we had acquired the habit of arguing about everything else. What was better: dogs or cats, rock or jazz, Cubs or Sox, tacos or egg rolls, right or left, night or day?—we could argue about anything.

It no longer required arguing or necking to summon the drowned woman; everywhere we went she surfaced by her own volition: at Rocky's Italian Beef, at Lindo Mexico, at the House of Dong, our favorite Chinese restaurant, a place we still frequented because when we'd first started seeing each other they had let us sit and talk until late over tiny cups of jasmine tea and broken fortune cookies. We would always kid about going there. "Are you in the mood for Dong tonight?" I'd whisper conspiratorially. It was a dopey joke, meant for you to roll your eyes at its repeated dopiness. Back then, in winter, if one of us ordered the garlic shrimp we would both be sure to eat them so that later our mouths tasted the same when we kissed.

Even when she wasn't mentioned, she was there with her drowned body—so dumpy next to yours—and her sad breasts, with their wrinkled nipples and sour milk—so saggy beside yours, which were still budding—with her swollen belly and her pubic bush colorless in the glare of electric light, with her tangled, slimy hair and her pouting, placid face—so lifeless beside yours—and her skin a pallid white, lightning-flash white, flashbulb white, a whiteness that couldn't be duplicated in daylight—how I'd come to hate that pallor, so cold beside the flush of your skin.

There wasn't a particular night when we finally broke up, just as there wasn't a particular night when we began going together, but it was a night in fall when I guessed that it was over. We were parked in the Rambler at the dead end of the street of factories that had been our lovers' lane, listening to a drizzle of rain and dry leaves sprinkle the hood. As always, rain revitalized the smells of smoked fish and kielbasa in the upholstery. The radio was on too low to hear, the windshield wipers swished at intervals as if we were driving, and the windows were steamed as if we'd been making out. But we'd been arguing, as usual, this time about a woman poet who had committed suicide, whose work you were reading. We were sitting, no longer talking or touching, and I remember thinking that I didn't want to argue with you anymore. I didn't want to sit like this in hurt silence; I wanted to talk excitedly all night as we once had. I wanted to find some way that wasn't corny sounding to tell you how much fun I'd had in your company, how much knowing you had meant to me, and how I had suddenly realized that I'd been so intent on becoming lovers that I'd overlooked how close we'd been as friends. I wanted you to know that. I wanted you to like me again.

"It's sad," I started to say, meaning that I was sorry we had reached the point of silence, but before I could continue you challenged the statement.

"What makes you so sure it's sad?"

"What do you mean, what makes me so sure?" I asked, confused by your question.

You looked at me as if what was sad was that I would never understand. "For all either one of us knows," you said, "death could have been her triumph!"

Maybe when it really ended was the night I felt we had just reached the beginning, that one time on the beach in the summer when our bodies rammed so desperately together that for a moment I thought we did it, and maybe in our hearts we did, although for me, then, doing it in one's heart didn't quite count. If it did, I supposed we'd all be Casanovas.

We rode home together on the El train that night, and I felt sick and defeated in a way I was embarrassed to mention. Our mute reflections emerged like negative exposures on the dark, greasy window of the train. Lightning branched over the city, and when the train entered the subway tunnel, the lights inside flickered as if the power was disrupted, though the train continued rocketing beneath the Loop.

When the train emerged again we were on the South Side of the city and it was pouring, a deluge as if the sky had opened to drown the innocent and guilty alike. We hurried from the El station to your house, holding the Navajo blanket over our heads until, soaked, it collapsed. In the dripping doorway of your apartment building, we said good night. You were shivering. Your bikini top showed through the thin blouse plastered to your skin. I swept the wet hair away from your face and kissed you lightly on the lips, then you turned and went inside. I stepped into the rain, and you came back out, calling after me.

"What?" I asked, feeling a surge of gladness to be summoned back into the doorway with you.

"Want an umbrella?"

I didn't. The downpour was letting up. It felt better to walk back to the station feeling the rain rinse the sand out of my hair, off my legs, until the only places where I could still feel its grit were in the crotch of my cutoffs and each squish of my shoes. A block down the street, I passed a pair of jockey shorts lying in a puddle and realized they were mine, dropped from my back pocket as we ran to your house. I left them behind, wondering if you'd see them and recognize them the next day.

By the time I had climbed the stairs back to the El platform, the rain had stopped. Your scent still hadn't washed from my fingers. The station—the entire city it seemed—dripped and steamed. The summer sound of crickets and nighthawks echoed from the drenched neighborhood. Alone, I could admit how sick I felt. For you, it was a night that would haunt your dreams. For me, it was another night when I waited, swollen and aching, for what I had secretly nicknamed the Blue Ball Express.

Literally lovesick, groaning inwardly with each lurch of the train and worried that I was damaged for good, I peered out at the passing yellow-lit stations, where lonely men stood posted before giant advertisements, pictures of glamorous models defaced by graffiti—the same old scrawled insults and pleas: *Fuck you, eat me.* At this late hour the world seemed given over to men without women, men waiting in abject patience for something indeterminate, the way I waited for our next times. I avoided their eyes so that they wouldn't see the pity in mine, pity for them because I'd just been with you, your scent was still on my hands, and there seemed to be so much future ahead.

For me it was another night like that, and by the time I

reached my stop I knew I would be feeling better, recovered enough to walk the dark street home making up poems of longing that I never wrote down. I was the D.H. Lawrence of not doing it, the voice of all the would-be lovers who ached and squirmed. From our contortions in doorways, on stairwells, and in the bucket seats of cars we could have composed a Kama Sutra of interrupted bliss. It must have been that night when I recalled all the other times of walking home after seeing you, so that it seemed as if I was falling into step behind a parade of my former selves—myself walking home on the night we first kissed, myself on the night when I unbuttoned your blouse and kissed your breasts, myself on the night when I lifted your skirt above your thighs and dropped to my knees—each succeeding self another step closer to that irrevocable moment for which our lives seemed poised.

But we didn't, not in the moonlight, or by the phosphorescent lanterns of lightning bugs in your backyard, not beneath the constellations we couldn't see, let alone decipher, or in the dark glow that replaced the real darkness of night, a darkness already stolen from us, not with the skyline rising behind us while a city gradually decayed, not in the heat of summer while a Cold War raged, despite the freedom of youth and the license of first love—because of fate, karma, luck, what does it matter?—we made not doing it a wonder, and yet we didn't, we didn't, we never did.

ABOUT THE CONTRIBUTORS

NELSON ALGREN (1909–1981) was the author of five major novels, two short fiction collections, a book-length poem, and several collections of reportage. Algren's powerful voice rose from the urban wilderness of postwar Chicago, to which he returned again and again in his work. He was the recipient of the first National Book Award for fiction and was lauded by Hemingway as "one of the two best authors in America."

Library of Congress

SHERWOOD ANDERSON (1876–1941) was an American novelist and short story writer. Born and raised in Ohio, he moved to Chicago in 1912 to become a writer after suffering a nervous breakdown. His best-known work is *Winesburg, Ohio* (1919), a collection of short stories based in the small farm town where he grew up. He was a great influence on the generation of American writers who came after him, especially William Faulkner and Ernest Hemingway.

Courtesy of the Estate

FREDRIC BROWN (1906–1972) is probably the only writer to have achieved equally great prominence in two distinct genres: science fiction and the mystery. Winner of the Edgar Award for Best First Novel (*The Fabulous Clipjoint*), his mysteries are all still in print over four decades after his death and his 1949 science fiction novel *What Mad Universe* is regarded as a classic. His short stories are often reprinted and several of his novels have been adapted for film.

Alan Goldfarb

SANDRA CISNEROS is the author of the novels *The House on Mango Street* and *Caramelo*; the short story collection *Woman Hollering Creek*; and the poetry collections *My Wicked Wicked Ways* and *Loose Woman*. Her most recent books are *Bravo Bruno!*, a children's book, and *Have You Seen Marie?*, an illustrated book for adults. She is the recipient of numerous awards, including a MacArthur, and is the founder of the Alfredo Cisneros del Moral Foundation.

John Deason

MAX ALLAN COLLINS is the author of the Shamus Award–winning Nathan Heller historical thrillers and the graphic novel *Road to Perdition*, the basis for the Academy Award–winning film. His innovative 1970s series, Quarry, has been revived by Hard Case Crime and he is developing novels from unfinished Mickey Spillane manuscripts. Collins wrote and directed the Lifetime movie *Mommy* and the documentary *Mike Hammer's Mickey Spillane.*

STUART DYBEK is the author of three books of fiction: *I Sailed with Magellan, The Coast of Chicago,* and *Childhood and Other Neighborhoods.* His work has appeared in the *New Yorker, Harper's,* the *Atlantic, Tin House,* and many other magazines. Among Dybek's numerous honors are a PEN/Malamud Award, a Whiting Writers' Award, and several O. Henry Prizes. He is currently a Distinguished Writer in Residence at Northwestern University.

Tiago Russo Pinto

BARRY GIFFORD is the author of more than forty published works of fiction, nonfiction, and poetry. He has been the recipient of awards from PEN, the National Endowment for the Arts, the American Library Association, the Writers Guild of America, and the Christopher Isherwood Foundation. His novel *Wild at Heart: The Story of Sailor and Lula* was made into a major motion picture which won the Palme d'Or at the Cannes Film Festival.

First Light Creative

LIBBY FISCHER HELLMANN left a career in broadcast news in Washington, DC, and moved to Chicago thirty-five years ago, where she, naturally, began to write gritty crime fiction. Eleven published novels and twenty short stories later, she claims they'll take her out of the Windy City feetfirst. She has been nominated for many awards in the mystery writing community and has even won a few.

Marion Ettlinger

PATRICIA HIGHSMITH (1921–1995) was the author of more than twenty novels, including *Strangers on a Train, The Price of Salt,* and *The Talented Mr. Ripley,* as well as numerous short stories.

HUGH HOLTON (1946–2001) was a thirty-year veteran and commander of the Chicago Police Department. He served as the Midwest chapter president of the Mystery Writers of America and wrote several best-selling novels, including *Time of the Assassins, The Left Hand of God, Violent Crimes,* and *Windy City.* At the time of his death, Hugh Holton was the highest-ranking active police officer writing novels in America.

Jean-Luc Vallet

STUART M. KAMINSKY (1934–2009) was a Chicago-born crime fiction writer of over sixty novels, as well as story collections and nonfiction works. He is best known for three long-running series of mystery novels. His novels have earned seven Edgar Award nominations, and his Inspector Rostnikov novel *A Cold Red Sunrise* won the Edgar Award in 1989. He was a film professor at Northwestern University for sixteen years.

Columbia University's Rare Book Library

HARRY STEPHEN KEELER (1890–1967) was the author of more than seventy mystery novels known for their highly intricate "webwork" plots. He was born and spent most of his life in Chicago, the setting for many of his books. Among his works are *The Skull of the Waltzing Clown* (1935), *The Case of the Barking Clock* (1947), and *The Mystery of the Fiddling Cracksman* (1934).

Joe Wigdahl

JOE MENO (editor) is a fiction writer and playwright who lives in Chicago. He is the winner of the Nelson Algren Literary Award, a Pushcart Prize, the Great Lakes Book Award, and a finalist for the Story Prize. He is the author of six novels including the best sellers *Hairstyles of the Damned* and *The Boy Detective Fails,* and his latest, *Marvel and a Wonder.* He is a professor in the Department of Creative Writing at Columbia College Chicago.

Steven Gross

SARA PARETSKY revolutionized the mystery world in 1982 when she introduced her detective V.I. Warshawski in *Indemnity Only.* Since then, her *New York Times* best-selling novels have been published in thirty countries. In 1986 she created Sisters in Crime, a worldwide organization to support women crime writers, which earned her *Ms.* magazine's 1987 Woman of the Year award. Her many accolades also include the 2011 Mystery Writers of America Grand Master Award for lifetime achievement.

Shirley Parker

PERCY SPURLARK PARKER was born and raised in Chicago. He became a published author in April 1972 when *Ellery Queen Mystery Magazine* published his story entitled "Block Party." He has served as Midwest chapter president of the Mystery Writers of America, and has been a member of the Private Eye Writers of America since its inception.

Carl Van Vechten

RICHARD WRIGHT (1908–1960) was born in Mississippi and moved to Chicago in 1927, where he worked at a post office and studied the works of other writers. His writing is widely believed to have helped change race relations in the United States in the mid-twentieth century. He is best known for his memoir *Black Boy* (1945) and his novel *Native Son* (1940).

For J.V.

Thank you to Koren, Lucia, Nicolas. Thanks to Johnny Temple, Johanna Ingalls, Ibrahim Ahmad, Aaron Petrovich, and everyone at Akashic for their unending courage and unflagging support. Thank you to Jon Resh for his enduring friendship and design acumen. Thanks to my family. Thanks to the Department of Creative Writing at Columbia College Chicago, its faculty, staff, and students. Thank you to the authors, their representatives, and their estates for allowing us to reprint their work.